1 MONTH OF
FREE
READING

at

www.ForgottenBooks.com

By purchasing this book you are eligible for one month membership to ForgottenBooks.com, giving you unlimited access to our entire collection of over 1,000,000 titles via our web site and mobile apps.

To claim your free month visit:

www.forgottenbooks.com/free227001

ISBN 978-0-266-21745-9
PIBN 10227001

This book is a reproduction of an important historical work. Forgotten Books uses
state-of-the-art technology to digitally reconstruct the work, preserving the original format
whilst repairing imperfections present in the aged copy. In rare cases, an imperfection in
the original, such as a blemish or missing page, may be replicated in our edition. We do,
however, repair the vast majority of imperfections successfully; any imperfections that
remain are intentionally left to preserve the state of such historical works.

CROOKED TRAILS AND STRAIGHT

BY

WILLIAM MacLEOD RAINE

AUTHOR OF

BRAND BLOTTERS, BUCKY O'CONNOR, MAVERICKS, WYOMING, RIDGWAY OF MONTANA, A TEXAS RANGER, Etc.

ILLUSTRATIONS BY

D. C. HUTCHISON

GROSSET & DUNLAP
PUBLISHERS   NEW YORK

Crooked Trails and Straight

CONTENTS

CONTENTS

Crooked Trails and Straight

PART I

CURLY

CHAPTER I

FOLLOWING A CROOKED TRAIL

ACROSS Dry Valley a dust cloud had been moving for hours. It rolled into Saguache at the brisk heels of a bunch of horses just about the time the town was settling itself to supper. At the intersection of Main and La Junta streets the cloud was churned to a greater volume and density. From out of the heart of it cantered a rider, who swung his pony as on a half dollar, and deflected the remuda toward Chunn's corral.

The rider was in the broad-rimmed felt hat, the gray shirt, the plain leather chaps of a vaquero. The alkali dust of Arizona lay thick on every exposed inch of him, but youth bloomed inextinguishably through the grime. As he swept forward with a whoop to turn the lead horses it rang in his voice, announced itself in his carriage, was apparent in the modeling of his slim, hard body. 'Under other conditions he might have been a college freshman for age, but the competent confidence of manhood sat easily on his broad shoulders. He was already a graduate of that school of experience which always holds open session on the baked desert. Curly Flandrau had more than once looked into the chill eyes of death.

The leaders of the herd dribbled into the corral through the open gate, and the others crowded on their heels. Three more riders followed Curly into the enclosure. Upon them, too, the desert had sifted its white coat. The stained withers of the animals they rode told of long, steady travel. One of them, a red-haired young fellow of about the same age as Curly, swung stiffly from the saddle.

"Me for a square meal first off," he gave out promptly.

"Not till we've finished this business, Mac. We'll put a deal right through if Warren's here," decided a third member of the party. He was a tough-looking customer of nearly fifty. From out of his leathery sun-and-wind beaten face, hard eyes looked without expression. "Bad Bill" Cranston he was called, and the man looked as if he had earned his sobriquet.

"And what if he ain't here?" snarled the fourth. "Are you aiming to sit down and wait for him?"

"We'll cross that bridge when we come to it," Bad Bill answered. "Curly, want to ride up to the hotel and ask if Mr. Dave Warren is there? Bring him right down if he is."

"And say, young fellow, don't shout all over the place what your business is with him," ordered the previous speaker sulkily. Lute Blackwell, a squat heavily muscled man of forty, had the manner of a bully. Unless his shifty eyes lied he was both cruel and vindictive.

Curly's gaze traveled over him leisurely. Not a muscle in the boyish face moved, but in the voice one might have guessed an amused contempt. "All right. I won't, since you mention it, Lute."

The young man cantered up the dusty street toward the hotel. Blackwell trailed toward the windmill pump.

"Thought you'd fixed it with this Warren to be right on the spot so's we could unload on him prompt," he grumbled at Cranston without looking toward the latter.

"I didn't promise he'd be hanging round your neck soon as you hit town," Cranston retorted coolly. "Keep your shirt on, Lute. No use getting in a sweat."

The owner of the corral sauntered from the stable

and glanced over the bunch of horses milling around.

"Been traveling some," he suggested to Bad Bill.

"A few. Seen anything of a man named Warren about town to-day?"

"He's been down here se-ve-re-al times. Said he was looking for a party with stock to sell. Might you be the outfit he's expecting?"

"We might." Bad Bill took the drinking cup from Blackwell and drained it. "I reckon the dust was caked in my throat an inch deep."

"Drive all the way from the Bar Double M?" asked the keeper of the corral, his eyes on the brand stamped on the flank of a pony circling past.

"Yep."

Bad Bill turned away and began to unsaddle. He did not intend to volunteer any information, though on the other hand he did not want to stir suspicion by making a mystery for gossips to chew on.

"Looks like you been hitting the road at a right lively gait."

Mac cut in. "Shoulder of my bronc's chafed from the saddle. Got anything that'll heal it?"

"You bet I have." The man hurried into the stable and the redheaded cowpuncher winked across the back of his horse at Bill.

The keeper of the stable and the young man were

still busy doctoring the sore when Curly arrived with Warren. The buyer was a roundbodied man with black gimlet eyes that saw much he never told. The bargain he drove was a hard one, but it did not take long to come to terms at about one-third the value of the string he was purchasing. Very likely he had his suspicions, but he did not voice them. No doubt they cut a figure in the price. He let it be understood that he was a supply agent for the rebels in Mexico. Before the bills were warm in the pockets of the sellers, his vaqueros were mounted and were moving the remuda toward the border.

Curly and Mac helped them get started. As they rode back to the corral a young man came out from the stable. Flandrau forgot that there were reasons why he wanted just now to be a stranger in the land with his identity not advertised. He let out a shout.

"Oh you, Slats Davis!"

"Hello, Curly! How are things a-comin'?"

"Fine. When did you blow in to Saguache? Ain't you off your run some?"

They had ridden the range together and had frolicked around on a dozen boyish larks. Their ways had suited each other and they had been a good deal more than casual bunkies. To put it mildly the meeting was likely to prove embarrassing.

"Came down to see about getting some cows for the old man from the Fiddleback outfit," Davis explained. "Didn't expect to bump into friends 'way down here. You riding for the Bar Double M?"

There was a momentary silence. Curly's vigilant eyes met those of his old side partner. What did Slats know? Had he been in the stable while the remuda was still in the corral? Had he seen them with Bad Bill and Blackwell? Were his suspicions already active?

"No, I'm riding for the Map of Texas," Flandrau answered evenly.

"Come on, Curly. Let's go feed our faces," Mac called from the stable.

Flandrau nodded. "You still with the Hashknife?" he asked Davis.

"Still with 'em. I've been raised to assistant foreman."

"Bully for you. That's great. All right, Mac. I'm coming. That's sure great, old hoss. Well, see you later, Slats."

Flandrau followed Mac, dissatisfied with himself for leaving his friend so cavalierly. In the old days they had told each other everything, had talked things out together before many a campfire. He guessed Slats would be hurt, but he had to think of his partners in this enterprise.

After supper they took a room at the hotel and divided the money Warren had paid for the horses. None of them had slept for the last fifty hours and Mac proposed to tumble into bed at once.

Bad Bill shook his head. "I wouldn't, Mac. Let's hit the trail and do our sleeping in the hills. There's too many telephone lines into this town to suit me."

"Sho! We made a clean getaway, and we're plumb wore out. Our play isn't to hike out like we were scared stiff of something. What we want to do is to act as if we could look every darned citizen in the face. Mac's sure right," Curly agreed.

"You kids make me tired. As if you knew anything about it. I'm going to dust *muy pronto*," Blackwell snarled.

"Sure. Whenever you like. You go and we'll stay. Then everybody'll be satisfied. We got to split up anyhow," Mac said.

Bad Bill looked at Blackwell and nodded. "That's right. We don't all want to pull a blue streak. That would be a dead give away. Let the kids stay if they want to."

"So as they can round on us if they're nabbed," Blackwell sneered.

Cranston called him down roughly. "That'll be enough along that line, Lute. I don't stand for any more cracks like it."

Blackwell, not three months out from the peni‧tentiary, faced the other with an ugly look in his eyes. He was always ready to quarrel, but he did not like to fight unless he had a sure thing. He knew Bad Bill was an ugly customer when he once got started.

"Didn't mean any harm," the ex-convict growled. "But I don't like this sticking around town. I tell you straight I don't like it."

"Then I wouldn't stay if I were you," Curly suggested promptly. "Mac and I have got a different notion. So we'll tie to Saguache for a day or two."

As soon as the older men had gone the others tumbled into bed and fell asleep at once. Daylight was sifting in through the open window before their eyes opened. Somebody was pounding on the bedroom door, which probably accounted for Flandrau's dream that a sheriff was driving nails in the lid of a coffin containing one Curly.

Mac was already out of bed when his partner's feet hit the floor.

"What's up, Mac?"

The eyes of the redheaded puncher gleamed with excitement. His six-gun was in his hand. By the look of him he was about ready to whang loose through the door.

"Hold your horses, you chump," Curly sang out. "It's the hotel clerk. I left a call with him."

But it was not the hotel clerk after all. Through the door came a quick, jerky voice.

"That you, Curly? For God's sake, let me in."

Before he had got the words out the door was open. Slats came in and shut it behind him. He looked at Mac, the forty-five shaking in the boy's hand, and he looked at Flandrau.

"They're after you," he said, breathing fast as if he had been running.

"Who?" fired Curly back at him.

"The Bar Double M boys. They just reached town."

"Put up that gun, Mac, and move into your clothes immediate," ordered Curly. Then to Davis: "Go on. Unload the rest. What do they know?"

"They inquired for you and your friend here down at the Legal Tender. The other members of your party they could only guess at."

"Have we got a chance to make our getaway?" Mac asked.

Davis nodded. "Slide out through the kitchen, cut into the alley, and across lots to the corral. We'll lock the door and I'll hold them here long as I can."

"Good boy, Slats. If there's a necktie party you'll get the first bid," Curly grinned.

Slats looked at him, cold and steady. Plainer than words he was telling his former friend that he would not joke with a horse thief. For the sake of old times he would save him if he could, but he would call any bluffs about the whole thing being a lark.

Curly's eyes fell away. It came to him for the first time that he was no longer an honest man. Up till this escapade he had been only wild, but now he had crossed the line that separates decent folks from outlaws. He had been excited with liquor when he joined in this fool enterprise, but that made no difference now. He was a rustler, a horse thief. If he lived a hundred years he could never get away from the disgrace of it.

Not another word was said while they hurried into their clothes. But as Curly passed out of the door he called back huskily. "Won't forget what you done for us, Slats."

Again their eyes met. Davis did not speak, but the chill look on his face told Flandrau that he had lost a friend.

The two young men ran down the back stairs, passed through the kitchen where a Chinese cook was getting breakfast, and out into the bright sunlight. Before they cut across to the corral their eyes searched for enemies. Nobody was in sight except the negro janitor of a saloon busy putting empty bottles into a barrel.

"Won't do to be in any hurry. The play is we're gentlemen of leisure, just out for an amble to get the mo'ning air," Curly cautioned.

While they fed, watered, and saddled they swapped gossip with the wrangler. It would not do to leave the boy with a story of two riders in such a hurry to hit the trail that they could not wait to feed their bronchos. So they stuck it out while the animals ate, though they were about as contented as a two-pound rainbow trout on a hook. One of them was at the door all the time to make sure the way was still clear. At that they shaved it fine, for as they rode away two men were coming down the street.

"Kite Bonfils," Curly called to his partner.

No explanation was needed. Bonfils was the foreman of the Bar Double M. He let out a shout as he caught sight of them and began to run forward. Simultaneously his gun seemed to jump from its holster.

Mac's quirt sang and his pony leaped to a canter in two strides. A bullet zipped between them. Another struck the dust at their heels. Faintly there came to the fugitives the sound of the foreman's impotent curses. They had escaped for the time.

Presently they passed the last barb wire fence and open country lay before them. It did not greatly matter which direction they followed, so long as they headed into the desert.

"What we're looking for is a country filled with absentees," Curly explained with a grin.

Neither of them had ever been in serious trouble before and both regretted the folly that had turned their drunken spree into a crime. Once or twice they came to the edge of a quarrel, for Mac was ready to lay the blame on his companion. Moreover, he had reasons why the thing he had done loomed up as a heinous offense.

His reasons came out before the camp fire on Dry Sandy that evening. They were stretched in front of it trying to make a smoke serve instead of supper. Mac broke a gloomy silence to grunt out jerkily a situation he could no longer keep to himself.

"Here's where I get my walking papers I reckon. No rustlers need apply."

Curly shot a slant glance at him. "Meaning— the girl?"

The redheaded puncher nodded. "She'll throw me down sure. Why shouldn't she? I tell you I've ruined my life. You're only a kid. What you know about it?"

He took from his coat pocket a photograph and

showed it to his friend. The sweet clean face of a wholesome girl smiled at Curly.

"She's ce'tainly a right nice young lady. I'll bet she stands by you all right. Where's she live at?"

"Waits in a restaurant at Tombstone. We was going to be married soon as we had saved five hundred dollars." Mac swallowed hard. "And I had to figure out this short cut to the money whilst I was drunk. As if she'd look at money made that way. Why, we'd a-been ready by Christmas if I'd only waited."

Curly tried to cheer him up, but did not make much of a job at it. The indisputable facts were that Mac was an outlaw and a horse thief. Very likely a price was already on his head.

The redheaded boy rolled another cigarette despondently. "Sho! I've cooked my goose. She'll not look at me—even if they don't send me to the pen." In a moment he added huskily, staring into the deepening darkness: "And she's the best ever. Her name's Myra Anderson."

Abruptly Mac got up and disappeared in the night, muttering something about looking after the horses. His partner understood well enough what was the matter. The redheaded puncher was in a stress of emotion, and like the boy he was he did not want Curly to know it.

Flandrau pretended to be asleep when Mac returned half an hour later.

They slept under a live oak with the soundness of healthy youth. For the time they forgot their troubles. Neither of them knew that as the hours slipped away red tragedy was galloping closer to them.

CHAPTER II

CAMPING WITH OLD MAN TROUBLE

The sun was shining in his face when Curly wakened. He sat up and rubbed his eyes. Mac was nowhere in sight. Probably he had gone to get the horses.

A sound broke the stillness of the desert. It might have been the explosion of a giant firecracker, but Flandrau knew it was nothing so harmless. He leaped to his feet, and at the same instant Mac came running over the brow of the hill. A smoking revolver was in his hand.

From behind the hill a gun cracked—then a second—and a third. Mac stumbled over his feet and pitched forward full length on the ground. His friend ran toward him, forgetting the revolver that lay in its holster under the live oak. Every moment he expected to see Mac jump up, but the figure stretched beside the cholla never moved. Flandrau felt the muscles round his heart tighten. He had seen sudden death before, but never had it come so near home.

A bullet sent up a spurt of dust in front of him, another just on the left. Riders were making a half circle around the knoll and closing in on him. In his right mind Curly would have been properly frightened. But now he thought only of Mac lying there so still in the sand. Right into the fire zone he ran, knelt beside his partner, and lifted the red-thatched head. A little hole showed back of the left ear and another at the right temple. A bullet had plowed through the boy's skull.

Softly Flandrau put the head back in the sand and rose to his feet. The revolver of the dead puncher was in his hand. The attackers had stopped shooting, but when they saw him rise a rifle puffed once more. The riders were closing in on him now. The nearest called to him to surrender. Almost at the same time a red hot pain shot through the left arm of the trapped rustler. Someone had nipped him from the rear.

Curly saw red. Surrender nothing! He would go down fighting. As fast as he could blaze he emptied Mac's gun. When the smoke cleared the man who had ordered him to give up was slipping from his horse. Curly was surprised, but he knew he must have hit him by chance.

"We got him. His gun's empty," someone shouted.

Cautiously they closed in, keeping him covered all the time. Of a sudden the plain tilted up to meet the sky. Flandrau felt himself swaying on

his feet. Everything went black. The boy had
fainted.

When he came to himself strange faces were all
around him, and there were no bodies to go with
them. They seemed to float about in an odd casual
sort of way. Then things cleared.

"He's coming to all right," one said.

"Good. I'd hate to have him cheat the rope,"
another cried with an oath.

"That's right. How *is* Cullison?"

This was said to another who had just come up.

"Hard hit. Looks about all in. Got him in
the side."

The rage had died out of Curly. In a flash he
saw all that had come of their drunken spree: the
rustling of the Bar Double M stock, the discovery,
the death of his friend and maybe of Cullison, the
certain punishment that would follow. He was a
horse thief caught almost in the act. Perhaps he
was a murderer too. And the whole thing had
been entirely unpremeditated.

Flandrau made a movement to rise and they
jerked him to his feet.

"You've played hell," one of the men told the
boy.

He was a sawed-off little fellow known as Dutch.
Flandrau had seen him in the Map of Texas country a year or two before. The rest were strangers

25

to the boy. All of them looked at him out of hard hostile eyes. He was scarcely a human being to them; rather a wolf to be stamped out of existence as soon as it was convenient. A chill ran down Curly's spine. He felt as if someone were walking on his grave.

At a shift in the group Flandrau's eyes fell on his friend lying in the sand with face turned whitely to the sky he never would see again. It came over him strangely enough how Mac used to break into a little chuckling laugh when he was amused. He had quit laughing now for good and all. A lump came into the boy's throat and he had to work it down before he spoke.

"There's a picture in his pocket, and some letters I reckon. Send them to Miss Myra Anderson, Tombstone, care of one of the restaurants. I don't know which one."

"Send nothin'," sneered Dutch, and coupled it with a remark no decent man makes of a woman on a guess.

Because of poor Mac lying there with the little hole in his temple Curly boiled over. With a jerk his right arm was free. It shot out like a pile-driver, all his weight behind the blow. Dutch went down as if a charging bull had flung him.

Almost simultaneously Curly hit the sand hard. Before he could stir three men were straddled over his anatomy. One of them ground his head into the dust.

"You would, eh? We'll see about that. Jake, bring yore rope."

They tied the hands of the boy, hauled him to his feet, and set him astride a horse. In the distance a windmill of the Circle C ranch was shining in the morning sun. Toward the group of buildings clustered around this two of his captors started with Flandrau. A third was already galloping toward the ranch house to telephone for a doctor.

As they rode along a fenced lane which led to the house a girl came flying down the steps. She swung herself to the saddle just vacated by the messenger and pulled the horse round for a start. At sight of those coming toward her she called out quickly.

"How is dad?" The quiver of fear broke in her voice.

"Don' know yet, Miss Kate," answered one of the men. "He's right peart though. Says for to tell you not to worry. Don't you, either. We've got here the mangy son of a gun that did it."

Before he had finished she was off like an arrow shot from a bow, but not until her eyes had fallen on the youth sitting bareheaded and bloody between the guns of his guard. Curly noticed that she had given a shudder, as one might at sight of a mangled mad dog which had just bit a dear friend. Long after the pounding of her pony's hoofs had died away the prisoner could see the startled eyes of fear and horror that had rested on him. As Curly kicked his foot out of the stirrup to dismount a light spring wagon rolled past him. In its bed were a mattress and pillows. The driver whipped up the horse and went across the prairie toward Dry Sandy Creek. Evidently he was going to bring home the wounded man.

His guards put Flandrau in the bunk house and one of them sat at the door with a rifle across his knees. The cook, the stable boy, and redheaded Bob Cullison, a nephew of the owner of the ranch, peered past the *vaquero* at the captive with the same awe they would have yielded to a caged panther.

"Why, he's only a kid, Buck," the cook whispered.

Buck chewed tobacco impassively. "Old enough to be a rustler and a killer."

Bob's blue eyes were wide with interest. "I'll bet he's a regular Billy the Kid," murmured the half-grown boy to the other lad.

"Sure. Course he is. He's got bad eyes all right."

"I'll bet he's got notches on his gun. Say, if Uncle Luck dies—" Bob left the result to the imagination.

28

The excitement at the Circle C increased. Horses cantered up. Men shouted to each other the news. Occasionally some one came in to have a look at the "bad man" who had shot Luck Cullison. Young Flandrau lay on a cot and stared at the ceiling, paying no more attention to them than if they had been blocks of wood. It took no shrewdness to see that there burned in them a still cold anger toward him that might easily find expression in lynch law.

The crunch of wagon wheels over disintegrated granite drifted to the bunk house.

"They're bringing the boss back," Buck announced from the door to one of his visitors.

The man joined him and looked over his shoulder. "Miss Kate there too?"

"Yep. Say, if the old man don't pull through it will break her all up."

The boy on the bed turned his face to the wall. He had not cried for ten years, but now he would have liked the relief of tears. The luck had broken bad for him, but it would be the worst ever if his random shot were to make Kate Cullison an orphan. A big lump rose in his throat and would not stay down. The irony of it was that he was staged for the part of a gray wolf on the howl, while he felt more like a little child that has lost its last friend.

After a time there came again the crisp roll of wheels.

"Doc Brown," announced Buck casually to the other men in the bunk house.

There was more than one anxious heart at the Circle C waiting for the verdict of the bowlegged baldheaded little man with the satchel, but not one of them—no, not even Kate Cullison herself—was in a colder fear than Curly Flandrau. He was entitled to a deep interest, for if Cullison should die he knew that he would follow him within a few hours. These men would take no chances with the delays of the law.

The men at the bunk house had offered more than once to look at Curly's arm, but the young man declined curtly. The bleeding had stopped, but there was a throb in it as if someone were twisting a redhot knife in the wound. After a time Doctor Brown showed up in the doorway of the men's quarters.

"Another patient here, they tell me," he grunted in the brusque way that failed to conceal the kindest of hearts.

Buck nodded toward Flandrau.

"Let's have a look at your arm, young fellow," the doctor ordered, mopping his bald head with a big bandanna handkerchief.

"What about the boss?" asked Jake presently.

"Mighty sick man, looks like. Tell you more to-morrow morning."

"Do you mean that he—that he may not get well?" Curly pumped out, his voice not quite steady.

Doctor Brown looked at him curiously. Somehow this boy did not fit the specifications of the desperado that had been poured into his ears.

"Don't know yet. Won't make any promises." He had been examining the wound in a business-like way. "Looks like the bullet's still in there. Have to give you an anæsthetic while I dig it out."

"Nothin' doing," retorted Flandrau. "You round up the pill in there and I'll stand the grief. When this lead hypodermic jabbed into my arm it sorter gave me one of them annie-what-d'ye-call-'em—and one's a-plenty for me."

"It'll hurt," the little man explained.

"Expect I'll find that out. Go to it."

Brown had not been for thirty years carrying a medicine case across the dusty deserts of the frontier without learning to know men. He made no further protest but set to work.

Twenty minutes later Curly lay back on the bunk with a sudden faintness. He was very white about the lips, but he had not once flinched from the instruments.

The doctor washed his hands and his tools, pulled on his coat, and came across to the patient.

"Feeling like a fighting cock, are you? Ready to tackle another posse?" he asked.

"Not quite." The prisoner glanced toward his guards and his voice fell to a husky whisper. "Say, Doc. Pull Cullison through. Don't let him die."

"Hmp! Do my best, young fellow. Seems to me you're thinking of that pretty late."

Brown took up his medicine case and went back to the house.

CHAPTER III

AT THE END OF THE ROAD

Curly's wooden face told nothing of what he was thinking. The first article of the creed of the frontier is to be game. Good or bad, the last test of a man is the way he takes his medicine. So now young Flandrau ate his dinner with a hearty appetite, smoked cigarettes impassively, and occasionally chatted with his guards casually and as a matter of course. Deep within him was a terrible feeling of sickness at the disaster that had overwhelmed him, but he did not intend to play the quitter.

Dutch and an old fellow named Sweeney relieved the other watchers about noon. The squat puncher came up and looked down angrily at the boy lying on the bunk.

"I'll serve notice right now that if you make any breaks I'll fill your carcass full of lead," he growled.

The prisoner knew that he was nursing a grudge for the blow that had floored him. Not to be bluffed, Curly came back with a jeer. "Much obliged, my sawed-off and hammered-down friend. But what's the matter with your face? It looks some lopsided. Did a mule kick you?"

Sweeney gave his companion the laugh. "Better

33

let him alone, Dutch. If he lands on you again like he did before your beauty ce'tainly will be spoiled complete."

The little puncher's eyes snapped rage. "You'll get yours pretty soon, Mr. Curly Flandrau. The boys are fixin' to hang yore hide up to dry."

"Does look that way, doesn't it?" the boy agreed quietly.

As the day began to wear out it looked so more than ever. Two riders from the Bar Double M reached the ranch and were brought in to identify him as the horse thief. The two were Maloney and Kite Bonfils, neither of them friends of the young rustler. The foreman in particular was a wet blanket to his chances. The man's black eyes were the sort that never soften toward the follies and mistakes of youth.

"You've got the right man all right," he said to Buck without answering Flandrau's cool nod of recognition.

"What sort of a reputation has he got?" Buck asked, lowering his voice a little.

Kite did not take the trouble to lower his. "Bad. Always been a tough character. Friend of Bad Bill Cranston and Soapy Stone."

Dutch chipped in. "Shot up the Silver Dollar saloon onct. Pretty near beat Pete Schiff's head off another time."

34

Curly laughed rather wildly. "That's right. Keep a-coming, boys. Your turn now, Maloney."

"All right. Might as well have it all," Buck agreed.

"I don't know anything against the kid, barring that he's been a little wild," Maloney testified. "And I reckon we ain't any of us prize Sunday school winners for that matter."

"Are we all friends of Soapy Stone and Bad Bill? Do we all rustle stock and shoot up good citizens?" Dutch shrilled.

Maloney's blue Irish eyes rested on the little puncher for a moment, then passed on as if he had been weighed and found wanting.

"I've noticed," he said to nobody in particular, "that them hollering loudest for justice are most generally the ones that would hate to have it done to them."

Dutch bristled like a turkey rooster. "What do you mean by that?"

The Irishman smiled derisively. "I reckon you can guess if you try real hard."

Dutch fumed, but did no guessing out loud. His reputation was a whitewashed one. Queer stories had been whispered about him. He had been a nester, and it was claimed that calves certainly not his had been found carrying his brand. The man had been full of explanations, but there came a

35

time when explanations no longer were accepted. He was invited to become an absentee at his earliest convenience. This was when he had been living across the mountains. Curly had béen one of those who had given the invitation. He had taken the hint and left without delay. Now he was paying the debt he owed young Flandrau.

Though the rôle Curly had been given was that of the hardened desperado he could not quite live up to the part. As Buck turned to leave the bunk house the boy touched him on the arm.

"How about Cullison?" he asked, very low.

But Buck would not have it that way. "What about him?" he demanded out loud, his voice grating like steel when it grinds.

"Is he—how is he doing?"

"What's eatin' you? Ain't he dying fast enough to suit you?"

Flandrau shrank from the cruel words, as a schoolboy does from his teacher when he jumps at him with a cane. He understood how the men were feeling, but to have it put into words like this cut him deeply.

It was then that Maloney made a friend of the young man for life. He let a hand drop carelessly on Curly's shoulder and looked at him with a friendly smile in his eyes, just as if he knew that this was no wolf but a poor lost dog up against it hard.

"Doc thinks he'll make it all right."

But there were times when Curly wondered whether it would make any difference to him whether Cullison got well or not. Something immediate was in the air. Public opinion was sifting down to a decision. There were wise nods, and whisperings, and men riding up and going off again in a hurry. There had been a good deal of lawlessness of late, for which Soapy Stone's band of followers was held responsible. Just as plainly as if he had heard the arguments of Dutch and Kite Bonfils he knew that they were urging the others to make an example of him. Most of these men were well up to the average for the milk of human kindness. They were the squarest citizens in Arizona. But Flandrau knew they would snuff out his life just the same if they decided it was best. Afterward they might regret it, but that would not help him.

Darkness came, and the lamps were lit. Again Curly ate and smoked and chatted a little with his captors. But as he sat there hour after hour, feeling death creep closer every minute, cold shivers ran up and down his spine.

They began to question him, at first casually and

carelessly, so it seemed to Curly. But presently he discerned a drift in the talk. They were trying to find out who had been his partners in the rustling.

"And I reckon Soapy and Bad Bill left you lads at Saguache to hold the sack," Buck suggested sympathetically.

Curly grew wary. He did not intend to betray his accomplices. "Wrong guess. Soapy and Bad Bill weren't in this deal," he answered easily.

"We know there were two others in it with you. I guess they were Soapy and Bad Bill all right."

"There's no law against guessing."

The foreman of the Bar Double M interrupted impatiently, tired of trying to pump out the information by finesse. "You've got to speak, Flandrau. You've got to tell us who was engineering this theft. Understand?"

The young rustler looked at the grim frowning face and his heart sank. "Got to tell you, have I?"

"That's what?"

"Out with it," ordered Buck.

"Oh, I expect I'll keep that under my hat," Curly told them lightly.

They were crowded about him in a half circle, nearly a score of hard leather-faced plainsmen. Some of them were riders of the Circle C outfit. Others had ridden over from neighboring ranches.

All of them plainly meant business. They meant to stamp out rustling, and their determination had been given an edge by the wounding of Luck Cullison, the most popular man in the county.

"Think again, Curly," advised Sweeney quietly. "The boys ain't trifling about this thing. They mean to find out who was in the rustling of the Bar Double M stock."

"Not through me, they won't."

"Through you. And right now."

A dozen times during the evening Curly had crushed down the desire to beg for mercy, to cry out desperately for them to let him off. He had kept telling himself not to show yellow, that it would not last long. Now the fear of breaking down sloughed from his soul. He rose from the bed and looked round at the brown faces circled about him in the shine of the lamps.

"I'll not tell you a thing—not a thing."

He stood there chalk-faced, his lips so dry that he had to keep moistening them with the tip of his tongue. Two thoughts hammered in his head. One was that he had come to the end of his trail, the other that he would game it out without weakening.

Dutch had a new rope in his hand with a loop at one end. He tossed it over the boy's head **and** drew it taut. Two or three of the faces in the circle were almost as bloodless as that of the prisoner, but they were set to see the thing out.

"Will you tell now?" Bonfils asked.

Curly met him eye to eye. "No."

"Come along then."

One of the men caught his arm at the place where he had been wounded. The rustler flinched.

"Careful, Buck. Don't you see you're hurting his bad arm?" Sweeney said sharply.

"Sure. Take him right under the shoulder."

"There's no call to be rough with him."

"I didn't aim to hurt him," Buck defended himself.

His grip was loose and easy now. Like the others he was making it up to his conscience for what he meant to do by doing it in the kindest way possible.

Curly's senses had never been more alert. He noticed that Buck had on a red necktie that had got loose from his shirt and climbed up his neck. It had black polka dots and was badly frayed. Sweeney ,was chewing tobacco. He would have that chew in his mouth after they had finished what they were going to do.

"Ain't he the gamest ever?" someone whispered.

The rustler heard the words and they braced him

40

as a drink of whiskey does a man who has been on a bad spree. His heart was chill with fear, but he had strung his will not to let him give way.

"Better do it at the cotttonwoods down by the creek," Buck told Bonfils in a low voice.

The foreman of the Bar Double M moved his head in assent. "All right. Let's get it over quick as we can."

A sound of flying feet came from outside. Someone smothered an oath of surprise. Kate Cullison stood in the doorway, all out of breath and panting.

She took the situation in before she spoke, guessed exactly what they intended to do. Yet she flung her imperious question at them.

"What is it?"

They had not a word to say for themselves. In that room were some of the most callous hearts in the territory. Not one man in a million could have phased them, but this slender girl dumfounded them. Her gaze settled on Buck. His wandered for help to Sweeney, to Jake, to Kite Bonfils.

"Now look-a-here, Miss Kate," Sweeney began to explain.

But she swept his remonstrance aside.

"No—No—No!" Her voice gathered strength with each repetition of the word. "I won't have it. What are you thinking about?"

To the boy with the rope around his neck she was an angel from heaven as she stood there so slim and straight, her dark eyes shining like stars. Some of these men were old enough to be her father. Any of them could have crushed her with one hand. But if a thunderbolt had crashed in their midst it could not have disturbed the vigilantes more.

"He's a rustler, Miss Kate; belongs to Soapy Stone's outfit," Sweeney answered the girl.

"Can you prove it?"

"We got him double cinched."

"Then let the law put him in prison."

"He shot yore paw," Buck reminded her.

"Is that why you're doing it?"

"Yes'm," and "That's why," they nodded.

Like a flash she took advantage of their admission. "Then I've got more against him than you have, and I say turn him over to the law."

"He'd get a good lawyer and wiggle out," Dutch objected.

She whirled on the little puncher. "You know how that is, do you?"

Somebody laughed. It was known that Dutch had once been tried for stealing a sheep and had been acquitted.

Kite pushed forward, rough and overbearing; "Now see here. We know what we're doing and we know why we're doing it. This ain't any business for a girl to mix in. You go back to the house and nurse your father that this man shot."

"So it isn't the kind of business for a girl," she answered scornfully. "It's work for a man, isn't it? No, not for one. For nine—eleven—thirteen —seventeen big brave strong men to hang one poor wounded boy."

Again that amused laugh rippled out. It came from Maloney. He was leaning against the door jamb with his hands in his pockets. Nobody had noticed him before. He had come in after the girl. When Curly came to think it over later, if he had been given three guesses as to who had told Kate Cullison what was on the program he would have guessed Maloney each time.

"Now that you've relieved your mind proper, Miss Cullison, I expect any of the boys will be glad to escort you back to the house," Kite suggested with an acid smile.

"What have you got to do with this?" she flamed. "Our boys took him. They brought him here as their prisoner. Do you think we'll let you come over into this county and dictate everything we do?"

"I've got a notion tucked away that you're try-ing to do the dictating your own self," the Bar Double M man contradicted.

"I'm not. But I won't stand by while you get

43

these boys to do murder. If they haven't sense enough to keep them from it I've got to stop it myself."

Kite laughed sarcastically. "You hear your boss, boys."

"You've had yore say now, Miss Kate. I reckon you better say good-night," advised Buck.

She handed Buck and his friends her compliments in a swift flow of feminine ferocity.

Maloney pushed into the circle. "She's dead right, boys. There's nothing to this lynching game. He's only a kid."

"He's not such a kid but what he can do murder," Dutch spat out.

Kate read him the riot act so sharply that the little puncher had not another word to say. The tide of opinion was shifting. Those who had been worked up to the lynching by the arguments of Bonfils began to resent his activity. Flandrau was their prisoner, wasn't he? No use going off half cocked. Some of them were discovering that they were not half so anxious to hang him as they had supposed.

The girl turned to her friends and neighbors. "I oughtn't to have talked to you that way, but you know how worried I am about Dad," she apologized with a catch in her breath. "I'm sure you didn't think or you would never have done anything to trouble me more just now. You know I didn't half mean it." She looked from one to another, her eyes shiny with tears. "I know that no braver or kinder men live than you. Why, you're my folks. I've been brought up among you. And so you've got to forgive me."

Some said "Sure," others told her to forget it, and one grass widower drew a laugh by saying that her little spiel reminded him of happier days.

For the first time a smile lit her face. The boy for whose life she was pleading thought it was like sunshine after a storm.

"I'm so glad you've changed your minds. I knew you would when you thought it over," she told them chattily and confidentially.

She was taking their assent for granted. Now she waited and gave them a chance to chorus their agreement. None of them spoke except Maloney. Most of them were with her in sympathy but none wanted to be first in giving way. Each wanted to save his face, so that the others could not later blame him for quitting first.

She looked around from one to another, still cheerful and sure of her ground apparently. Two steps brought her directly in front of one. She caught him by the lapels of his coat and looked straight into his eyes. "You *have* changed your mind, haven't you, Jake?"

The big Missourian twisted his hat in embarrassment. "I reckon I have, Miss Kate. Whatever the other boys say," he got out at last.

"Haven't you a mind of your own, Jake?"

"Sure. Whatever's right suits me."

"Well, you know what is right, don't you?"

"I expect."

"Then you won't hurt this man, our prisoner?"

"I haven't a thing against him if you haven't."

"Then you won't hurt him? You won't stand by and let the other boys do it?"

"Now, Miss Kate—"

She burst into sudden tears. "I thought you were my friend, but now I'm in trouble you—you think only of making it worse. I'm worried to death about Dad—and you—you make me stay here —away from him—and torment me."

Jake gave in immediately and the rest followed like a flock of sheep. Two or three of the promises came hard, but she did not stop till each one individually had pledged himself. And all the time she was cajoling them, explaining how good it was of them to think of avenging her father, how in one way she did not blame them at all, though of course they had seen it would not do as soon as they gave the matter a second thought. Dad would be so pleased at them when he heard about it, and she wanted them to know how much she liked and admired them. It was quite a love feast.

The young man she had saved could not keep his eyes from her. He would have liked to kneel down and kiss the edge of her dress and put his curly head in the dust before her. The ice in his heart had melted in the warmth of a great emotion. She was standing close to him talking to Buck when he spoke in a low voice.

"I reckon I can't tell you—how much I'm obliged to you, Miss."

She drew back quickly as if he had been a snake about to strike, her hand instinctively gathering her skirts so that they would not brush against him.

"I don't want your thanks," she told him, and her voice was like the drench of an icy wave.

But when she saw the hurt in his eyes she hesitated. Perhaps she guessed that he was human after all, for an impulse carried her forward to take the rope from his neck. While his heart beat twice her soft fingers touched his throat and grazed his cheek. Then she turned and was gone from the room.

It was a long time before the bunk house quieted. Curly, faint with weariness, lay down and tried to sleep. His arm was paining a good deal and he felt feverish. The men of the Circle C and their guests sat down and argued the whole thing over. But after a time the doctor came in and had the patient carried to the house. He was put in a good clean bed and his arm dressed again.

The doctor brought him good news. "Cullison is doing fine. He has dropped into a good sleep. He'd ought to make it all right."

Curly thought about the girl who had fought for his life.

"You'll not let him die, Doc," he begged.

"He's too tough for that, Luck Cullison is."

Presently Doctor Brown gave him a sleeping powder and left him. Soon after that Curly fell asleep and dreamed about a slim dark girl with fine longlashed eyes that could be both tender and ferocious.

CHAPTER IV

THE CULLISONS

Curly was awakened by the sound of the cook beating the call to breakfast on a triangle. Buck was standing beside the bed.

"How're they coming this glad mo'ning, son?" he inquired with a grin.

"Fine and dandy," grinned back Flandrau.

So he was, comparatively speaking. The pain in his arm had subsided. He had had a good sleep. And he was lying comfortably in a clean bed instead of hanging by the neck from the limb of one of the big cottonwoods on the edge of the creek.

A memory smote him and instantly he was grave again.

"How is Cullison?"

"Good as the wheat, doc says. Mighty lucky for Mr. C. Flandrau that he is. Say, I'm to be yore valley and help you into them clothes. Git a wiggle on you."

Buck escorted his prisoner over to the ranch mess house. The others had finished breakfast but Maloney was still eating. His mouth was full of

49

hot cakes, but he nodded across at Curly in a casual friendly way.

"How's the villain in the play this mo'ning?" he inquired.

Twenty-one usually looks on the cheerful side of life. Curly had forgotten for the moment about what had happened to his friend Mac. He did not remember that he was in the shadow of a penitentiary sentence. The sun was shining out of a deep blue sky. The vigor of youth flowed through his veins. He was hungry and a good breakfast was before him. For the present these were enough.

"Me, I'm feeling a heap better than I was last night," he admitted.

"Came pretty near losing him out of the cast, didn't we?"

"Might a-turned out that way if the stage manager had not remembered the right cue in time."

Curly was looking straight into the eyes twinkling across the table at him. Maloney knew that the young fellow was thanking him for having saved his life. He nodded lightly, but his words still seemed to make a jest of the situation.

"Enter the heroine. Spotlight. Sa-a-ved," he drawled.

The heart of the prisoner went out to this man who was reaching a hand to him in his trouble. He had always known that Maloney was true and steady as a snubbing post, but he had not looked for any kindness from him.

"Kite just got a telephone message from Saguache," the Bar Double M man went on easily. "Your friends that bought the rustled stock didn't get away with the goods. Seems they stumbled into a bunch of *rurales* unexpected and had to pull their freight sudden. The boys from the ranch happened along about then, claimed ownership and got possession."

"If the men bought the stock why didn't they stop and explain?" asked Buck.

"That game of buying stolen cattle is worn threadbare. The *rurales* and the rangers have had their eye on those border flitters for quite some time. So they figured it was safer to dust."

"Make their getaway?" Curly inquired as indifferently as he could. But in spite of himself a note of eagerness crept into his voice. For if the men had escaped that would be two less witnesses against him.

"Yep."

"Too bad. If they hadn't I could have proved by them I was not one of the men who sold them the stock," Flandrau replied.

"Like hell you could," Buck snorted, then grinned at his prisoner in a shamefaced way: "You're a good one, son."

"Luck has been breaking bad for me, but when things are explained——"

"It sure will take a lot of explaining to keep you out of the pen. You'll have to be slicker than Dutch was."

Jake stuck his head in at the door. "Buck, you're needed to help with them two-year-olds. The old man wants to have a talk with the rustler. Doc says he may. Maloney, will you take him up to the house? I'll arrange to have you relieved soon as I can."

Maloney had once ridden for the Circle C and was friendly with all the men on the place. He nodded. "Sure."

A Mexican woman let them into the chamber where the wounded man lay. It was a large sunny southeast room with French windows opening upon a long porch. Kate was bending over the bed rearranging the pillows, but she looked up quickly when the two men entered. Her eyes were still gentle with the love that had been shining down from them upon her father.

Cullison spoke. "Sit down, Dick." And to his prisoner: "You too."

Flandrau saw close at hand for the first time the man who had been Arizona's most famous fighting sheriff. Luck Cullison was well-built and of medium height, of a dark complexion, clean shaven, wiry and muscular. Already past fifty, he looked not a day more than forty. One glance was enough to tell Curly the kind of man this was. The power 'of him found expression in the gray steel-chilled eyes that bored into the young outlaw. A child could have told he was not one to trifle with.

"You have begun early, young fellow," he said quietly.

"Begun what?" Curly asked, having nothing better to say.

"You know what. But never mind that. I don't ask you to convict yourself. I sent for you to tell you I don't blame you for this." He touched the wound in his side.

"Different with your boys, sir."

"So the boys are a little excited, are they?"

"They were last night anyhow," Curly answered, with a glimmer of a smile.

Cullison looked quickly at Maloney and then at his daughter.

"I'll listen to what you've been hiding from me," he told them.

"Oh, the boys had notions. Miss Kate argued with them and they saw things different," the Bar Double M rider explained.

But Cullison would not let it go at that. He made them tell him the whole story. When Curly and Maloney had finished he buried his daughter's

53

little hand in his big brown fist. His eyes were dancing with pride, but he gave her not a word of spoken praise.

Kate, somewhat embarrassed, changed the subject briskly. "Now you're talking too much, Dad. Doctor Brown said you might see him for just a few minutes. But you're not to tire yourself, so I'll do the talking for you."

He took his orders with the smiling submission of the man who knows his mistress.

Kate spoke to Curly. "Father wants me to tell you that we don't blame you for shooting at him. We understand just how it was. Your friend got excited and shot as soon as he saw he was surrounded. We are both very sorry he was killed. Father could not stop the boys in time. Perhaps you remember that he tried to get you to surrender."

The rustler nodded. "Yes, I heard him holler to me to put my gun down, but the others blazed away at me."

"And so you naturally defended yourself. That's how we understand it. Father wants it made clear that he feels you could have done nothing else."

"Much obliged. I've been sorry ever since I hit him, and not only on my own account."

"Then none of us need to hold hard feelings." The girl looked at her father, who answered her appeal with a grim nod, and then she turned again to the young rustler a little timidly. "I wonder if you would mind if I asked you a question."

"You've earned the right to ask as many as you like."

"It's about—— We have been told you know the man they call Soapy Stone. Is that true?"

Flandrau's eyes took on a stony look. It was as if something had sponged all the boyishness from his face. Still trying to get him to give away his partners in the rustling, were they? Well, he would show them he could take his medicine without squealing.

"Maybe it is and maybe it isn't."

"Oh, but you don't see what we mean. It isn't that we want to hurt you." She spoke in a quick eager voice of protest.

"No, you just want me to squeal on my friends to save my own hide. Nothing doing, Miss Cullison."

"No. You're wrong. Why are you so suspicious?"

Curly laughed bitterly. "Your boys were asking that question about Soapy last night. They had a rope round my neck at the time. Nothing unfriendly in the matter, of course. Just a casual interest in my doings."

Cullison was looking at him with the steel eyes

that bored into him like a gimlet. Now he spoke sharply.

"I've got an account running with Soapy Stone. Some day I'll settle it likely. But that ain't the point now. Do you know his friends—the bunch he trails with?"

Wariness still seemed to crouch in the cool eyes of Flandrau.

"And if I say yes, I'll bet your next question will be about the time and the place I last saw them."

Kate picked up a photograph from the table and handed it to the prisoner. "We're not interested in his friends—except one of them. Did you ever see the boy that sat for that picture?"

The print was a snapshot of a boy about nineteen, a good looking handsome fellow, a little sulky around the mouth but with a pair of straight honest eyes.

Curly shook his head slowly. Yet he was vaguely reminded of someone he knew. Glancing up, he found instantly the clew to what had puzzled him. The young man in the picture was like Kate Cullison, like her father too for that matter.

"He's your brother." The words were out before Flandrau could stop them.

"Yes. You've never met him?"

"No."

Cullison had been watching the young man steadily. "Never saw him with Soapy Stone?"

"No."

"Never heard Stone speak of Sam Cullison?"

"No. Soapy doesn't talk much about who his friends are."

The ex-sheriff nodded. "I've met him."

Of course he had met him. Curly knew the story of how in one drive he had made a gather of outlaws that had brought fame to him. Soapy had broken through the net, but the sheriff had followed him into the hills alone and run him to earth. What passed between the men nobody ever found out. Stone had repeatedly given it out that he could not be taken alive. But Cullison had brought him down to the valley bound and cowed. In due season the bandits had gone over the road to Yuma. Soapy and the others had sworn to get their revenge some day. Now they were back in the hills at their old tricks. Was it possible that Cullison's son was with them, caught in a trap during some drunken frolic just as Curly had been? In what way could Stone pay more fully the debt of hate he owed the former sheriff than by making his son a villain?

The little doctor came briskly into the room.

"Everybody out but the nurse. You've had company enough for one day, Luck," he announced cheerily.

Kate followed Maloney and his prisoner to the porch.

"About the letters of your friend that was shot," she said to Curly. "Doctor Brown was telling me what you said. I'll see they reach Miss Anderson. Do you know in what restaurant she works?"

"No. Mac didn't tell me." The boy gulped to swallow an unexpected lump in his throat. "They was expecting to get married soon."

"I—I'll write to her," Kate promised, her eyes misty.

"I'd be obliged, Miss. Mac was a good boy. Anyone will tell you that. And he was awful fond of her. He talked about her that last night before the camp fire. I led him into this."

"I'll tell her what you say."

"Do. Tell her he felt bad about what he had done. Bad companions got him going wrong, but he sure would have settled down into a good man. That's straight goods, too. You write it strong."

The girl's eyes were shiny with tears. "Yes," she answered softly.

"I ain't any Harvard A. B. Writing letters ain't my long suit. I'm always disremembering whether a man had ought to say have went and have knew. Verbs are the beatingest things. But I know you'll fix it up right so as to let that little girl down easy."

"I've changed my mind. I'll not write but go to see her."

Curly could only look his thanks. Words seemed strangely inadequate. But Kate understood the boy's unspoken wish and nodded her head reassuringly as he left the room.

CHAPTER V

LAURA LONDON

Kite Bonfils and Maloney took Curly back to Saguache and turned him over to Sheriff Bolt.

"How about bail?" Maloney asked.

The sheriff smiled. He was a long lean leather-faced man with friendly eyes from which humorous wrinkles radiated.

"You honing to go bail for him, Dick?"

"How much?"

"Oh, say two thousand."

"You're on."

"What!"

A cowpuncher with fifty dollars two weeks after pay day was a rarity. No wonder Bolt was surprised.

"It's not my money. Luck Cullison is going bail for him," Maloney explained.

"Luck Cullison!" Maloney's words had surprised the exclamation from Curly. Why should the owner of the Circle C of all men go bail for him?

The sheriff commented dryly on the fact. "I thought this kid was the one that shot him."

"That was just a happenstance. Curly shot to save his bacon. Luck don't hold any grudge."

"So I should judge. Luck gave you his check, did he?"

Bolt belonged to the political party opposed to Cullison. He had been backed by Cass Fendrick, a sheepman in feud with the cattle interests and in particular with the Circle C outfit. But he could not go back on his word. He and Maloney called together on the district attorney. An hour later Dick returned to the jail.

"It's all right, kid," he told Curly. "You can shake off the dust of Saguache from your hoofs till court meets in September."

To Flandrau the news seemed too good for the truth. Less than twenty-four hours ago he had been waiting for the end of the road with a rope around his neck. Now he was free to slip a saddle on his pony Keno and gallop off as soon as he pleased. How such a change had been brought about he did not yet understand.

While he and Maloney were sitting opposite each other at the New Orleans Hash House waiting for a big steak with onions he asked questions.

"I don't savvy Cullison's play. Whyfor is he digging up two thousand for me? How does he know I won't cut my stick for Mexico?"

"How do I know it?"

"Well, do you?"

Maloney helped himself to the oyster crackers to pass the time. "Sure I do."

"How?"

"Search me. But I know you'll be here in September if you're alive and kicking."

Flandrau persisted. "But Luck don't owe me anything, except one pill sent promiscuous to his address. What's he going down into his jeans for? Will you tell me that? And shove them crackers north by east. Got to fill up on something."

"Ain't you as good a guesser as I am, Curly?"

"Well then, here's my guess. Miss Kate made him."

"I reckon maybe she influenced him. But why did she? You don't figure that curly topknot of yours is disturbing her dreams any, do you?"

"Quit your joshing and tell me why."

"I can't tell you for sure. But here's my guess. Don't cost you a cent if you ain't satisfied with it. First off, there was poor Mac shot by the Circle C boys. Course Mac was a horse thief, but then he was a kid too. That worried the little girl some. She got to thinking about brother Sam and how he might be in the same fix one of these days as you are now. He's on her mind a good deal, Sam is. Same way with the old man too, I reckon, though he don't say much. Well, she decided Soapy Stone had led you astray like he's doing with Sam.

It got to worrying her for fear her brother might need a friend some time. So she handed over her worry to the old man and made him dig up for you."

"That's about it. Tell me what you know of Sam. Is he as white as the rest of the family?"

"Sam is all right, but he has got off wrong foot first. He and the old man got to kind of disagreeing, for the kid was a wild colt. Come by it honestly from the old man too. Well, they had a row one time when Sam got into trouble. Luck told him he never wanted to see him again. Sam lit out, and next folks knew he was trailing with Soapy's gang. Consequence is, Sam's hitting the toboggan for Tophet by all accounts."

"Looks like some one ought to be able to pry him loose from that bunch," Curly mused aloud.

Maloney grinned across at him. "You try it, son. You've always led a good pious life. He sure would listen to you."

He had said it as a jest, but Curly did not laugh. Why not? Why shouldn't he hunt up Sam and let him know how his folks were worrying about him? What was to hinder him from trying to wipe out some of the big debt he owed the Cullison family? He was footloose till September and out of a job. For he could not go back to the Map of Texas with his hat in his hand and a repentant whine on his lips. Why not take a hike into the hills and round up the boy? Of course Sam might not listen to him, but he could not tell that till he had tried. It had taken him scarcely a moment to make up his mind. The smile had not yet died out of Maloney's eyes when he spoke.

"Damn if I don't take a crack at it."

The man on the other side of the table stared at him.

"Meaning that, are you?"

"Yep."

"Might be some lively if Soapy gets wise to your intentions," he said in a casual sort of way.

"I don't aim to declare them out loud."

That was all they said about it at the time. The rest of the evening was devoted to pleasure. After dinner they took in a moving picture show. The first film was a Western melodrama and it pleased them both immensely.

"I'd be afraid to live in a country where guns popped like they do in moving picture land," Curly drawled. "Where is it anyhow? It ain't Texas, nor Oklahoma, nor Wyoming, nor Montana, nor any of the spots in between, because I've been in all of them."

Maloney laughed. "Day before yesterday that's the way I'd a-talked my own self, but now I know better. What about your little stunt? Wasn't that

CROOKED TRAILS AND STRAIGHT

warm enough for you? Didn't guns pop enough? Don't you talk about moving pictures!"

After the picture show there were other things. But both of them trod the narrow path, Maloney because he was used to doing so and Flandrau because his experiences had sobered him.

"I'm on the water wagon, Dick." He grinned ruefully at his friend. "Nothing like locking the stable after your bronc's been stole. I'd a-been a heap better off if I'd got on the wagon a week ago."

Since their way was one for several miles Maloney and Curly took the road together next morning at daybreak. Their ponies ambled along side by side at the easy gait characteristic of the Southwest. Steadily they pushed into the brown baked desert. Little dust whirls in the shape of inverted cones raced across the sand wastes. The heat danced along the road in front of them in shimmering waves.

Your plainsman is a taciturn individual. These two rode for an hour without exchanging a syllable. Then Curly was moved to talk.

"Can you tell me how it is a man can get fond of so Godforsaken a country? Cactus and greasewood and mesquite, and for a change mesquite and greasewood and cactus! Nothing but sand washes and sand hills, except the naked mountains 'way off with their bones sticking through. But in the mo'ning like this, when the world's kind o'. smiley with the sunshine, or after dark when things are sorter violet soft and the mountains lose their edges—say, would you swap it for any other country on earth?"

Maloney nodded. He had felt that emotion a hundred times, though he had never put it into words.

At Willow Wash their ways diverged. They parted with a casual "So-long; see you later." Curly was striking for the headwaters of Dead Cow Creek, where Soapy Stone had a horse ranch.

He put up that night at the place of a nester in the foothills. His host looked at him curiously when he mentioned his destination, but he did not say anything. It was none of his business how many young fellows rode to Soapy's ranch.

Flandrau took the trail again next morning after breakfast. About two o'clock he reached a little park in the hills, in the middle of which, by a dry creek, lay a ranch.

The young man at first thought the place was deserted for the day, but when he called a girl appeared at the door. She smiled up at him with the lively interest any ranch girl may be expected to feel in a stranger who happens to be both young and good looking.

She was a young person of soft curves and engaging dimples. Beneath the brown cheeks of Arizona was a pink that came and went very attractively.

Curly took off his dusty gray hat. *"Buenos tardes, senorita!* I'll bet I'm too late to draw any dinner."

"Buenos, senor," she answered promptly. "I'll bet you'd lose your money."

He swung from the saddle. "That's good hearing. When a fellow has had his knees clamped to the side of a bronch for seven hours he's sure ready for the dinner bell."

"You can wash over there by the pump. There's a towel on the fence."

She disappeared into the house, and Curly took care of his horse, washed, and sauntered back to the porch. He could smell potatoes frying and could hear the sizzling of ham and eggs.

While he ate the girl flitted in and out, soft-footed and graceful, replenishing his plate from time to time.

Presently he discovered that her father was away hunting strays on Sunk Creek, that the nearest neighbor was seven miles distant, and that Stone's ranch was ten miles farther up Dead Cow.

"Ever meet a lad called Sam Cullison?" the guest asked carelessly.

Curly was hardly prepared to see the color whip into her cheeks or to meet the quick stabbing look she fastened on him.

"You're looking for him, are you?" she said.

"Thought while I was here I'd look him up. I know his folks a little."

"Do you know him?"

He shook his head. She looked at him very steadily before she spoke.

"You haven't met him yet but you want to. Is that it?"

"That's it."

"Will you have another egg?"

Flandrau laughed. "No, thanks. Staying up at Stone's, is he?"

"How should I know who's staying at Stone's?"

It was quite plain she did not intend to tell anything that would hurt young Cullison.

"Oh, well, it doesn't matter. I ain't lost him any to speak of," the young man drawled.

"Are you expecting to stop in the hills long— or just visiting?"

"Yes," Curly answered, with his most innocent blank wall look.

"Yes which?"

"Why, whichever you like, Miss London. What's worrying you? If you'll ask me plain out I'll know how to answer you."

"So you know my name?"

"Anything strange about that? The Bar 99 is the London brand. I saw your calves in the corral with their flanks still sore. Naturally I assume the young lady I meet here is Miss Laura London."

She defended her suspicions. "Folks come up here with their mysterious questions. A person would think nobody lived on Dead Cow but outlaws and such, to hear some of you valley people tell it."

"There's nothing mysterious about me and my questions. I'm just a lunkheaded cowpuncher out of a job. What did you think I was?"

"What do you want with Sam Cullison? Are you friendly to him? Or aren't you?"

"Ladies first. Are *you* friendly to him? Or aren't you?"

Curly smiled gaily across the table at her. A faint echo of his pleasantry began to dimple the corners of her mouth. It lit her eyes and spread from them till the prettiest face on the creek wrinkled with mirth. Both of them relaxed to peals of laughter, and neither of them quite knew the cause of their hilarity.

"Oh, you!" she reproved when she had sufficiently recovered.

"So you thought I was a detective or a deputy sheriff. That's certainly funny."

"For all I know yet you may be one."

"I never did see anyone with a disposition so dark-complected as yours. If you won't put them suspicions to sleep I'll have to table my cards." From his pocket he drew a copy of the Saguache Sentinel and showed her a marked story. "Maybe that will explain what I'm doing up on Dead Cow."

This was what Laura London read:

From Mesa comes the news of another case of bold and flagrant rustling. On Friday night a bunch of horses belonging to the Bar Double M were rounded up and driven across the mountains to this city. The stolen animals were sold here this morning, after which the buyers set out at once for the border and the thieves made themselves scarce. It is claimed that the rustlers were members of the notorious Soapy Stone outfit. Two of the four were identified, it is alleged, as William Cranston, generally known as "Bad Bill," and a young vaquero called "Curly" Flandrau.

At the time of going to press posses are out after both the outlaws and the stolen horses. Chances of overtaking both are considered excellent. All likely points and outlying ranches have been notified by telephone whenever possible.

In case the guilty parties are apprehended the *Sentinel* hopes an example will be made of them that will deter others of like stamp from a practice that has of late been far too common. Lawlessness seems to come in cycles. Just now the southern tier of counties appears to be suffering from such a sporadic attack. Let all good men combine to stamp it out. The time has passed when Arizona must stand as a synonym for anarchy.

She looked up at the young man breathlessly, her pretty lips parted, her dilated eyes taking him in solemnly. A question trembled on her lips.

"Say it," advised Flandrau.

The courage to ask what she was thinking came back in a wave. "Then I will. Are you a rustler?"

"That's what the paper says, don't it?"

"Are you this man mentioned here? What's his name—'Curly' Flandrau?"

"Yes."

"And you're a rustler?"

"What do you think? Am I more like a rustler than a deputy sheriff? Stands to reason I can't be both."

Her eyes did not leave him. She brushed aside his foolery impatiently. "You don't even deny it."

"I haven't yet. I expect I will later."

"Why do men do such things?" she went on, letting the hands that held the paper drop into her lap helplessly. "You don't look bad. Anyone would think——"

Her sentence tailed out and died away. She was still looking at Curly, but he could see that her mind had flown to someone else. He would have bet a month's pay that she was thinking of another lad who was wild but did not look bad.

Flandrau rose and walked round the table to her. "Much obliged, Miss Laura. I'll shake hands on that with you. You've guessed it. Course, me being so 'notorious' I hate to admit it, but I ain't bad any more than he is."

She gave him a quick shy look. He had made a center shot she was not expecting. But, woman-like, she did not admit it.

"You mean this 'Bad Bill'?"

"You know who I mean all right. His name is Sam Cullison. And you needn't to tell me where' he is. I'll find him."

"I know you don't mean any harm to him." But she said it as if she were pleading with him.

"C'rect. I don't. Can you tell me how to get to Soapy Stone's horse ranch from here, Miss London?"

She laughed. Her doubts were vanishing like mist before the sunshine. "Good guess. At least he was there the last I heard."

"And I expect your information is pretty recent."

That drew another little laugh accompanied by a blush.

"Don't you think I have told you enough for one day, Mr. Flandrau?"

"That 'Mr.' sounds too solemn. My friends call me 'Curly,' " he let her know.

She remembered that he was a stranger and a rustler and she drew herself up stiffly. This pleasant young fellow was too familiar.

"If you take this trail to the scrub pines above, then keep due north for about four miles, you'll strike the creek again. Just follow the trail along it to the horse ranch."

With that she turned on her heel and walked into the kitchen.

Curly had not meant to be "fresh." He was always ready for foolery with the girls, but he was not the sort to go too far. Now he blamed himself for having moved too fast. He had offended her sense of what was the proper thing.

There was nothing for it but to saddle and take the road.

CHAPTER VI

A BEAR TRAP

The winding trail led up to the scrub pines and from there north into the hills. Curly had not traveled far when he heard the sound of a gun fired three times in quick succession. He stopped to listen. Presently there came a faint far call for help.

Curly cantered around the shoulder of the hill and saw a man squatting on the ground. He was stooped forward in an awkward fashion with his back to Flandrau.

"What's up?"

At the question the man looked over his shoulder. Pain and helpless rage burned in the deep-set black eyes.

"Nothing at all. Don't you see I'm just taking a nap?" he answered quietly.

Curly recognized him now. The man was Soapy Stone. Behind the straight thin-lipped mouth a double row of strong white teeth were clamped tightly. Little beads of perspiration stood out all over his forehead. A glance showed the reason. One of his hands was caught in a bear trap fastened to a cottonwood. Its jaws held him so that he could not move.

The young man swung from the back of Keno. He found the limb of a cottonwood about as thick as his forearm below the elbow. This he set close to the trap.

"Soon as I get the lip open shove her in," he told Stone.

The prisoner moistened his dry lips. It was plain that he was in great pain.

The rescuer slipped the toes of his boots over the lower lip and caught the upper one with both hands. Slowly the mouth of the trap opened. Stone slipped in the wooden wedge and withdrew his crushed wrist. By great good fortune the steel had caught on the leather gauntlet he was wearing. Otherwise it must have mangled the arm to a pulp.

Even now he was suffering a good deal.

"You'll have to let a doc look at it," Curly suggested.

Stone agreed. "Reckon I better strike for the Bar 99." He was furious at himself for having let such an accident happen. The veriest tenderfoot might have known better.

His horse had disappeared, but Curly helped him to the back of Keno. Together they took the trail for the Bar 99. On the face of the wounded man gathered the moisture caused by intense pain. His jaw was clenched to keep back the groans.

"Hard sledding, looks like," Curly sympathized.

"Reckon I can stand the grief," Stone grunted.

Nor did he speak again until they reached the ranch and Laura London looked at him from a frightened face.

"What is it?"

"Ran a sliver in my finger, Miss Laura. Too bad to trouble you," Soapy answered with a sneer on his thin lips.

A rider for the Bar 99 had just ridden up and Laura sent him at once for the doctor. She led the way into the house and swiftly gathered bandages, a sponge, and a basin of water. Together she and Curly bathed and wrapped the wound. Stone did not weaken, though he was pretty gray about the lips.

Laura was as gentle as she could be.

"I know I'm hurting you," she said, her fingers trembling.

"Not a bit of it. Great pleasure to have you for a nurse. I'm certainly in luck." Curly did not understand the bitterness in the sardonic face and he resented it.

"If the doctor would only hurry," Laura murmured.

"Yes, I know I'm a great trouble. Too bad Curly found me."

She was busy with the knots of the outer wrapping and did not look up. "It is no trouble."

"I'm too meddlesome. Serves me right for being inquisitive about your father's trap."

"He'll be sorry you were caught."

"Yes. He'll have to climb the hill and reset it."

That something was wrong between them Curly could see. Soapy was very polite in spite of his bitterness, but his hard eyes watched her as a cat does a mouse. Moreover, the girl was afraid of him. He could tell that by the timid startled way she had of answering. Now why need she fear the man? It would be as much as his life was worth to lift a hand to hurt her.

After the doctor had come and had attended to the crushed wrist Curly stepped out to the porch to find Laura. She was watering her roses and he went across the yard to her.

"I'm right sorry for what I said, Miss Laura. Once in a while a fellow makes a mistake. If he's as big a chump as I am it's liable to happen a little oftener. But I'm not really one of those smart guys."

Out came her gloved hand in the firmest of grips.

"I know that now. You didn't think. And I made a mistake. I thought you were taking advantage because I had been friendly. I'm glad you spoke about it. We'll forget it."

"Then maybe we'll be friends after all, but I

77

"Reckon I can stand the gr█   Stone g█

Nor did he speak again u█   they rea█
ranch and Laura London lo█   █ at him
frightened face.

"What is it?"

"Ran a sliver in my fing█ Miss Laura.
bad to trouble you," Soapy █   ered with a
on his thin lips.

A rider for the Bar 99 h█ ust ridden u█
Laura sent him at once for th█ octor. She l█
way into the house and swif█ gathered band
a sponge, and a basin of wat█. Together she
Curly bathed and wrapped t█ wound. Stone
not weaken, though he was █etty gray about
lips.

Laura was as gentle as sh█ould be.

"I know I'm hurting you, she said, her █
trembling.

"Not a bit of it. Great p█sure █
a nurse. I'm certainly in
understand the bitterness █
he resented it.

"If the doctor w█
mured.

"Yes, I know I'n
found me."

She was busy █
ping and did not l

"How do you

he had been
ses.
ough him?"

and get him
once. And
s an Indian.
n him, folks

he make a

completely
e broke a
a girl. He
n't let me
the way
d, one
e who

e friend
r good?"

him con-

e in the

sha'n't tell you what my friends call me," he answered gaily.

She laughed out in a sudden bubbling of mirth. "Take care."

"Oh, I will. I won't even spell it."

He helped her with the watering. Presently she spoke, with a quick look toward the house.

"There's something I want to say."

"Yes."

"Something I want you to do for me."

"I expect maybe I'll do it."

She said nothing more for a minute, then the thing that was troubling her burst from the lips of the girl as a flame leaps out of a pent fire.

"It's about that boy he has up there." She gave a hopeless little gesture toward the hills.

"Sam Cullison?"

"Yes."

"What about him?"

"He's bent on ruining him, always has been ever since he got a hold on him. I can't tell you how I know it, but I'm sure—— And now he's more set on it than ever."

Curly thought he could guess why, but he wanted to make sure. "Because you are Sam's friend?"

The pink flooded her cheeks. "Yes."

"And because you won't be Soapy Stone's friend?"

78

She flashed a startled look at him. "How do you know?"

"Jealous, is he?"

Her face, buried in the blooms she had been cutting, was of the same tint as the roses.

"And so he wants to hurt you through him?" Flandrau added.

"Yes. If he can drag Sam down and get him into trouble he'll pay off two grudges at once. And he will too. You'll see. He's wily as an Indian. For that matter there is Apache blood in him, folks say."

"What about young Cullison? Can't he make a fight for himself?"

"Oh, you know how boys are. Sam is completely under this man's influence." Her voice broke a little. "And I can't help him. I'm only a girl. He won't listen to me. Besides, Dad won't let me have anything to do with him because of the way he's acting. What Sam needs is a man friend, one just as strong and determined as Soapy but one who is good and the right sort of an influence."

"Are you picking me for that responsible friend who is to be such a powerful influence for good?" Curly asked with a smile.

"Yes—yes, I am." She looked up at him confidently.

"Haven't you forgotten that little piece in the

79

Sentinel? How does it go? An example had ought to be made of the desperadoes, and all the rest of it."

"I don't care what it says. I've seen you."

"So had the editor."

She waved his jests aside. "Oh, well! You've done wrong. What of that? Can't I tell you are a man? And I don't care how much fun you make of me. You're good too."

Curly met her on the ground of her own serious-ness. "I'll tell you something, Miss Laura. Maybe you'll be glad to know that the reason I'm going to the horse ranch is to help Sam Cullison if I can."

He went on to tell her the whole story of what the Cullisons had done for him. In all that he said there was not one word to suggest such a thing, but Laura London's mind jumped the gaps to a knowledge of the truth that Curly himself did not have. The young man was in love with Kate Cullison. She was sure of it. Also, she was his ally in the good cause of romance.

When Curly walked back into the house, Stone laid down the paper he had been reading.

"'I see the *Sentinel* hints that Mr. Curly Flandrau had better be lynched," he jeered.

"The *Sentinel* don't always hit the bull's-eye, Soapy," returned the young man evenly. "It thinks

I belong to the Soapy Stone outfit, but we know I haven't that honor."

"There's no such outfit—not in the sense he means," snapped the man on the lounge. "What are your plans? Where you going to lie low? Picked a spot yet?"

"I don't know where I'm going, but I'm on the way," Curly assured him gaily.

Soapy frowned at him under the heavy eyebrows that gave him so menacing an effect.

"Better come back with me to the ranch till you look around."

"Suits me right down to the ground if it does you."

Someone came whistling into the house and opened the door of the room. He was a big lank fellow with a shotgun in his hands. "From Missouri" was stamped all over his awkward frame. He stood staring at his unexpected guests. His eyes, clashing with those of Stone, grew chill and hard.

"So you're back here again, are you?" he asked, looking pretty black.

Stone's lip smile mocked him. "I don't know how you guessed it, but I sure am here."

"Didn't I tell you to keep away from the Bar 99 —you and your whole cursed outfit?"

"Seems to me you did mention something of

that sort. But how was I to know whether you meant it unless I came back to see?"

Laura came into the room and ranged herself beside her father. Her hand rested lightly on his forearm.

"He got caught in one of your bear traps and this young man brought him here to wait for the doctor," she explained.

"Hmp!"

The Missourian stared without civility at his guest, turned on his heel, and with his daughter beside him marched out of the room. He could not decently tell Stone to leave while he was under the care of a doctor, but he did not intend to make him welcome. London was a blunt grizzled old fellow who said what he thought even about the notorious Soapy Stone.

"We'll pull our freights right away, Curly," Stone announced as soon as his host had gone.

The young man went to the stable and saddled Keno. While he was tightening the cinch a shadow fell across his shoulder. He did not need to look round to see whose it was.

"I'm so glad you're going to the horse ranch. You will look out for Sam. I trust you. I don't know why, but I have the greatest confidence in you," the owner of the shadow explained sweetly.

Curly smiled blandly over his shoulder at her.

"Fine! That's a good uplifting line of talk, Miss Laura. Now will you please explain why you're feeding me this particular bunch of taffy? What is it I'm to do for you?"

She blushed and laughed at the same time. Her hand came from behind her back. In it was a letter.

"But I do mean it, every word of it."

"That's to be my pay for giving Master Sam his billy doo, is it?"

"How did you guess? It *is* a letter to Sam."

"How did I guess it? Shows I'm sure a wiz, don't it?"

She saw her father coming and handed him the letter quickly.

"Here. Take it." A spark of mischief lit her eye and the dimples came out on her cheeks. "Good-by, *Curly*."

CHAPTER VII

BAD MEDICINE

The house at the horse ranch was a long, low L-shaped adobe structure. The first impression Curly received was that of negligence. In places the roof sagged. A door in the rear hung from one hinge. More than one broken pane of glass was stuffed with paper. The same evidence of shiftlessness could be seen on every hand. Fences had collapsed and been repaired flimsily. The woodwork of the well was rotting. The windmill wheezed and did its work languidly for lack of oil.

Two men were seated on the porch playing seven up. One was Bad Bill, the other Blackwell. At sight of Curly they gave up their game.

"Hello, kid! Where did you drop from?" Cranston asked.

A muscle twitched in Flandrau's cheek. "They got Mac."

"Got him! Where? At Saguache?"

"Ran us down near the Circle C. Mac opened fire. They—killed him."

"Shot him, or——?" Curly was left to guess the other half of the question.

"Shot him, and took me prisoner."

"They couldn't prove a thing, could they?"

"They could prove I wounded Cullison. That was enough for them. They set out to hang me. Later they changed their minds."

"How come you here? Did you escape?"

"Nope. Friends dug up bail."

Cranston did not ask what friends. He thought he knew. Alec Flandrau, an uncle of Curly, owned a half interest in the Map of Texas ranch. No doubt he had come to the aid of the young scapegoat.

"I'll bet the old man was sore at having to ante," was Big Bill's comment.

"Say, Soapy has been telling me that the Cullison kid is up here. I reckon we better not say anything about my mixup with his folks. I'm not looking for any trouble with him."

"All right, Curly. That goes with me. How about you, Blackwell?"

"Sure. What Sam don't know won't hurt him."

Curly sat down on the porch and told an edited story of his adventures to them. Before he had finished a young fellow rode up and dismounted. He had a bag of quail with him which he handed over to the Mexican cook. After he had unsaddled and turned his pony into a corral he joined the card players on the porch.

By unanimous consent the game was changed to poker. Young Cullison had the chair next to Flandrau. He had, so Curly thought, a strong family resemblance to his father and sister. "His eye jumps straight at you and asks its questions right off the reel," the newcomer thought. Still a boy in his ways, he might any day receive the jolt that would transform him into a man.

The cook's "Come and get it" broke up the game for a time. They trooped to supper, where for half an hour they discussed without words fried quail, cornbread and coffee. Such conversation as there was held strictly to necessary lines and had to do with the transportation of edibles.

Supper over, they smoked till the table was cleared. Then coats were removed and they sat down to the serious business of an all night session of draw.

Curly was not playing to win money so much as to study the characters of those present. Bill he knew already fairly well as a tough nut to crack, game to the core, and staunch to his friends. Blackwell was a bad lot, treacherous, vindictive, slippery as an eel. Even his confederates did not trust him greatly. But it was Soapy Stone and young Cullison that interested Flandrau most. The former played like a master. He chatted carelessly, but he overlooked no points. Sam had the qualities that

86

go to make a brilliant erratic player, but he lacked the steadiness and the finesse of the veteran.

The last play before they broke up in the gray dawn was a flashlight on Stone's cool audacity. The limit had long since been taken off. Blackwell and Stone had been the winners of the night, and the rest had all lost more or less.

Curly was dealing. Cranston opened the pot.

"She's cracked," he announced.

Blackwell, sitting next to him, had been waiting his turn with palpable eagerness. "Got to boost her, boys, to protect Bill," he explained as his raise went in.

Sam, who had drunk more than was good for him, raised in his turn. "Kick her again, gentlemen. Me, I'm plumb tired of that little song of mine, 'Good here'."

Stone stayed. Curly did not come in.

Cranston showed his openers and laid down his hand. Blackwell hesitated, then raised again.

"Reckon I'm content to trail along," Cullison admitted, pushing in the necessary chips.

Soapy rasped his stubby chin, looked sideways at Sam and then at Blackwell, and abruptly shoved in chips enough to call the raise.

"Cards?" asked Curly.

"I'll play these," Blackwell announced.

Sam called for two and Stone one.

Blackwell raised. Sam, grumbling, stayed.

"Might as well see what you've got when I've gone this far," he gave as a reason for throwing good money after bad.

Soapy took one glance at his new card and came in with a raise.

Blackwell slammed his fist down on the table. "Just my rotten luck. You've filled."

Stone smiled, then dropped his eyes to his cards. Suddenly he started. What had happened was plain. He had misread his hand.

With a cheerful laugh Blackwell raised in his turn.

"Lets me out," Sam said.

For about a tenth of a second one could see triumph ride in Soapy's eyes. "Different here," he explained in a quiet businesslike way. All his chips were pushed forward to the center of the table.

On Blackwell's face were mapped his thoughts. Curly saw his stodgy mind working on the problem, studying helplessly the poker eyes of his easy placid enemy. Was Soapy bluffing? Or had he baited a hook for him to swallow? The faintest glimmer of amusement drifted across the face of Stone. He might have been a general whose plans have worked out to suit him, waiting confidently for certain victory. The longer the convict looked at him the surer he was that he had been trapped.

88

With an oath he laid down his hand. "You've got me beat. Mine is only a jack high straight."

Stone put down his cards and reached for the pot.

Curly laughed.

Blackwell whirled on him.

"What's so condemned funny?"

"The things I notice."

"Meaning?"

"That I wouldn't have laid down my hand."

"Betcher ten plunks he had me beat."

"You're on." Curly turned to Soapy. "Object to us seeing your hand?"

Stone was counting his chips. He smiled. "It ain't poker, but go ahead. Satisfy yourselves."

"You turn the cards," Flandrau said.

A king of diamonds showed first, then a ten-spot and a six-spot of the same suit.

"A flush," exulted Blackwell.

"I've got just one more ten left, but it says you're wrong."

The words were not out of Curly's mouth before the other had taken the bet. Soapy looked at Flandrau with a new interest. Perhaps this boy was not such a youth as he had first seemed.

The fourth card turned was a king of hearts, the last a six of spades. Stone had had two pair to go on and had not bettered at the draw.

Blackwell tossed down two bills and went away furious.

That night was like a good many that followed. Sam was at an impressionable age, inclined to be led by any man whom he admired. Curly knew that he could gain no influence over him by preaching. He had to live the rough-and-tumble life of these men who dwelt beyond the pale of the law, to excel them at the very things of which they boasted. But in one respect he held himself apart. While he was at the horse ranch he did not touch a drop of liquor.

Laura London's letter was not delivered until the second day, for, though she had not told her messenger to give it to Sam when he was alone, Curly guessed this would be better. The two young men had ridden down to Big Tree spring to get quail for supper.

"Letter for you from a young lady," Flandrau said, and handed it to Cullison.

Sam did not read his note at once, but put it in his pocket carelessly, as if it had been an advertisement. They lay down in the bushes about twenty yards apart, close to the hole where the birds flew every evening to water. Hidden by the mesquite, Sam ran over his letter two or three times while he was waiting. It was such a message as any brave-hearted, impulsive girl might send to the man she loved when he seemed to her to walk in danger.

Cullison loved her for the interest she took in him, even while he ridiculed her fears.

Presently the quails came by hundreds on a bee-line for the water hole. They shot as many as they needed, but no more, for neither of them cared to kill for pleasure.

As they rode back to the ranch, Curly mentioned that he had seen Sam's people a day or two before.

Cullison asked no questions, but he listened intently while the other told the story of his first rustling and of how Miss Kate and her father had stood by him in his trouble. The dusk was settling over the hills by this time, so that they could not see each other's faces clearly.

"If I had folks like you have, the salt of the earth, and they were worrying their hearts out about me, seems to me I'd quit helling around and go back to them," Curly concluded.

"The old man sent you to tell me that, did he?" Hard and bitter came the voice of the young man out of the growing darkness.

"No, he didn't. He doesn't know I'm here. But he and your sister have done more for me than I ever can pay. That's why I'm telling you this."

Sam answered gruffly, as a man does when he is moved. "Much obliged, Curly, but I reckon I can look out for myself."

"Just what *I* thought, and in September I have to

go to the penitentiary. Now I have mortgaged it away, my liberty seems awful good to me."

"You'll get off likely."

"Not a chance. They've got me cinched. But with you it's different. You haven't fooled away your chance yet. There's nothing to this sort of life. The bunch up here is no good. Soapy don't mean right by you, or by any young fellow he trails with."

"I'll not listen to anything against Soapy. He took me in when my own father turned against me."

"To get back at your father for sending him up the road."

"That's all right. He has been a good friend to me. I'm not going to throw him down."

"Would it be throwing him down to go back to your people?"

"Yes, it would. We've got plans. Soapy is re-lying on me. No matter what they are, but I'm not going to lie down on him. And I'm not going back to the old man. He told me he was through with me. Once is a-plenty. I'm not begging him to take me back, not on your life."

Curly dropped the matter. To urge him fur-ther would only make the boy more set in his de-cision. But as the days passed he kept one thing in his mind, not to miss any chance to win his

HE WAS THE MADDEST MAN IN ARIZONA

friendship. They rode together a good deal, and Flandrau found that Sam liked to hear him talk about the Circle C and its affairs. But often he was discouraged, for he made no progress in weaning him from his loyalty to Stone. The latter was a hero to him, and gradually he was filling him with wrong ideas, encouraging him the while to drink a great deal. That the man had some definite purpose Curly was sure. What it was he meant to find out.

Meanwhile he played his part of a wild young cow-puncher ready for any mischief, but beneath his obtuse good humor Flandrau covered a vigilant wariness. Soapy held all the good cards now, but if he stayed in the game some of them would come to him. Then he would show Mr. Stone whether he would have everything his own way.

CHAPTER VIII

A REHEARSED QUARREL

Because he could not persuade him to join in their drinking bouts, Stone nicknamed Curly the good bad man.

"He's the prize tough in Arizona, only he's promised his ma not to look on the wine when it is red," Blackwell sneered.

Flandrau smiled amiably, and retorted as best he could. It was his cue not to take offence unless it were necessary.

It was perhaps on account of this good nature that Blackwell made a mistake. He picked on the young man to be the butt of his coarse pleasantries. Day after day he pointed his jeers at Curly, who continued to grin as if he did not care.

When the worm turned, it happened that they were all sitting on the porch. Curly was sewing a broken stirrup leather. Blackwell had a quirt in his hand, and from time to time flicked it at the back of his victim. Twice the lash stung, not hard, but with pepper enough to hurt. Each time the young man asked him to stop.

Blackwell snapped the quirt once too often.

When he picked himself out of the dust five seconds later, he was the maddest man in Arizona. Like a bull he lowered his head and rushed. Curly side-stepped and lashed out hard with his left.

The convict whirled, shook the hair out of his eyes, and charged again. It was a sledge-hammer bout, with no rules except to hit the other man often and hard. Twice Curly went down from chance blows, but each time he rolled away and got to his feet before his heavy foe could close with him. Blackwell had no science. His arms went like flails. Though by sheer strength he kept Flandrau backing, the latter hit cleaner and with more punishing effect.

Curly watched his chance, dodged a wild swing, and threw himself forward hard with his shoulder against the chest of the convict. The man staggered back, tripped on the lowest step of the porch, and went down hard. The fall knocked the breath out of him.

"Had enough?" demanded Curly.

For answer Blackwell bit his thumb savagely.

"Since you like it so well, have another taste." Curly, now thoroughly angry, sent a short-arm jolt to the mouth.

The man underneath tried to throw him off, but Flandrau's fingers found his hairy throat and tight-

"You're killing me," the convict gasped.

"Enough?"

"Y-yes."

Curly stepped back quickly, ready either for a knife or a gunplay. Blackwell got to his feet, and glared at him.

"A man is like a watermelon; you can't most generally tell how good he is till you thump him," Sam chuckled.

Cranston laughed. "Curly was not so ripe for picking as you figured, Lute. If you'd asked me, I could a-told you to put in yore spare time letting him alone. But a fellow has to buy his own experience."

The victor offered his hand to Blackwell. "I had a little luck. We'll call it quits if you say so."

"I stumbled over the step," the beaten man snarled.

"Sure. I had all the luck."

"Looked to me like you were making yore own luck, kid," Bad Bill differed.

The paroled convict went into the house, swearing to get even. His face was livid with fury.

"You wouldn't think a little thing like a whaling) given fair and square would make a man hold a grudge. My system has absorbed se-ve-real without doing it any harm." Sam stooped to inspect a rapidly discoloring eye. "Say, Curly, he hung a peach of a lamp on you."

Soapy made no comment in words, but he looked at Flandrau with a new respect. For the first time a doubt as to the wisdom of letting him stay at the ranch crossed his mind.

His suspicion was justified. Curly had been living on the edge of a secret for weeks. Mystery was in the air. More than once he had turned a corner to find the other four whispering over something. The group had disintegrated at once with a casual indifference that did not deceive. Occasionally a man had ridden into the yard late at night for private talk with Stone, and Curly was morally certain that the man was the little cowpuncher Dutch of the Circle C.

Through it all Curly wore a manner of open confidence. The furtive whisperings did not appear to arouse his curiosity, nor did he intercept any of the knowing looks that sometimes were exchanged. But all the time his brain was busy with questions. What were they up to? What was it they had planned?

Stone and Blackwell rode away one morning. To Curly the word was given that they were going to Mesa. Four days later Soapy returned alone. Lute had found a job, he said.

"That a paper sticking out of your pocket?" Flandrau asked.

Soapy, still astride his horse, tossed the *Saguache Sentinel* to him as he turned toward the stable.

"Lie number one nailed," Curly said to himself. "How came he with a Saguache paper if he's been to Mesa?"

Caught between the folds of the paper was a raiload time table. It was a schedule of the trains of the Texas, Arizona & Pacific for July. This was the twenty-ninth of June. Certainly Soapy had lost no time getting the new folder as soon as it was issued. Why? He might be going traveling. If so, what had that to do with the mystery agitating him and his friends?

Curly turned the pages idly till a penciled marking caught his eye. Under Number 4's time was scrawled, just below Saguache, the word Tin Cup, and opposite it the figures 10:19. The express was due to leave Saguache at 9:57 in the evening. From there it pushed up to the divide and slid down with air brakes set to Tin Cup three thousand feet lower. Soapy could not want to catch the train fifteen miles the other side of Saguache. But this note on the margin showed that he was interested in the time it reached the water tank. There must be a reason for it.

Stone came back hurriedly from the corral, to find Curly absorbed in the *Sentinel*.

"Seen anything of a railroad folder? I must a-dropped it."

"It was stuck in the paper. I notice there's liable to be trouble between Fendrick and the cattle in, terests over his sheep," the reader answered casually.

"Yep. Between Fendrick and Cullison, anyhow." Stone had reclaimed and pocketed his time table.

Incidentally Flandrau's doubt had been converted into a lively suspicion. Presently he took a gun, and strolled off to shoot birds. What he really wanted was to be alone so that he could think the matter over. Coming home in the dusk, he saw Stone and young Cullison with their heads together down by the corral. Curious to see how long this earnest talk would last, Curly sat down on a rock, and watched them, himself unobserved. They appeared to be rehearsing some kind of a scene, of which Soapy was stage director.

The man on the rock smiled grimly. "They're having a quarrel, looks like. . . . Now the kid's telling Soapy to go to Guinea, and Soapy's pawing around mad as a bull moose. It's all a play. They don't mean it. But why? I reckon this dress rehearsal ain't for the calves in the corral."

Curly's mind was so full of guesses that his poker was not up to par that night. About daybreak he began to see his way into the maze. His first gleam of light was when a row started between Soapy and Cullison. Before anyone could say a word to stop them they were going through with that identical corral quarrel.

Flandrau knew now they had been preparing it for his benefit. Cranston chipped in against Sam, and to keep up appearances Curly backed the boy. The quarrel grew furious. At last Sam drove his fist down on the table and said he was through with the outfit and was going back to Saguache.

"Yo tambien," agreed Curly. "Not that I've got anything against the horse ranch. That ain't it. But I'm sure pining for to bust the bank at Bronson's.

> 'Round and round the little ball goes,
> Where it will land nobody knows.'

I've got forty plunks burning my jeans. I've got to separate myself from it or make my roll a thousand."

The end of it was that both Sam and Curly went down to the corral and saddled their ponies. To the last the conspirators played up to their parts.

"Damned good riddance," Stone called after them as they rode away.

"When I find out I'm doing business with four-flushers, I quit them cold," Sam called back angrily.

Curly was amused. He wanted to tell his friend that they had pulled off their little play very well. But he did not.

Still according to program, Sam sulked for the first few miles of their journey. But before they reached the Bar 99 he grew sunny again.

"I'm going to have a talk with Laura while I'm so near," he explained.

"Yes, that will be fine. From the way the old man talked when I was there, I expect he'll kill the fatted yearling for you."

"I don't figure on including the old man in my call. What's the use of having a friend along if you don't use him? You drift in . . . just happen along, you know. I'll stay in the scrub pines up here. If the old man is absent scenery, you wave your bandanna real industrious. If he is at home, give Laura the tip and she'll know where to find me."

The owner of the ranch, as it happened, was cutting trail over by Agua Caliente.

"Do you want to see him very bad, Mr. Flandrau?" asked Miss Laura demurely.

"My friends call me Curly."

"I meant to say Curly."

"That's what I thought. No, I can't say I've lost Mr. London."

"You inquired for him."

"Hmp! That's different. When I used to come home from the swimming hole contrary to orders, I used to ask where Dad was, but I didn't want to see him."

"I see. Did you just come down from the horse ranch?"

"You've guessed it right."

"Then I'm sorry I can't ask you to 'light. Dad's orders."

"You've got lots of respect for his orders, haven't you?" he derided.

"Yes, I have." She could not quite make up her mind whether to laugh or become indignant.

"Then there's no use trying to tell you the news from the ranch."

A smile dimpled her cheeks and bubbled in her eyes. "If you should tell me, I suppose I couldn't help hearing."

"But I'm trying to figure out my duty. Maybe I oughtn't to tempt you."

"While you're making up your mind, I'll run back into the kitchen and look at the pies in the oven."

Curly swung from the saddle, and tossed the bridle rein to the ground. He followed her into the house. She was taking an apple pie from the oven, but took time to be saucy over her shoulder.

"I'm not allowed to invite you into the house, sir."

"Anything in the by-laws about me inviting myself in?"

"No, that wasn't mentioned."

"Anything in them about you meeting one of the lads from the horse ranch up on the hillside where it is neutral ground?"

"Did Sam come with you?" she cried.

"Who said anything about Sam?"

Glints of excitement danced in the brown pupils of her eyes. "He's here. Oh, I know he's here."

"What do I get for bringing good news?"

"I didn't say it was good news."

"Sho! Your big eyes are shouting it."

"Was that the news from the horse ranch?"

"That's part of it, but there is more. Sam and Curly are on their way to Saguache to spend the Fourth of July. Sam is going for another reason, but I'm not sure yet what it is."

"You mean——?"

"There's something doing I don't *savez,* some big deal on foot that's not on the level. Sam is in it up to the hocks. To throw me off the scent they fixed up a quarrel among them. Sam is supposed to be quitting Soapy's outfit for good. But I know better."

White to the lips, she faced him bravely. "What sort of trouble is he leading Sam into?"

"I've got a kind of a notion. But it won't bear talking about yet. Don't you worry, little girl. I'm going to stand by Sam. And don't tell him what I've told you, unless you want to spoil my chance of helping him."

"I won't," she promised; then added, with quick eagerness: "Maybe I can help you. I'm going down to Saguache to visit on the fourth. I'm to be there two weeks."

"I'll look you up. Trouble is that Sam is hell bent on ruining himself. Seems to think Soapy is his best friend. If we could show him different things might work out all right."

While she climbed the hill to Sam, Curly watered his horse and smoked a cigarette. He was not hired to chaperone lovers. Therefore, it took him three-quarters of an hour to reach the scrub pine belt on the edge of the park.

At once he saw that they had been having a quarrel. The girl's eyes were red, and she was still dabbing at them with her handkerchief when he came whistling along. Sam looked discouraged, but stubborn. Very plainly they had been disagreeing about his line of conduct.

The two young men took the trail again. The moroseness of Sam was real and not affected this time. He had flared up because the girl could not let him alone about his friendship for Soapy Stone. In his heart the boy knew he was wrong, that he was moving fast in the wrong direction. But his pride would neither let him confess it or go back on his word to the men with whom he had been living.

About noon the next day they reached Saguache. After they had eaten, Curly strolled off by himself to the depot.

"Gimme a ticket to Tin Cup for this evening. I want to go by the express," he told the agent.

The man looked at him and grinned. "I saw you at Mesa in the bucking broncho doings last year, didn't I?"

"Maybe you did and maybe you didn't. Why?"

"You certainly stay with the bad bronchs to a fare-you-well. If I'd been judge you'd a-had first place, Mr. Flandrau."

"Much obliged. And now you've identified me sufficient, how about that ticket?"

"I was coming to that. Sure you can get a ticket. Good on any train. You're so darned active, maybe you could get off Number 4 when she is fogging along sixty miles per. But most folks couldn't, not with any comfort."

"Meaning that the Flyer doesn't stop?"

"Not at Tin Cup."

"Have to take the afternoon train then?"

"I reckon." He punched a ticket and shoved it through the window toward Curly. "Sixty-five cents, please."

Flandrau paid for and pocketed the ticket he did not intend to use. He had found out what he wanted to know. The express did not stop at Tin Cup. Why, then, had Soapy marked the time of its arrival there? He was beginning to guess the reason. But he would have to do more than guess.

Curly walked back to the business section from the depot. Already the town was gay with banners in preparation for the Fourth. On the program were broncho-busting, roping, Indian dances, races, and other frontier events. Already visitors were gathering for the festivities. Saguache, wide open for the occasion, was already brisk with an assorted population of many races. Mexicans, Chinese, Indians of various tribes brushed shoulders with miners, tourists and cattlemen. Inside the saloons faro, chuckaluck and roulette attracted each its devotees.

Flandrau sauntered back to the hotel on the lookout for Sam. He was not there, but waiting for him was a boy with a note for the gentleman in Number 311.

"Kid looking for you," the clerk called to the cow-puncher.

"Are you Mr. Soapy Stone's friend, the one just down from Dead Cow creek?" asked the boy.

Taken as a whole, the answer was open to debate. But Curly nodded and took the note.

This was what he read:

> Sam, come to Chalkeye's place soon as you get this. There we will talk over the business.
>
> You Know Who.

Though he did not know who, Curly thought he could give a pretty good guess both as to the author and the business that needed talking over.

Through the open door of the hotel he saw Sam approaching. Quickly he sealed the flap of the envelope again, and held it pressed against his fingers while he waited.

"A letter for you, Sam."

Cullison tore open the envelope and read the note.

"A friend of mine has come to town and wants to see me," he explained.

To help out his bluff, Curly sprang the feeble-minded jest on him. "Blonde or brunette?"

"I'm no lady's man," Sam protested, content to let the other follow a wrong scent.

"Sure not. It never is a lady," Flandrau called after him as he departed.

But Sam had no more than turned the corner before Curly was out of a side door and cutting through an alley toward Chalkeye's place. Reaching the back door of the saloon, he opened it a few inches and peered in. A minute later Sam opened the front screen and asked a question of the man in the apron. The bartender gave a jerk of his thumb. Sam walked toward the rear and turned in at the second private booth.

Curly slipped forward quietly, and passed unobserved into the third stall. The wall which divided one room from another was of pine boarding and did not reach the ceiling. As the eavesdropper slid to a seat a phonograph in front began the Merry Widow waltz. Noiselessly Flandrau stood on the cushioned bench with his ear close to the top of the dividing wall. He could hear a murmur of voices but could not make out a word. The record on the instrument wheezed to silence, but immediately a rag-time tune followed.

Presently the music died away. Flattened against

the wall, his attention strained to the utmost, Curly began to catch words and phrases of the low-voiced speakers in the next compartment. His position was perilous in the extreme, but he would not leave now until he had found out what he wanted to know.

CHAPTER IX

EAVESDROPPING

Out of the murmur of voices came one that Curly recognized as that of Soapy Stone, alias You Know Who.

"......then you'll take the 9:57, Sam......"

After more whispering, "Yep, soon as you hear the first shot......cover the passengers......"

The listener lost what followed. Once he thought he heard the name Tin Cup, but he could not be sure. Presently another fragment drifted to him. "......make our getaway and cache the plunder ......"

The phonograph lifted up its voice again. This time it was "I love a lassie." Before the song was finished there came the sound of shuffling feet. One of the men in the next stall was leaving. Curly could not tell which one, nor did he dare look over the top of the partition to find out. He was playing safe. This adventure had caught him so unexpectedly that he had not found time to run back to his room for his six-gun. What would happen to him if he were caught listening was not a matter of doubt.   Soapy would pump lead into him till hᴶ quit kicking, slap a saddle on a broncho, and light out for the Sonora line.

As the phonograph finished unexpectedly—some-one had evidently interrupted the record—the frag-ment of a sentence seemed to jump at Curly.

".....so the kid will get his in the row."

It was the voice of Soapy, raised slightly to make itself heard above the music.

"Take care," another voice replied, and Flandrau would have sworn that this belonged to Blackwell.

Stone, who had been sitting on the other side of the table, moved close to the paroled convict.   Be-tween him and Curly there was only the thickness of a plank.   The young man was afraid that the knocking of his heart could be heard.

".....don't like it," Blackwell was objecting sullenly.

"Makes it safe for us.   Besides"—Stone's voice grated like steel rasping steel, every word distinct though very low—"I swore to pay off Luck Culli-son, and by God! I'm going to do it."

"Someone will hear you if you ain't careful," the convict protested anxiously.

"Don't be an old woman, Lute."

".....if you can do it safe.   I owe Luck Culli-son much as you do, but....."

Again they fell to whispers.   The next word that

III

came to Curly clearly was his own name. But it was quite a minute before he gathered what they were saying.

"Luck Cullison went his bail. I learnt it this mo'ning."

"The son-of-a-gun. It's a cinch he's a spy. And me wanting you to let him in so's he could hold the sack instead of Sam."

"Knew it wouldn't do, Lute. He's smart as a whip."

"Reckon he knows anything?"

"No. Can't."

"If I thought he did——"

"Keep your shirt on, Lute. He don't know a thing. And you get revenge on him all right. Sam will run with him and his friends while he's here. Consequence is, when they find the kid where we leave him they'll sure guess Curly for one of his pardners. Tell you his ticket is good as bought to Yuma. He's a horse thief. Why shouldn't he be a train robber, too. That's how a jury will argue."

Blackwell grumbled something under his breath.

Stone's voice grated harshly. "Me too. If he crosses my trail I'm liable to spoil his hide before court meets. No man alive can play me for a sucker and throw me down. Not Soapy Stone."

Once more the voices ran together indistinctly.

It was not till Blackwell suggested that they go get a drink that Curly understood anything more of what was being said.

The outlaws passed out of the little room and strolled forward to the bar.

Curly had heard more than he had expected to. Moreover, as he congratulated himself, his luck had stood up fine. Nobody in the sunburnt territory felt happier than he did that minute when he struck the good fresh air of the alley and knew that he had won through his hazardous adventure alive.

The first thing that Flandrau did was to walk toward the outskirts of the town where he could think it out by himself. But in this little old planet events do not always occur as a man plans them. Before he reached Arroyo street Curly came plump against his old range-mate Slats Davis.

The assistant foreman of the Hashknife nodded as he passed. He had helped Curly escape less than a month before, but he did not intend to stay friendly with a rustler.

Flandrau caught him by the arm. "Hello, Slats. You're the man I want."

"I'm pretty busy to-day," Davis answered stiffly.

"Forget it. This is more important."

"Well?"

"Come along and take a walk. I got something to tell you."

"Can't you tell it here?"

"I ain't going to, anyhow. Come along. I ain't got smallpox."

Reluctantly Davis fell in beside him. "All right. Cut it short. I've got to see a man."

"He'll have to wait." Curly could not help chuckling to himself at the evident embarrassment of the other. The impish impulse to "devil" him had its way. "You're a man of experience, Slats. Ever hold up a train?"

The foreman showed plainly his disgust at this foolishness. "Haven't you sense enough ever to be serious, Curly? You're not a kid any more. In age you're a grown man. But how do you act? Talk like that don't do you any good. You're in trouble good and deep. Folks have got their eyes on you. Now is the time to show them you have quit all that hell raising you have been so busy at."

"He sure is going good this mo'ning," Curly drawled confidentially to the scenery. "You would never guess, would you, that him and me had raised that crop in couples?"

"That's all right, too. I'm no sky pilot. But I know when to quit. Seemingly you don't. I hear you've been up at Stone's horse ranch. I want to tell you that won't do you any good if it gets out."

"Never was satisfied till I had rounded up all the trouble in sight. That's why I mentioned this train robbery. Some of my friends are aiming to hold up one shortly. If you'd like to get in I'll say a good word for you."

Davis threw at him a look that drenched like ice water. "I expect you and me are traveling different trails these days, Curly. You don't mean it of course, but the point is I'm not going to joke with you along that line. Understand?"

"Wrong guess, old hoss. I do mean it."

Davis stopped in his tracks. "Then you've said too much to me. We'll part right here."

"It takes two to agree to that, Slats."

"That's where you're wrong. One is enough. We used to be good friends, but those days are past. None of us can keep a man from being a durned fool if he wants to be one. Nor a scoundrel. You've got the bit in your teeth and I reckon you'll go till there is a smash. But you better understand this. When you choose Soapy Stone's crowd to run with that cuts out me and other decent folks. If they have sent you here to get me mixed up in their deviltry you go back and tell them there's nothing doing."

"Won't have a thing to do with them. Is that it?"

"Not till the call comes for citizens to get together and run them out of the country. Or to put them behind bars. Or to string them to a cottonwood. Then I'll be on the job."

He stood there quiet and easy, the look in his steady eyes piercing Curly's ironic smile as a summer sun does mackerel clouds in a clear sky. Not many men would have had the courage to send that message to Soapy and his outfit. For Stone was not only a man killer, but a mean one at that. Since he had come back from the penitentiary he had been lying pretty low, but he brought down from the old days a record that chilled the blood.

Curly sloughed his foolishness and came to the point.

"You're on, Slats. I'm making that call to you now."

The eyes of the two men fastened. Those of Flandrau had quit dancing and were steady as the sun in a blue sky. Surprise, doubt, wonder, relief filled in turn the face of the other man.

"I'm listening, Curly."

His friend told him the whole story from the beginning, just as he had been used to do in the old days. And Davis heard it without a word, taking the tale in quietly with a grim look settling on his face.

"So he aims to play traitor to young Cullison. The thing is damnable."

"He means to shut Sam's mouth for good and all. That is what he has been playing for from the start, to get even with Luck. He and his gang will get away with the haul and they will leave Sam dead on the scene of the hold-up. There will be some shooting, and it will be figured the boy was hit by one of the train crew. Nothing could be easier."

"If it worked out right."

"Couldn't help working out right. That's why Soapy didn't let me in on the proposition. To get rid of one would be no great trouble, but two— well, that's different. Besides, I could tell he was not sure of me. Now he aims to put me on the stand and prove by me that Sam and he had a quarrel and parted company mighty sore at each other hardly a week before the hold-up. He'll have an alibi too to show he couldn't have been in it. You'll see."

"You wouldn't think a white man could take a revenge like that on his enemy. It's an awful thing to do in cold blood."

"Soapy is no white man. He's a wolf. See how slick his scheme is. At one flip of the cards he kills the kid and damns his reputation. He scores Cullison and he snuffs out Sam, who had had the luck to win the girl Soapy fancies. The boy gets his and the girl is shown she can't love another man than Stone."

"Ever hear the story of French Dan?" asked Slats.

"Not to know the right of it."

"Soapy and Dan trained together in them days and went through a lot of meanness as side pardners. One day the Arivaca stage was held up by two men and the driver killed. In the scrap one of the men had his mask torn off. It was French Dan. Well, the outlaws had been too damned busy. Folks woke up and the hills were sprinkled with posses. They ran the fellows down and hunted them from place to place. Two—three times they almost nailed them. Shots were exchanged. A horse of one of the fugitives was killed and they could not get another. Finally one dark night the outlaws were surrounded. The posse lay down in the zacaton and waited for morning. In the night one of them heard a faint sound like the popping of a cork. When mo'ning broke the hunters crept forward through the thick grass. Guess what they found."

Curly's answer was prompt. "Gimme a harder one. There were two men and only one horse. The only chance was to slip through the line before day arrived. My guess is that they found French Dan with a little round hole in his skull—*and that the bullet making it had gone in from behind.* My guess also is that the posse didn't find the horse and the other man, just a trail through the zacaton back into the hills."

"Go to the head of the class. There was one man too many in that thicket for the horse. French Dan's pardner was afraid they might not agree about who was to have the bronch for a swift get-away. So he took no chances. There's only one man alive to-day can swear that Soapy was the man with French Dan lying in the zacaton. And he'll never tell, because he pumped the bullet into his friend. But one thing is sure. Soapy disappeared from Arizona for nearly two years. You can pick any reason you like for his going. That is the one I choose."

"Same here. And the man that would shoot one partner in the back would shoot another if he had good reasons. By his way of it Soapy has reasons a-plenty."

"I'm satisfied that is his game. Question is how to block it. Will you go to the sheriff?"

"No. Bolt would fall down on it. First off, he would not believe the story because I'm a rustler myself. Soapy and his friends voted for Bolt. He would go to them, listen to their story, prove part of it by me, and turn them loose for lack of evidence. Sam would go back to Dead Cow with them, and Stone would weave another web for the kid."

"You've got it about right," Slats admitted. "How about warning Sam?"

"No use. He would go straight to Soapy with it, and his dear friend would persuade him it was just a yarn cooked up to get him to throw down the only genuwine straight-up pal he ever had."

"Cullison then?"

"You're getting warm. I've had that notion myself. The point is, would he be willing to wait and let Soapy play his hand out till we called?"

"You would have to guarantee his boy would be safe meanwhile."

"Two of us would have to watch him day and night without Sam knowing it."

"Count me in."

"This is where we hit heavy traveling, Slats. For we don't know when the thing is going to be pulled off."

"We'll have to be ready. That's all."

"Happen to know whether Dick Maloney is here for the show?"

"Saw him this mo'ning. Luck is here too, him and his girl."

"Good. We've got to have a talk with them,

and it has to be on the q.t. You go back to town and find Dick. Tell him to meet us at the Del Mar, where Luck always puts up. Find out the number of Cullison's room and make an appointment. I'll be on El Molino street all mo'ning off and on. When you find out pass me without stopping, but tell me when we are to meet and just where."

Curly gave Slats a quarter of an hour before sauntering back to town. As he was passing the Silver Dollar saloon a voice called him. Stone and Blackwell were standing in the door. Flandrau stopped.

Soapy's deep-set eyes blazed at him. "You didn't tell me it was Luck Cullison went bail for you, Curly."

"You didn't ask me."

"So you and him are thick, are you?"

"I've met him once, if that's being thick. That time I shot him up."

"Funny. And then he went bail for you."

"Yes."

"Now I wonder why."

The eyes of the man had narrowed to red slits. His head had shot forward on his shoulders as that of a snake does. Curly would have given a good deal just then for the revolver lying on the bed of his room. For it was plain trouble was in sight. The desperado had been drinking heavily and was ready to do murder.

"That's easy to explain, Soapy. I shot him because I was driven to it. He's too much of a man to bear a grudge for what I couldn't help."

"That's it, is it? Does that explain why he dug up good money to turn loose a horse thief?"

"If I told you why, you would not understand."

"Let's hear you try."

"He did it because I was young, just as Sam is; and because he figured that some day Sam might need a friend, too."

"You're a liar. He did it because you promised to sneak up to my ranch and spy on us. That's why he did it."

With the last word his gun jumped into sight. That he was lashing himself into a fury was plain. Presently his rage would end in a tragedy.

Given a chance, Curly would have run for it. But Soapy was a dead shot. Of a sudden the anger in the boy boiled up over the fear. In two jumps he covered the ground and jammed his face close to the cold rim of the blue steel barrel.

"I'm not heeled. Shoot and be damned, you coward. And with my last breath I'll tell you that you're a liar."

Flandrau had called his bluff, though he had not meant it as one. A dozen men were in sight and were watching. They had heard the young man tell Stone he was not armed. Public opinion would hold him to account if he shot Curly down in cold blood. He hung there undecided, breathing fast, his jaw clamped tightly.

The lad hammered home his defiance. "Drop that gun, you four-flusher, and I'll whale you till you can't stand. *Sabe?* Call yourself a bad man, do you? Time I'm through with you there will be one tame wolf crawling back to Dead Cow with its tail between its legs."

The taunt diverted his mind, just as Curly had hoped it would. He thrust the revolver back into the holster and reached for his foe.

Then everybody, hitherto paralyzed by the sight of a deadly weapon, woke up and took a hand. They dragged the two men apart. Curly was thrust into a barber shop on the other side of the street and Stone was dragged back into the Silver Dollar.

In two minutes Flandrau had made himself famous, for he was a marked man. The last words of the struggling desperado had been that he would shoot on sight. Now half a dozen talked at once. Some advised Curly one thing, some another. He must get out of town. He must apologize at once to Stone. He must send a friend and explain.

The young man laughed grimly. "Explain nothing. I've done all the explaining I'm going to.

And I'll not leave town either. If Soapy wants me he'll sure find me."

"Don't be foolish, kid. He has got four notches on that gun of his. And he's a dead shot."

The tongues of those about him galloped. Soapy was one of these Billy-the-Kid killers, the only one left from the old days. He could whang away at a quarter with that sawed-off .45 of his and hit it every crack. The sooner Curly understood that no boy would have a chance with him the better it would be. So the talk ran.

"He's got you bluffed to a fare-you-well. You're tame enough to eat out of his hand. Didn't Luck Cullison go into the hills and bring him down all alone?" Flandrau demanded.

"Luck's another wonder. There ain't another man in Arizona could have done it. Leastways no other but Bucky O'Connor."

But Curly was excited, pleased with himself because he had stood up to the bogey man of the Southwest, and too full of strength to be afraid.

Maloney came into the barber shop and grinned at him.

"Hello, son!"

"Hello, Dick!"

"I hear you and Soapy are figuring on setting off some fireworks this Fourth."

It did Curly good to see him standing there so

easy and deliberate among the excitable town people.

"Soapy is doing the talking."

"I heard him; happened to be at the Silver Dollar when they dragged him in."

Maloney's eyebrows moved the least bit. His friend understood. Together they passed out of the back door of the shop into an alley. The others stood back and let them go. But their eyes did not leave Curly so long as he was in sight. Until this thing was settled one way or the other the young rustler would be one of the most important men in town. Citizens would defer to him that had never noticed him before. He carried with him a touch of the solemnity that is allowed only the dead or the dying.

Back to the hotel the two ran. When Curly buckled on his revolver and felt it resting comfortably against his thigh he felt a good deal better.

"I've seen Slats Davis," Maloney explained. "He has gone to find Luck, who is now at the Del Mar. At least he was an hour ago."

"Had any talk with Slats?"

"No. He said you'd do the talking."

"I'm to wait for him on El Molino street to learn where I'm to meet Cullison."

"That won't do. You'd make too tempting a target. I'll meet him instead."

That suited Curly. He was not hunting trouble

just now, even though he would not run away from it. For he had serious business on hand that could not take care of itself if Soapy should kill him.

Nearly an hour later Maloney appeared again.

"We're to go right over to the Del Mar. Second floor, room 217. You are to go down El Molino to Main, then follow it to the hotel, keeping on the right hand side of the street. Slats will happen along the other side of the street and will keep abreast of you. Luck will walk with me behind you. Unless I yell your name don't pay any attention to what is behind you. Soon as we reach the hotel Slats will cross the road and go in by the side door. You will follow him a few steps behind; and we'll bring up the rear casually as if we hadn't a thing to do with you."

"You're taking a heap of pains, seems to me."

"Want to keep you from getting spoilt till September term of court opens. Didn't I promise Bolt you would show up?"

They moved down the street as arranged. Every time a door opened in front of him, every time a man came out of a store or a saloon, Curly was ready for that lightning lift of the arm followed by a puff of smoke. The news of his coming passed ahead of him, so that windows were crowded with spectators. These were doomed to disappointment.

Nothing happened. The procession left behind it the Silver Dollar, the Last Chance, Chalkeye's Place and Pete's Palace.

Reaching the hotel first, Davis disappeared according to program into the side door. Curly followed, walked directly up the stairs, along the corridor, and passed without knocking into Room 217.

A young woman was sitting there engaged with some fancy work. Slender and straight, Kate Cullison rose and gave Curly her hand. For about two heartbeats her fingers lay cuddled in his big fist. A strange stifling emotion took his breath.

Then her arm fell to her side and she was speaking to him.

"Dad has gone to meet you. We've heard about what happened this morning."

"You mean what didn't happen. Beats all how far a little excitement goes in this town," he answered, embarrassed.

Her father and Maloney entered the room. Cullison wrung his hand.

"Glad to see you, boy. You're in luck that convict did not shoot you up while he had the chance. Saguache is sure buzzing this mo'ning with the way you stood up to him. That little play of yours will help with the jury in September."

Curly thanked him for going bail.

Luck fixed his steel-spoked eyes on him. "By what Dick tells me you've more than squared that account."

Kate explained in her soft voice. "Dick told us why you went up to Dead Cow creek."

"Sho! I hadn't a thing to do, so I just ran up there. Sam's in town with me. We're rooming together."

"Oh, take me to him," Kate cried.

"Not just now, honey," her father said gently. "This young man came here to tell us something. Or so I gathered from his friend Davis."

Flandrau told his story, or all of it that would bear telling before a girl. He glossed over his account of the dissipation at the horse ranch, but he told all he knew of Laura London and her interest in Sam. But it was when he related what he had heard at Chalkeye's place that the interest grew most tense. While he was going over the plot to destroy young Cullison there was no sound in the room but his voice. Luck's eyes burned like live coals. The color faded from the face of his daughter so that her lips were gray as cigar ash. Yet she sat up straight and did not flinch.

When he had finished the owner of the Circle C caught his hand. "You've done fine, boy. Not a man in Arizona could have done it better."

Kate said nothing in words but her dark long-lashed eyes rained thanks upon him.

They talked the situation over from all angles. Always it simmered down to one result. It was Soapy's first play. Until he moved they could not. They had no legal evidence except the word of Curly. Nor did they know on what night he had planned to pull off the hold-up. If they were to make a complete gather of the outfit, with evidence enough to land them in the penitentiary, it could only be after the hold-up.

Meanwhile there was nothing to do but wait and take what precautions they could against being caught by surprise. One of these was to see that Sam was never for an instant left unguarded either day or night. Another was to ride to Tin Cup and look the ground over carefully. For the present they could do no more than watch events, attracting no attention by any whispering together in public.

Before the conference broke up Kate came in with her protest.

"That's all very well, but what about Mr. Flandrau? He can't stay in Saguache with that man threatening to kill him on sight."

"Don't worry about me, Miss Kate;" and Curly looked at her and blushed.

Her father smiled grimly. "No, I wouldn't, Kate. He isn't going to be troubled by that wolf just now."

"Doesn't stand to reason he'd spoil all his plans just to bump me off."

"But he might. He forgot all about his plans this morning. How do we know he mightn't a second time?"

"Don't you worry, honey. I've got a card up my sleeve," Luck promised.

CHAPTER X

"STICK TO YOUR SADDLE"

The old Arizona fashion of settling a difference of opinion with the six-gun had long fallen into disuse, but Saguache was still close enough to the stark primeval emotions to wait with a keen interest for the crack of the revolver that would put a period to the quarrel between Soapy Stone and young Flandrau. It was known that Curly had refused to leave town, just as it was known that Stone and that other prison bird Blackwell were hanging about the Last Chance and Chalkeye's Place drinking together morosely. It was observed too that whenever Curly appeared in public he was attended by friends. Sometimes it would be Maloney and Davis, sometimes his uncle Alec Flandrau, occasionally a couple of the Map of Texas vaqueros.

It chanced that "Old Man" Flandrau, drifting into Chalkeye's Place, found in the assembled group the man he sought. Billie Mackenzie, grizzled owner of the Fiddleback ranch, was with him, and it was in the preliminary pause before drinking that Alec made his official announcement.

"No, Mac, I ain't worrying about that any. Curly

is going to get a square deal. We're all agreed on that. If there's any shooting from cover there'll be a lynching *pronto.* That goes."

Flandrau, Senior, did not glance at the sullen face of Lute Blackwell hovering in the background, but he knew perfectly well that inside of an hour word would reach Soapy Stone that only an even break with Curly would be allowed.

The day passed without a meeting between the two. Curly grew nervous at the delay.

"I'm as restless as a toad on a hot skillet," he confessed to Davis. "This thing of never knowing what minute Soapy will send me his leaden compliments ain't any picnic. Wisht it was over."

"He's drinking himself blind. Every hour is to the good for you."

Curly shrugged. "Drunk or sober Soapy always shoots straight."

Another day passed. The festivities had begun and Curly had to be much in evidence before the public. His friends had attempted to dissuade him from riding in the bucking broncho contest, but he had refused to let his name be scratched from the list of contestants.

A thousand pair of eyes in the grandstand watched the boy as he lounged against the corral· fence laughing and talking with his friends. A dozen people were on the lookout for the approach of

Stone. Fifty others had warned the young man to be careful. For Saguache was with him almost to a man.

Dick Maloney heard his voice called as he was passing the grandstand. A minute later he was in the Cullison box shaking hands with Kate.

"Is—is there anything new?" she asked in a low voice.

Her friend shook his head. "No. Soapy may drift out here any minute now."

"Will he——?" Her eyes finished the question.

He shook his head. "Don't know. That's the mischief of it. If they should meet just after Curly finishes riding the boy won't have a chance. His nerves won't be steady enough."

"Dad is doing something. I don't know what it is. He had a meeting with a lot of cattlemen about it—— I don't see how that boy *can* sit there on the fence laughing when any minute——"

"Curly's game as they make 'em. He's a prince, too. I like that boy better every day."

"He doesn't seem to me so——wild. But they say he's awfully reckless." She said it with a visible reluctance, as if she wanted him to deny the charge.

"Sho! Curly needs explaining some. That's all. Give a dog a bad name and hang him. That saying is as straight as the trail of a thirsty cow. The kid got off wrong foot first, and before he'd hardly

took to shaving respectable folks were hunting the
dictionary to find bad names to throw at him. He
was a reprobate and no account. Citizens that
differed on everything else was unanimous about
that. Mothers kinder herded their young folks in
a corral when he slung his smile their way."

"But why?" she persisted. "What had he done?"

"Gambled his wages, and drank some, and beat
up Pete Schiff, and shot the lights out of the Legal
Tender saloon. That's about all at first."

"Wasn't it enough?"

"Most folks thought so. So when Curly bumped
into them keep-off-the-grass signs parents put up
for him he had to prove they were justified. That's
the way a kid acts. Half the bad men are only
coltish cowpunchers gone wrong through rotten
whiskey and luck breaking bad for them."

"Is Soapy that kind?" she asked, but not because
she did not know the answer.

"He's the other kind, bad at the heart. But Curly
was just a kid crazy with the heat when he made
that fool play of rustling horses."

A lad made his way to them with a note. Kate
read it and turned to Dick. Her eyes were shining
happily.

"I've got news from Dad. It's all right. Soapy
Stone has left town."

"Why?"

"A dozen of the big cattlemen signed a note and sent it to Stone. They told him that if he touched Curly he would never leave town alive. He was given word to get out of town at once."

Maloney slapped his hand joyously on his thigh. "Fine! Might a-known Luck would find a way out. I tell you this thing has been worying me. Some of us wanted to take it off Curly's hands, but he wouldn't have it. He's a man from the ground up, Curly is. But your father found a way to butt in all right. Soapy couldn't stand out against the big ranchmen when they got together and meant business. He had to pull his freight."

"Let me tell him the good news, Dick," she said, eagerly.

"Sure. I'll send him right up."

Bronzed almost to a coffee brown, with the lean lithe grace of youth garbed in the picturesque regalia of the *vaquero,* Flandrau was a taking enough picture to hold the roving eye of any girl. A good many centered upon him now, as he sauntered forward toward the Cullison box cool and easy and debonair. More than one pulse quickened at sight of him, for his gallantry, his peril and his boyishness combined to enwrap him in the atmosphere of romance. Few of the observers knew what a wary vigilance lay behind that careless manner.

135

Kate gathered her skirts to make room for him beside her.

"Have you heard? He has left town."

"Who?"

"Soapy Stone. The cattlemen served notice on him to go. So he left."

A wave of relief swept over the young man. "That's your father's fine work."

"Isn't it good?" Her eyes were shining with gladness.

"I'm plumb satisfied," he admitted. "I'm not hankering to shoot out my little difference with Soapy. He's too handy with a six-gun."

"I'm so happy I don't know what to do."

"I suppose now the hold-up will be put off. Did Sam and Blackwell go with him?"

"No. He went alone."

"Have you seen Sam yet?"

"No, but I've seen Laura London. She's all the nice things you've said about her."

Curly grew enthusiastic. "Ain't she the dandiest girl ever? She's the right kind of a friend. And pretty—with that short crinkly hair the color of ripe nuts! You would not think one person could own so many dimples as she does when she laughs. It's just like as if she had absorbed sunshine and was warming you up with her smile."

"I see she has made a friend of you."

136

"You bet she has."

Miss Cullison shot a swift slant glance at him. "If you'll come back this afternoon you can meet her. I'm going to have all those dimples and all that sunshine here in the box with me."

"Maybe that will draw Sam to you."

"I'm hoping it will. But I'm afraid not. He avoids us. When they met he wouldn't speak to Father."

"That's the boy of it. Just the same he feels pretty bad about the quarrel. I reckon there's nothing to do but keep an eye on him and be ready for Soapy's move when he makes it."

"I'm so afraid something will happen to Sam."

"Now don't you worry, Miss Kate. Sam is going to come out of this all right. We'll find a way out for him yet."

Behind her smile the tears lay close. "You're the *best* friend. How can we ever thank you for what you're doing for Sam?"

A steer had escaped from the corral and was galloping down the track in front of the grandstand with its tail up. The young man's eyes followed the animal absently as he answered in a low voice.

"Do you reckon I have forgot how a girl took a rope from my neck one night? Do you reckon I ever forget that?"

"It was nothing. I just spoke to the boys."

"Or that I don't remember how the man I had shot went bail for a rustler he did not know?"

"Dick knew you. He told us about you."

"Could he tell you any good about me? Could he say anything except that I was a worthless no-'count——?"

She put her hand on his arm and stopped him. "Don't! I won't have you say such things about yourself. You were just a boy in trouble."

"How many would have remembered that? But you did. You fought good for my life that night. I'll pay my debt, part of it. The whole I never could pay."

His voice trembled in spite of the best he could do. Their eyes did not meet, but each felt the thrill of joy waves surging through their veins.

The preliminaries in the rough riding contest took place that afternoon. Of the four who won the right to compete in the finals, two were Curly Flandrau and Dick Maloney. They went together to the Cullison box to get the applause due them.

Kate Cullison had two guests with her. One was Laura London, the other he had never seen. She was a fair young woman with thick ropes of yellow hair coiled round her head. Deep-breasted and robust-loined, she had the rich coloring of the Scandinavian race and much of the slow grace peculiar to its women.

The hostess pronounced their names. "Miss Anderson, this is Mr. Flandrau. Mr. Flandrau—Miss Anderson."

Curly glanced quickly at Kate Cullison, who nodded. This then was the sweetheart of poor Mac.

Her eyes filled with tears as she took the young man's hand. To his surprise Curly found his throat choking up. He could not say a word, but she understood the unspoken sympathy. They sat together in the back of the box.

"I'd like to come and talk to you about—Mac. Can I come this evening, say?"

"Please."

Kate gave them no more time for dwelling on the past.

"You did ride so splendidly," she told Curly.

"No better than Dick did," he protested.

"I didn't say any better than Dick. You both did fine."

"The judges will say you ride better. You've got first place cinched," Maloney contributed.

"Sho! Just because I cut up fancy didoes on a horse. Grandstand stunts are not riding. For straight stick-to-your-saddle work I know my boss, and his name is Dick Maloney."

"We'll know to-morrow," Laura London summed up.

As it turned out, Maloney was the better prophet.

Curly won the first prize of five hundred dollars and the championship belt. Dick took second place.

Saguache, already inclined to make a hero of the young rustler, went wild over his victory. He could have been chosen mayor that day if there had been an election. To do him justice, Curly kept his head remarkably well.

"To be a human clothes pin ain't so much," he explained to Kate. "Just because a fellow can stick to the hurricane deck of a bronch without pulling leather whilst it's making a milk shake out of him don't prove that he has got any more brains or decency than the law allows. Say, ain't this a peach of a mo'ning."

A party of young people were taking an early morning ride through the outskirts of the little city. Kate pulled her pony to a walk and glanced across at him. He had taken off his hat to catch the breeze, and the sun was picking out the golden lights in his curly brown hair. She found herself admiring the sure poise of the head, the flat straight back, the virile strength of him.

It did not occur to her that she herself made a picture to delight the heart. The curves of her erect tiger-lithe young body were modeled by nature to perfection. Radiant with the sheer pleasure of life, happy as God's sunshine, she was a creature vividly in tune with the glad morning.

"Anyhow, I'm glad you won."

Their eyes met. A spark from his flashed deep into hers as a star falls through the heavens on a summer night. Each looked away. After one breathless full-pulsed moment she recovered her-self.

"Wouldn't it be nice if——?"

His gaze followed hers to two riders in front of them. One was Maloney, the other Myra Ander-son. The sound of the girl's laughter rippled back to them on the light breeze.

Curly smiled. "Yes, that would be nice. The best I can say for her—and it's a whole lot—is that I believe she's good enough for Dick."

"And the best I can say for him is that he's good enough for her," the girl retorted promptly.

"Then let's hope——"

"I can't think of anything that would please me more."

He looked away into the burning sun on the edge of the horizon. "I can think of one thing that would please me more," he murmured.

She did not ask him what it was, nor did he volunteer an explanation. Perhaps it was from the rising sun her face had taken its swift glow of warm color.

PART II

LUCK

CHAPTER I

AT THE ROUND UP CLUB

A big game had been in progress all night at the Round Up Club. Now the garish light of day streamed through the windows, but the electric cluster still flung down its yellow glare upon the table. Behind the players were other smaller tables littered with cigars, discarded packs, and glasses full or empty. The men were in their shirt sleeves. Big broad-shouldered fellows they were, with the marks of the outdoors hardriding West upon them. No longer young, they were still full of the vigor and energy of unflagging strength. From bronzed faces looked steady unwinking eyes with humorous creases around the corners, hard eyes that judged a man and his claims shrewdly and with good temper. Most of them had made good in the land, and their cattle fed upon a thousand hills.

The least among them physically was Luck Cullison, yet he was their recognized leader. There was some innate quality in this man with the gray, steel-chilled eyes that marked him as first in whatever company he chose to frequent. A good friend and a good foe, men thought seriously before they opposed him. He had made himself a power in the Southwest because he was the type that goes the limit when aroused. Yet about him, too, there was the manner of a large amiability, of the easy tolerance characteristic of the West.

While Alec Flandrau shuffled and dealt, the players relaxed. Cigars were relit, drinks ordered. Conversation reverted to the ordinary topics that interested Cattleland. The price of cows, the good rains, the time of the fall roundup, were touched upon.

The door opened to let in a newcomer, a slim, graceful man much younger than the others present, and one whose costume and manner brought additional color into the picture. Flandrau, Senior, continued to shuffle without turning his head. Cullison also had his back to the door, but the man hung his broad-rimmed gray hat on the rack—beside an exactly similar one that belonged to the owner of the Circle C—and moved leisurely forward till he was within range of his vision.

"Going to prove up soon on that Del Oro claim of yours, Luck?" asked Flandrau.

He was now dealing, his eyes on the cards, so that he missed the embarrassment in the faces of those about him.

"On Thursday, the first day the law allows," Cullison answered quietly.

Flandrau chuckled. "I reckon Cass Fendrick will be some sore."

"I expect." Cullison's gaze met coolly the black, wrathful eyes of the man who had just come in.

"Sort of put a crimp in his notions when you took up the cañon draw," Flandrau surmised.

Something in the strained silence struck the dealer as unusual. He looked up, and showed a momentary confusion.

"Didn't know you were there, Cass. Looks like I put my foot in it sure that time. I ce'tainly thought you were an absentee," he apologized.

"Or you wouldn't have been talking about me," retorted Fendrick acidly. The words were flung at Flandrau, but plainly they were meant as a challenge for Cullison.

A bearded man, the oldest in the party, cut in with good-natured reproof. "I shouldn't wonder, Cass, but your name is liable to be mentioned just like that of any other man."

"Didn't know you were in this, Yesler," Fendrick drawled insolently.

"Oh, well, I butted in," the other laughed easily.

He pushed a stack of chips toward the center of the table. "The pot's open."

Fendrick, refused a quarrel, glared at the impassive face of Cullison, and passed to the rear room for a drink. His impudence needed fortifying, for he knew that since he had embarked in the sheep business he was not welcome at this club, that in fact certain members had suggested his name be dropped from the books. Before he returned to the poker table the drink he had ordered became three.

The game was over and accounts were being straightened. Cullison was the heavy loser. All night he had been bucking hard luck. His bluffs had been called. The others had not come in against his strong hands. On a straight flush he had drawn down the ante and nothing more. To say the least, it was exasperating. But his face had showed no anger. He had played poker too many years, was too much a sport in the thorough-going frontier fashion, to wince when the luck broke badly for him.

The settlement showed that the owner of the Circle C was twenty-five hundred dollars behind the game. He owed Mackenzie twelve hundred, Flandrau four hundred, and three hundred to Yesler.

With Fendrick sitting in an easy chair just across

the room, he found it a little difficult to say what otherwise would have been a matter of course.

"My bank's busted just now, boys. Have to ask you to let it stand for a few days. Say, till the end of the week."

Fendrick laughed behind the paper he was pretending to read. He knew quite well that Luck's word was as good as his bond, but he chose to suggest a doubt.

"Maybe you'll explain the joke to us, Cass," the owner of the Circle C said very quietly.

"Oh, I was just laughing at the things I see, Luck," returned the younger man with airy offense, his eyes on the printed sheet.

"Meaning for instance?"

"Just human nature. Any law against laughing?"

Cullison turned his back on him. "See you on Thursday if that's soon enough, boys."

"All the time you want, Luck. Let mine go till after the roundup if you'd rather," Mackenzie suggested.

"Thursday suits me."

Cullison rose and stretched. He had impressed his strong, dominant personality upon his clothes, from the high-heeled boots to the very wrinkles in the corduroy coat he was now putting on. He had enemies, a good many of them, but his friends were legion.

"Don't hurry yourself."

"Oh, I'll rustle the money, all right. Coming down to the hotel?" Luck was reaching for his hat, but turned toward his friends as he spoke.

Without looking again at Fendrick, he led the way to the street.

The young man left alone cursed softly to himself, and ordered another drink. He knew he was overdoing it, but the meeting with Cullison had annoyed him exceedingly. The men had never been friends, and of late years they had been leaders of hostile camps. Both of them could be overbearing, and there was scarcely a week but their interests overlapped. Luck was capable of great generosity, but he could be obstinate as the rock of Gibraltar when he chose. There had been differences about the ownership of calves, about straying cattle, about political matters. Finally had come open hostility. Cass leased from the forestry department the land upon which Cullison's cattle had always run free of expense. Upon this he had put sheep, a thing in itself of great injury to the cattle interests. The stockmen had all been banded together in opposition to the forestry administration of the new régime, and Luck regarded Fendrick's action as treachery to the common cause.

148

He struck back hard. In Arizona the open range is valuable only so long as the water holes also are common property or a private supply available. The Circle C cattle and those of Fendrick came down from the range to the Del Oro to water at a point where the cañon walls opened to a spreading valley. This bit of meadow Luck homesteaded and fenced on the north side, thus cutting the cattle of his enemy from the river.

Cass was furious. He promptly tore down the fence to let his cattle and sheep through. Cullison rebuilt it, put up a shack at a point which commanded the approach, and set a guard upon it day and night. Open warfare had ensued, and one of the sheepherders had been beaten because he persisted in crossing the dead line.

Now Cullison was going to put the legal seal on the matter by making final proof on his homestead. Cass knew that if he did so it would practically put him out of business. He would be at the mercy of his foe, who could ruin him if he pleased. Luck would be in a position to dictate terms absolutely.

Nor did it make his defeat any more palatable to Cass that he had brought it on himself by his bad-tempered unneighborliness and by his overreaching disposition. A hundred times he had blacknamed himself for an arrant fool because he had not anticipated the move of his enemy and homesteaded on his own account.

He felt that there must be some way out of the trap if he could only find it. Whenever the thought of eating humble pie to Luck came into his mind, the rage boiled in him. He swore he would not do it. Better a hundred times to see the thing out to a fighting finish.

Taking the broad-rimmed gray hat he found on the rack, Cass passed out of the clubhouse and into the sun-bathed street.

CHAPTER II

LUCK MEETS AN OLD ACQUAINTANCE

Cullison and his friends proceeded down Papago
street to the old plaza where their hotel was lo-
cated. Their transit was an interrupted one, for
these four cattlemen were among the best known
in the Southwest. All along the route they scattered nods of recognition, friendly greetings, and
genial banter. One of them—the man who had
formerly been the hard-riding, quick-shooting
sheriff of the county—met also scowls once or
twice, to which he was entirely indifferent. Luck
had no slavish respect for law, had indeed, if rumor were true, run a wild and stormy course in his
youth. But his reign as sheriff had been a terror
to lawbreakers. He had made enemies, desperate
and unscrupulous ones, who had sworn to wipe him
from among the living, and one of these he was
now to meet for the first time since the man had
stood handcuffed before him, livid with fury, and
had sworn to cut his heart out at the earliest chance.

It was in the lobby of the hotel that Cullison
came plump against Lute Blackwell. For just a
moment they stared at each other before the former
sheriff spoke.

"Out again, eh, Blackwell?" he said easily.

From the bloodshot eyes one could have told at a glance the man had been drinking heavily. From whiskey he had imbibed a Dutch courage just bold enough to be dangerous.

"Yes, I'm out—and back again, just as I promised, Mr. Sheriff," he threatened.

The cattleman ignored his manner. "Then I'll give you a piece of advice gratis. Papago County has grown away from the old days. It has got past the two-gun man. He's gone to join the antelope and the painted Indian. You'll do well to remember that."

The fellow leaned forward, sneering so that his ugly mouth looked like a crooked gash. "How about the one-gun man, Mr. Sheriff?"

"He doesn't last long now."

"Doesn't he?"

The man's rage boiled over. But Luck was far and away the quicker of the two. His left hand shot forward and gripped the rising wrist, his right caught the hairy throat and tightened on it. He shook the convict as if he had been a child, and flung him, black in the face, against the wall, where he hung, strangling and sputtering.

"I—I'll get you yet," the ruffian panted. But he did not again attempt to reach for the weapon in his hip pocket.

"You talk too much with your mouth."

With superb contempt, Luck slapped him, turned on his heel, and moved away, regardless of the raw, stark lust to kill that was searing this man's elemental brain.

Across the convict's rage came a vision. He saw a camp far up in the Rincons, and seated around a fire five men at breakfast, all of them armed. Upon them had come one man suddenly. He had dominated the situation quietly, had made one disarm the others, had handcuffed the one he wanted and taken him from his friends through a hostile country where any hour he might be shot from ambush. Moreover, he had traveled with his prisoner two days, always cheerful and matter of fact, not at all uneasy as to what might lie behind the washes or the rocks they passed. Finally he had brought his man safely to Casa Grande, from whence he had gone over the road to the penitentiary. Blackwell had been the captured man, and he held a deep respect for the prowess of the officer who had taken him. The sheer pluck of the adventure had alone made it possible. For such an unflawed nerve Blackwell knew his jerky rage was no match.

The paroled convict recovered his breath and slunk out of the hotel.

Billie Mackenzie, owner of the Fiddleback ranch, laughed even while he disapproved. "Some day,

Luck, you'll get yours when you are throwing chances at a coyote like this. You'll guess your man wrong, or he'll be one glass drunker than you figure on, and then he'll plug you through and through."

"The man that takes chances lives longest, Mac," his friend replied, dismissing the subject carelessly. "I'm going to tuck away about three hours of sleep. So long." And with a nod he was gone to his room.

"All the same Luck's too derned rash," Flandrau commented. "He'll run into trouble good and hard one of these days. When I'm in Rattlesnake Gulch I don't aim to pick posies too unobservant."

Mackenzie looked worried. No man lived whom he admired so much as Luck Cullison. "And he hadn't ought to be sitting in these big games. He's hard up. Owes a good bit here and there. Always was a spender. First thing he'll have to sell the Circle C to square things. He'll pay us this week like he said he would. That's dead sure. He'd die before he'd fall down on it, now Fendrick has got his back up. But I swear I don't know where he'll raise the price. Money is so tight right now."

That afternoon Luck called at every bank in Saguache. All of the bankers knew him and were friendly to him, but in spite of their personal regard they could do nothing for him.

154

"It's this stringency, Luck," Jordan of the Cat-tlemen's National explained to him. "We can't let a dollar go even on the best security. You know I'd like to let you have it, but it wouldn't be right to the bank. We've got to keep our reserve up. Why, I'm lying awake nights trying to figure out a way to call in more of our money."

"I'm not asking much, Jack."

"Luck, I'd let you have it if I dared. Why, we're running close to the wind. Public confidence is a mighty ticklish thing. If I·didn't have twenty thousand coming from El Paso on the Flyer to-night I'd be uneasy for the bank."

"Twenty thousand on the Flyer. I reckon you ship by express, don't you?"

"Yes. Don't mention it to anyone. That twenty thousand would come handy to a good many people in this country these times."

"It would come right handy to me," Luck laughed ruefully. "I need every cent of it. After the beef round-up, I'll be on Easy Street, but it's going to be hard sledding to keep going till then."

"You'll make a turn somehow. It will work out. Maybe when money isn't so tight I'll be able to do something for you."

Luck returned to the hotel morosely, and tried to figure a way out of his difficulties. He was not going to be beaten. He never had accepted defeat, even in the early days when he had sometimes taken a lawless short cut to what he wanted. By God, he would not lose out after all these years of fighting. It had been his desperate need of money that had made him sit in last night's poker game. But he had succeeded only in making a bad situation worse. He knew his debts by heart, but he jotted them down on the back of an envelope and added them again.

Mortgage on ranch (due Oct. 1), $13,000
Note to First National,   3,500
Note to Reynolds,   1,750
I O U to Mackenzie,   1,200
Same to Flandrau,   400
Same to Yesler,   300
                        Total, $20,150

Twenty thousand was the sum he needed, and mighty badly, too. Absentmindedly he turned the envelope over and jotted down one or two other things. Twenty thousand dollars! Just the sum Jordan had coming to the bank on the Flyer. Subconsciously, Luck's fingers gave expression to his thoughts. $20,000. Half a dozen times they penciled it, and just below the figures, "W. & S. Ex. Co." Finally they wrote automatically the one word, "To-night."

Luck looked at what he had written, laughed grimly, and tore the envelope in two. He threw the pieces in the waste paper basket.

CHAPTER III

AN INITIALED HAT

Mackenzie was reading the *Sentinel* while he ate a late breakfast. He had it propped against the water bottle, so that it need not interfere with the transportation of sausages, fried potatoes, hot cakes, and coffee to their common destination.

Trying to do two things at once has its disadvantages. A startling headline caught his eyes just as the cup was at his lips. Hot coffee, precipitately swallowed, scalded his tongue and throat. He set down the cup, swore mildly, and gave his attention to the news that had excited him. The reporter had run the story to a column, but the leading paragraph gave the gist of it:

> While the citizens of Saguache were peacefully sleeping last night, a lone bandit held up the messengers of the Western and Southern Express Company, and relieved them of $20,000 just received from El Paso on the Flyer.
>
> Perry Hawley, the local manager of the company, together with Len Rogers, the armed guard, had just returned from the

depot, where the money had been turned over to them and receipted for. Hawley had unlocked the door of the office and had stepped in, followed by Rogers, when a masked desperado appeared suddenly out of the darkness, disarmed the guard and manager, took the money, passed through the door and locked it after him, and vanished as silently as he had come. Before leaving, he warned his victims that the place would be covered for ten minutes and at any attempt to call for help they would be shot. Notwithstanding this, the imprisoned men risked their lives by raising the alarm.

Further down the page Mackenzie discovered that the desperado was still at large, but that Sheriff Bolt expected shortly to lay hands on him.

"I'll bet a dollar Nick Bolt didn't make any such claim to the reporter. He ain't the kind that brags," Mackenzie told himself.

He folded the paper and returned to his room to make preparation to return to his ranch. The buzz of the telephone called him to the receiver. The voice of Cullison reached him.

"That you, Mac. I'll be right up. No, don't come down. I'd rather see you alone."

The owner of the Circle C came right to business. "I've made a raise, Mac, and while I've got it I'm going to skin off what's coming to you."

He had taken a big roll of bills from his pocket, and was counting off what he had lost to his friend. The latter noticed that it all seemed to be in twenties.

"Twelve hundred. That squares us, Mac."

The Scotchman was vaguely uneasy without a definite reason for his anxiety. Only last night Cullison had told him not a single bank in town would advance him a dollar. Now he had money in plenty. Where had he got it?

"No hurry at all, Luck. Pay when you're good and ready."

"That's now."

"Because I'll only put it in the Cattlemen's National. It's yours if you need it."

"I'll let you know if I do," his friend nodded.

Mackenzie's eye fell on a copy of the *Sentinel* protruding from the other's pocket. "Read about the hold-up of the W. & S. Express? That fellow had his nerve with him."

"Sho! This hold-up game's the easiest yet. He got the drop on them, and there was nothing to it. The key was still in the lock of the door. Well, when he gets through he steps out, turns the key, and rides away."

"How did he know there was money coming in last night?"

"There's always a leak about things of that sort.

Somebody talks. I knew it myself for that matter."

"You knew! Who told you?"

"That's a secret, Mac. Come to think of it, I
wish you wouldn't tell anybody that I knew. I
don't want to get the man who told me in trouble."

"Sure I won't." He passed to another phase of
the subject. "The *Sentinel* says Bolt expects to
catch the robber. Think he will?"

"Not if the fellow knows his business. Bolt has
nothing to go on. He has the whole Southwest to
pick from. For all he knows, it was you."

"Yes, but——"

"Or more likely me." The gray eyes of the
former sheriff held a frosty smile.

In spite of that smile, or perhaps because of it,
Mackenzie felt again that flash of doubt. "What's
the use of talking foolishness, Luck? Course you
didn't do it. Anybody would know that. Man, I
whiles wonder at you," he protested, relapsing into
his native tongue as he sometimes did when excited.

"I didn't say I did it. I said I might have done
it."

"Oh, well! You didn't. I know you too well."

But the trouble was Mackenzie did not know him
well enough. Cullison was hard up, close to the
wall. How far would he go to save himself?

Thirty years before when they had been wild young lads these two had hunted their fun together. Luck had always been the leader, had always been ready for any daredeviltry that came to his mind. He had been the kind to go the limit in whatever he undertook, to play it to a finish in spite of opposition. And what a man is he must be to the end. In his slow, troubled fashion, Mac wondered if his old side partner's streak of lawlessness would take him as far as a hold-up. Of course it would not, he assured himself; but he could not get the ridiculous notion out of his head. It drew his thoughts, and at last his steps toward the express office where the hold-up had taken place.

He opened a futile conversation with Hawley, while Len Rogers, the guard who had not made good, looked at him with a persistent, hostile eye.

"Hard luck," the cattleman condoled.

"That's what you think, is it? You and your friends, too, I reckon."

Mackenzie looked at the guard, who was plainly sore in every humiliated crevice of his brain. "I ain't speaking for my friends, Len, but for myself," he said amiably.

Rogers laughed harshly. "Didn't know but what you might be speaking for one of your friends."

"They can all speak for themselves when they have got anything to say."

Hawley sent a swift, warning look toward his subordinate. The latter came to time sulkily. "I didn't say they couldn't."

Mackenzie drifted from this unfriendly atmosphere to the courthouse. He found Sheriff Bolt in his office. It was that official's busy day, but he found time not only to see the owner of the Fiddleback, but to press upon him cordially an invitation to sit down and smoke. The Scotchman wanted to discuss the robbery, but was shy about attacking the subject. While he boggled at it, Bolt was off on another tack.

Inside of a quarter of an hour the sheriff had found out all he wanted to know about the poker game, Cullison's financial difficulties, and the news that Luck had liquidated his poker debt since breakfast time. He had turned the simple cattleman's thoughts inside out, was aware of the doubt Billie had scarcely admitted to himself, and knew all he did except the one point Luck had asked him not to mention. Moreover, he had talked so casually that his visitor had no suspicion of what he was driving at.

Mackenzie attempted a little sleuthing of his own. "This hold-up fellow kind of slipped one over on you last night, Bolt."

"Maybe so, and maybe not."

"Got a clew, have you?"

"Oh, yes—yes." The sheriff looked straight at him. "I've a notion his initials are L. C."

Billie felt himself flushing. "What makes you think that, Nick?"

Bolt walked to a cupboard and unlocked it. His back was toward the cattleman, but the latter could see him take something from a shelf. Turning quickly, the sheriff tossed a hat upon the table.

"Ever see this before?"

Mac picked it up. His fingers were not quite steady, for a great dread drenched his heart like a rush of icy water. Upon that gray felt hat with the pinched crown was stamped the individuality— and the initials—of Luck Cullison.

"Don't know as I recognize it," he lied, not very readily. "Not to know it. Why?"

"Thought perhaps you might know it. The hold-up dropped it while getting away."

Mackenzie's eyes flinched. "Dropped it. How was that?"

"A man happened to come along San Miguel street just as the robber swung to his horse. He heard the cries of the men inside, guessed what was doing, and exchanged shots with the miscreant. He shot this hat off the fellow's head."

"The *Sentinel* didn't tell any such a story."

163

"I didn't give that detail to the editor."

"Who was the man that shot the robber?"

"Cass Fendrick."

"But he didn't claim to recognize the hold-up?" Mackenzie forced himself to ask this in spite of his fears.

"Not for certain."

"Then he—he had a guess."

"Yes, Mac. He guessed a man whose initials are the same as those in that hat."

"Who do you mean, Nick?"

"I don't need to tell you that. You know who."

"If you mean Luck Cullison, it's a damned lie," exploded the cattleman. He was furious with himself, for he felt now that he had been unsuspectingly helping to certify the suspicions of the sheriff. Like an idiot, he had let out much that told heavily against his friend.

"I hope so."

"Cass Fendrick is not on good terms with him. We all know that. Luck has got him in a hole. I wouldn't put it a bit above Cass to lie if he thought it would hurt Luck. Tell you it's a damned conspiracy. Man, can't you see that?"

"What about this hat, with the two holes shot through the rim?"

"Sho! We all wear hats just like that. Look at mine." Billie held it out eagerly.

"Has yours an L. C. stamped in the sweat band?" Bolt asked with a smile.

"I know you ain't his friend, Nick. But you want to be fair to him even if he did oppose your election." Mackenzie laid an appealing hand on the knee of the man seated opposite him.

"I'm sheriff of Papago County. It doesn't make any difference who worked for or against me, Billie. I was elected, and I'm going to enforce the law."

"And you think Luck would do a fool thing like this?"

"I didn't say I thought so, but it's my business not to overlook any bets."

"But you do believe it. Now, don't you?"

"Since you've got to have an answer—yes, I do."

"By heaven, I'd as lief think I did it myself."

"You're a good friend," Bolt conceded. "By the way, I've got to pay for some supplies this morning. Can you cash a check for a hundred?"

"I reckon so." Mackenzie drew from his pocket the roll Cullison had given him two hours before. He peeled five twenties from it. The sheriff observed that the prevailing denomination was the same.

"Get these from Luck?" he asked carelessly.

The cattleman stared at him, and the suspicion grew on him that he had been trapped again.

"Why do you ask?"

"Because it happens the bills stolen from the W. & S. were all twenties."

"No, I didn't get them from Cullison. This is money I had," he answered sullenly.

"Then I dare say you can let me see the money you got from him."

"He paid me by check."

"Banked it yet?"

"That's my business, Nick."

"And mine, Billie. I can find out from the bank if you have. Besides, I happen to know that Luck's bank account is overdrawn."

"Some one has been at you to prejudice you, Bolt."

"Nobody but Luck Cullison himself—and his actions."

From the office of the sheriff, Mackenzie wandered to the club in search of Luck. He was thoroughly dispirited, both dreaded to meet Luck, and yet was anxious to do so. For he wanted to warn him, wanted to see him fall into one of his chill rages when he told him there were suspicions against him.

Cullison had left the club, but Alec Flandrau was still there. Billie drew him into a corner, and learned that Luck had just settled with him.

"Anyone see him give it to you, Alec?"

"No. He took me upstairs to the library and paid me."

"In bills?"

"Yes—in twenties."

"For God's sake, don't tell anybody that." In a dozen jerky sentences the owner of the Fiddleback told Flandrau of the suspicions of the sheriff.

Together they went in search of Luck. But though they looked for him all day, he was not to be found. They might have concluded he had ridden out to the ranch, but his horse was still at the stable where he had left it.

The last that had been seen of him Luck was walking along the plaza toward the hotel, not a hundred and fifty yards from the latter. A dozen men had spoken to him in the distance of a block. But he had not been seen to reach his hotel. He had not called for his room key. Somehow he had vanished, and none could tell how or where.

To Bolt his disappearance was as good as a confession of guilt. He searched Luck's room at the hotel. Among other things, he found an old envelope with interesting data penciled on it.

Before nightfall the word was whispered all over Saguache that Luck Cullison, pioneer cattleman and former sheriff, was suspected of the W. & S. Express robbery and had fled to save himself from arrest. At first men marveled that one so well

known and so popular, one who had been so prominent in affairs, could be suspected of such a crime,
but as they listened to the evidence and saw it fall
like blocks of a building into place, the conviction
grew that he was the masked bandit wanted by the
sheriff.

CHAPTER IV

KATE USES HER QUIRT

Red-headed Bob Cullison finished making the diamond hitch and proudly called his cousin Kate to inspect the packhorse.

"You never saw the hitch thrown better, sis," he bragged, boy-like. "Uncle Luck says I do it well as he can."

"It's fine, Bob," his cousin agreed, with the proper enthusiasm in her dark eyes. "You'll have to teach me how to do it one of these days."

She was in a khaki riding skirt, and she pulled herself to the saddle of her own horse. From this position she gave him final instructions before leaving. "Stay around the house, Bob. Dad will call the ranch up this morning probably, and I want you to be where you can hear the 'phone ring. Tell him about that white-faced heifer, and to be sure to match the goods I gave him. You'll find dinner set out for you on the dining-room table."

It had been on Wednesday morning that Luck Cullison disappeared from the face of the earth. Before twenty-four hours the gossip was being whispered in the most distant cañons of Papago County. The riders of the Circle C knew it, but none of them had yet told either Bob or Kate.

Now it was Friday morning and Kate was beginning to wonder why her father did not call her up. Could it be that Soapy Stone was pulling off his train robbery at Tin Cup and her father so busy that he could not take time to ride to a telephone station? She did not like to leave the ranch just now, even for a few hours, but other business called her away. Sweeney was holding down the fort at the Del Oro against Fendrick's sheepherders, and his weekly supply of provisions had to be taken to him. Since she wanted to see with her own eyes how things were getting along at the cañon, she was taking the supplies in person.

It was a beautiful morning, even for Arizona. The soft air was at its winiest best. The spring rains had carpeted the hills with an unusually fine grass, and the summer suns had not yet burnt this to the crisp brown of August. Her young heart expanded with the very joy of life. Oh, how good it was to be alive in a world of warm sunshine, of blue, unflecked sky, and of cool, light breezes. Swifts basked on the rocks or darted like arrows for safety, and lay palpitating with suspense. The clear call of the quails sounded to right and left of her. To her eager consciousness it was as if some bath of splendor had poured down overnight upon the old earth.

She rode from sunlight into shadow and from shadow to sunlight again, winding along the hill trail that took her toward the Del Oro. After hours of travel she came to the saddle from which one looked down to the gap in the cañon walls that had been the common watering place of all men's cattle, but now was homesteaded by her father. Far below her it lay, a dwarfed picture with detail blurred to a vague impressionistic map. She could see the hut, the fence line running parallel to the stream on the other side, some grazing cattle, Sweeney's horse in the corral.

The piteous bleating of a lamb floated to her. Kate dismounted and made her way toward the sound. A pathetic little huddle of frightened life tried to struggle free at her approach. The slim leg of the lamb had become wedged at the intersection of several rocks in such a way that it could not be withdrawn.

Kate pulled the boulder away, and released the prisoner. It looked at her and bleated without attempting to move. She took the soft, woolly creature in her arms, and examined the wounded limb, all torn and raw from its efforts to escape. A wound, she recalled, ought to be washed with cold water and bound. Returning to her horse, she put the little animal in front of the saddle and continued on the trail that led down to the river.

Sweeney came out from the cabin and hailed her. He was a squat, weather-beaten man, who had ridden for her father ever since she could remember.

"What in Mexico you got there?" he asked in surprise.

She explained the circumstances under which she had found the lamb.

"And what you aiming to do with it?"

"I'm going to tie up its leg and take it across the river. Some of the C. F. herders are sure to find it before night."

"Sho! What are you fooling with Cass Fendrick's sheep for?" he grumbled.

"It isn't a sheep, but a lamb. And I'm not going to see it suffer, no matter who owns it."

She was already walking toward the river. Protestingly he followed, and lent a hand at tying up the leg with the girl's handkerchief.

"I'll just ride across and leave it outside the fence," she said.

"Lemme go. I know the river better."

Sweeney did not wait for her assent, but swung to the saddle. She handed him the lamb, and he forded the stream. At no place did the water come above the fetlocks of the horse.

172

"I'm so glad you know the dangerous places. Be careful you don't drown," she mocked.

The rider's laughter rang back to her. One of her jokes went a long way with Sweeney. The danger of the river had been the flimsiest of excuses. What he had been afraid of was that one of Fendrick's herders might be lurking in some arroyo beyond the fence. There was little chance that he would dare hurt her, but he might shout something unpleasant.

In point of fact, Sweeney saw some one disappear into a wash as he reached the fence. The rider held up the lamb, jabbered a sentence of broncho Spanish at the spot where the man had been, put down his bleating burden, and cantered back to his own side of the river without unnecessary delay. No bullets had yet been fired in the Cullison-Fendrick feud, but a "greaser" was liable to do anything, according to the old puncher's notion. Anyhow, he did not want to be a temptation to anyone with a gun in his hand.

An hour later, Kate, on the return trip, topped the rise where she had found the lamb. Pulling up her pony, to rest the horse from its climb, she gazed back across the river to the rolling ridges among which lay the C. F. ranch. Oddly enough, she had never seen Cass Fendrick. He had come to Papago County a few years before, and had bought the place from an earlier settler. In the disagreement that had fallen between the two men, she was wholly on the side of her father. Sometimes she had wondered what manner of man this Cass Fendrick might be; disagreeable, of course, but after precisely what fashion.

"Your property, I believe, Miss Cullison."

She turned at sound of the suave, amused drawl, and looked upon a dark, slim young man of picturesque appearance. He was bowing to her with an obvious intention of overdoing it. Voice and manner had the habit of the South rather than of the West. A kind of indolent irony sat easily upon the swarthy face crowned with a black sleek head of hair.

Her instinct told the girl who he was. She did not need to ask herself any longer what Cass Fendrick looked like.

He was holding out to her the bloodstained kerchief that had been tied to the lamb's leg.

"I didn't care to have it returned," she told him with cold civility.

"Now, if you'd only left a note to say so, it would have saved me a quite considerable climb," he suggested.

In spite of herself a flicker of amusement lit her eyes. She had a sense of humor. "I did not think

174

of that, and since you have troubled to return it to me, I can only say thank you."

She held out her hand for the kerchief, but he did not move. "I don't know but what I'll keep it, after all, for a souvenir. Just to remind me that Luck Cullison's daughter went out of her way to help one of Cass Fendrick's sheep."

She ignored his sardonic mockery. "I don't let live creatures suffer when I can help it. Are you going to give me my handkerchief?"

"Haven't made up my mind yet. Perhaps I'll have it washed and bring it home to you."

She decided that he was trying to flirt with her, and turned the head of her horse to start.

"Now your father has pulled his freight, I expect it will be safe to call," he added.

The bridle rein tightened. "What nonsense are you saying about my father?"

"No news, Miss Cullison; just what everybody is saying, that he has gone to cover on account of the hold-up."

A chill fear drenched her heart. "Do you mean the hold-up of the Limited at Tin Cup?"

"No, I don't." He looked at her sharply. "Mean to say you haven't heard of the hold-up of the W. & S. Express Company at Saguache?"

"No. When was it?"

"Tuesday night. The man got away with twenty thousand dollars."

"And what has my father to do with that?" she demanded haughtily.

A satisfied spleen purred in his voice. "My dear young lady, that is what everyone is asking."

"What do you mean? Say it." There was fear as well as anger in her voice. Had her father somehow got into trouble trying to save Sam?"

"Oh, I'm saying nothing. But what Sheriff Bolt means is that when he gets his handcuffs on Luck Cullison, he'll have the man that can tell him where that twenty thousand is."

"It's a lie."

He waved his hand airily, as one who declined responsibility in the matter, but his dark, saturnine face sparkled with malice.

"Maybe so. Seems to be some evidence, but I reckon he can explain that away—when he comes back. The hold-up dropped a hat with the initials L. C. in the band, since identified as his. He had lost a lot of money at poker. Next day he paid it. He had no money in the bank, but maybe he found it growing on a cactus bush."

"You liar!" she panted, eyes blazing.

"I'll take that from you, my dear, because you look so blamed pretty when you're mad; but I wouldn't take it from him—from your father, who is hiding out in the hills somewhere."

Anger uncurbed welled from her in an inarticulate cry. He had come close to her, and was standing beside the stirrup, one bold hand upon the rein. Her quirt went swiftly up and down, cut like a thin bar of red-hot iron across his uplifted face. He stumbled back, half blind with the pain. Before he could realize what had happened the spur on her little boot touched the side of the pony, and it was off with a bound. She was galloping wildly down the trail toward home.

He looked after her, fingers caressing the welt that burned his cheek.

"You'll pay for that, Kate Cullison," he said aloud to himself.

Anger stung him, but deeper than his rage was a growing admiration. How she had lashed out at him because he had taunted her of her father. By Jove, a girl like that would be worth taming! His cold eyes glittered as he put the bloodstained kerchief in his pocket. She was not through with him yet—not by a good deal.

CHAPTER V

"AIN'T SHE THE GAMEST LITTLE THOR-OUGHBRED?"

Kate galloped into the ranch plaza around which the buildings were set, slipped from her pony, and ran at once to the telephone. Bob was on a side porch mending a bridle.

"Have you heard anything from dad?" she cried through the open door.

"Nope," he answered, hammering down a rivet.

Kate called up the hotel where Maloney was staying at Saguache, but could not get him. She tried the Del Mar, where her father and his friends always put up when in town. She asked in turn for Mackenzie, for Yesler, for Alec Flandrau.

While she waited for an answer, the girl moved nervously about the room. She could not sit down or settle herself at anything. For some instinct told her that Fendrick's taunt was not a lie cut out of whole cloth.

The bell rang. Instantly she was at the telephone. Mackenzie was at the other end of the line.

"Oh, Uncle Mac." She had called him uncle ever since she could remember. "What is it they are saying about dad? Tell me it isn't true," she begged.

"A pack of lees, lassie." His Scotch idiom and accent had succumbed to thirty years on the plains, but when he became excited it rose triumphant through the acquired speech of the Southwest.

"Then is he there—in Saguache, I mean."

"No-o. He's not in town."

"Where is he?"

"Hoots! He'll just have gone somewhere on business."

He did not bluff well. Through the hearty assurance she pierced to the note of trouble in his voice.

"You're hiding something from me, Uncle Mac. I won't have it. You tell me the truth—the whole truth."

In three sentences he sketched it for her, and when he had finished he knew by the sound of her voice that she was greatly frightened.

"Something has happened to him. I'm coming to town."

"If you feel you'd rather. Take the stage in tomorrow."

"No. I'm coming to-night. I'll bring Bob. Save us two rooms at the hotel."

"Better wait till to-morrow. Forty miles is a long ride, lass."

"No, I can't wait. Have Curly Flandrau come to the Del Mar if he's in town—and Dick Maloney, too. That's all. Good-by."

She turned to her cousin, who was standing big-eyed at her elbow.

"What is it, Kate? Has anything happened to Uncle Luck?"

She swallowed a lump in her throat. "Dad's gone, Bob. Nobody knows where. They say—the liars—that he robbed the W. & S. Express Company."

Suddenly her face went down into her forearm on the table and sobs began to rack her body. The boy, staggered at this preposterous charge, could only lay his hand on her shoulder and beg her not to cry.

"It'll be all right, Kate. Wait till Uncle Luck comes back. He'll make 'em sick for talking about him."

"But suppose he—suppose he——" She dared not complete what was in her mind, that perhaps he had been ambushed by some of his enemies and killed.

"You bet they'll drop into a hole and pull it in after them when Uncle Luck shows up," the boy bragged with supreme confidence.

His cousin nodded, choking down her sobs. "Of course. It—it'll come out all right—as soon as he finds out what they're saying. Saddle two horses right away, Bob."

"Sure. We'll soon find where he is, I bet you."

The setting sun found their journey less than half done. The brilliant rainbow afterglow of sunset faded to colder tints, and then disappeared. The purple saw-toothed range softened to a violet hue. With the coming of the moon the hard, dry desert lost detail, took on a loveliness of tone and outline that made it an idealized painting of itself. Myriads of stars were out, so that the heavens seemed sown with them as an Arizona hillside is in spring with yellow poppies.

Kate was tortured with anxiety, but the surpassing beauty that encompassed them was somehow a comfort to her. Deep within her something denied that her father could be gone out of a world so good. And if he were alive, Curly Flandrau would find him—Curly and Dick between them. Luck Cullison had plenty of good friends who would not stand by and see him wronged.

Any theory of his disappearance that accepted his guilt did not occur to her mind for an instant. The two had been very close to each other. Luck had been in the habit of saying smilingly that she was his majordomo, his right bower. Some share of his lawless temperament she inherited; enough to feel sure that this particular kind of wrongdoing was impossible for him. He was reckless, sometimes passionate, but she did not need to reassure herself that he was scrupulously honest.

This brought her back to the only other tenable hypothesis—foul play. And from this she shrank with a quaking heart. For surely if his enemies wished to harm him they would destroy him, and this was a conclusion against which she fought desperately.

The plaza clock boomed ten strokes as they rode into Saguache. Mackenzie was waiting for them on the steps of the hotel.

"Have they—has anything been——?"

The owner of the Fiddleback shook his grizzled head. "Not yet. Didn't you meet Curly?"

"No."

"He rode out to come in with you, but if he didn't meet you by ten he was to come back. You took the north road, I reckon?"

"Yes."

His warm heart was wrung for the young woman whose fine eyes stared with dumb agony from a face that looked very white in the shining moonlight. He put an arm around her shoulders, and drew her into the hotel with cheerful talk.

"Come along, Bob. We're going to tuck away a good supper first off. While you're eating, I'll tell you all there is to be told."

Kate opened her lips to say that she was not hungry and could not possibly eat a bite, but she thought better of it. Bob had tasted nothing since noon, and of course he must be fed.

The lad fell to with an appetite grief had not dulled. His cousin could at first only pick at what was set before her. It seemed heartless to be sitting down in comfort to so good a supper while her father was in she knew not how great distress. Grief swelled in her throat, and forced back the food she was trying to eat.

Mackenzie broke off his story to remonstrate. "This won't do at all, Kate. If you're going to help find Luck, you've got to keep yourself fit. Now, you try this chicken, honey."

"I—just can't, Uncle Mac."

"But you need it."

"I know," the girl confessed, and as she said it broke down again into soft weeping.

Mac let her have her cry out, petting her awkwardly. Presently she dried her eyes, set at her supper in a business-like way, heard the story to an end quietly, and volunteered one heartbroken comment.

"As if father *could* do such a thing."

The cattleman agreed eagerly. There were times when he was full of doubt on that point, but he was not going to let her know it.

Curly came into the room, and the girl rose to meet him. He took her little hand in his tanned, muscular one, and somehow from his grip she gathered strength. He would do all that could be done to find her father, just as he had done so much to save her brother.

"I'm so glad you've come," she said simply.

"I'm glad you're glad," he smiled cheerfully.

He knew she had been crying, that she was suffering cruelly, but he offered her courage rather than maudlin sympathy. Hope seemed to flow through her veins at the meeting of the eyes. Whatever a man could do for her would be done by Curly.

They talked the situation over together.

"As it looks to me, we've got to find out two things—first, what has become of your father, and, second, who did steal that money."

"Now you're talking," Mackenzie agreed. "I always did say you had a good head, Curly."

"I don't see it yet, but there's some link between the two things. I mean between the robbery and his disappearance."

"How do you mean?" Kate asked.

"We'll say the robbers were his enemies—some of the Soapy Stone outfit maybe. They have got him out of the way to satisfy their grudge and to make people think he did it. Unfortunately there

184

is evidence that makes it look as if he might have done it—what they call corroborating testimony."

Billie Mackenzie scratched his gray poll. "Hold on, Curly. This notion of a link between the hold-up and Luck's leaving is what the other side is tying to. Don't we want to think different from them?"

"We do. They think he is guilty. We know he isn't."

"What does Sheriff Bolt think?"

Curly waved the sheriff aside. "It don't matter what he thinks, Miss Kate. He *says* he thinks Luck was mixed up in the hold-up. Maybe that's what he thinks, but we don't want to forget that Cass Fendrick made him sheriff and your father fought him to a fare-you-well."

"Then we can't expect any help from him."

"Not much. He ain't a bad fellow, Bolt ain't. He'll be square, but his notions are liable to be warped."

"I'd like to talk with him," the young woman announced.

"All right," Mackenzie assented. "To-morrow mo'ning——"

"No, to-night, Uncle Mac."

The cattleman looked at her in surprise. Her voice rang with decision. Her slight figure seemed compact of energy and resolution. Was this the

girl who had been in helpless tears not ten minutes before?

"I'll see if he's at his office. Maybe he'll come
up," Curly said.

"No. I'll go down to the courthouse if he's
there."

Flandrau got Bolt on the telephone at his room.
After a little grumbling he consented to meet Miss
Cullison at his office.

"Bob, you must go to bed. You're tired out,"
his cousin told him.

"I ain't, either," he denied indignantly. "Tired
nothing. I'm going with you."

Curly caught Kate's glance, and she left the boy
to him.

"Look here, Bob. We're at the beginning of a
big job. Some of us have to keep fresh all the
time. We'll work in relays. To-night you sleep so
as to be ready to-morrow."

This way of putting it satisfied the boy. He reluctantly consented to go to bed, and was sound
asleep almost as soon as his head struck the pillow.

At the office of the sheriff, Kate cut to essen-
tials as soon as introductions were over.

"Do you think my father robbed the W. & S.
Express Company, Mr. Bolt?" she asked.

Her plainness embarrassed the officer.

"Let's look at the facts, Miss Cullison," he began

amiably. "Then you tell me what you would think in my place. Your father needed money mighty bad. There's no doubt at all about that. Here's an envelope on which he had written a list of his debts. You'll notice they run to just a little more than twenty thousand. I found this in his bedroom the day he disappeared."

She took the paper, glanced at it mechanically, and looked at the sheriff again. "Well? Everybody wants money. Do they all steal it?"

"Turn that envelope over, Miss Cullison. Notice how he has written there half a dozen times in a row, '$20,000,' and just below it twice, 'W. & S. Ex. Co.' Finally, the one word, 'To-night.'"

She read it all, read it with a heart heavy as lead, and knew that there he had left in his own strong, bold handwriting convincing evidence against himself. Still, she did not doubt him in the least, but there could be no question now that he knew of the intended shipment, that absent-mindedly he had jotted down this data while he was thinking about it in connection with his own debts.

The sheriff went on tightening the chain of evidence in a voice that for all its kindness seemed to her remorseless as fate. "It turns out that Mr. Jordan of the Cattleman's National Bank mentioned this shipment to your father that morning. Mr. Cullison was trying to raise money from him, but he couldn't let him have it. Every bank in the city refused him a loan. Yet next morning he paid off two thousand dollars he owed from a poker game."

"He must have borrowed the money from some one," she said weakly.

"That money he paid in twenty-dollar bills. The stolen express package was in twenties. You know yourself that this is a gold country. Bills ain't so plentiful."

The girl's hand went to her heart. Faith in her father was a rock not to be washed away by any amount of evidence. What made her wince was the amount of circumstantial testimony falling into place so inexorably against him.

"Is that all?" she asked despairingly.

"I wish it were, Miss Cullison. But it's not. A man came round the corner and shot at the robber as he was escaping. His hat fell off. Here it is."

As Kate took the hat something seemed to tighten around her heart. It belonged to her father. His personality was stamped all over it. She even recognized a coffee stain on the under side of the brim. There was no need of the initials L. C. to tell her whose it had been. A wave of despair swept over her. Again she was on the verge of breaking down, but controlled herself as with a tight curb.

Bolt's voice went on. "Next day your father disappeared, Miss Cullison. He was here in town all morning. His friends knew that suspicion was fastening on him. The inference is that he daren't wait to have the truth come out. Mind, I don't say he's guilty. But it looks that way. Now, that's my case. If you were sheriff in my place, what would you do?"

Her answer flashed back instantly. "If I knew Luck Cullison, I would be sure there was a mistake somewhere, and I would look for foul play. I would believe anything except that he was guilty— anything in the world. You know he has enemies."

The sheriff liked her spirited defense no less because he could not agree with her. "Yes, I know that. The trouble is that these incriminating facts don't come in the main from his enemies."

"You say the robber had on his hat, and that somebody shot at him. Whoever it was must know the man wasn't father."

Gently Bolt took this last prop from her hope. 'He is almost sure the man was your father."

A spark of steel came into her dark eyes. "Who s the man?"

"His name is Fendrick."

"Cass Fendrick?" She whipped the word at him, leaning forward in her chair rigidly with her hands clenched on the arms of it. One could have guessed that the sound of the name had unleashed a dormant ferocity in her.

"Yes. I know he and your father aren't friends. They have had some trouble. For that reason he was very reluctant to give your father's name."

The girl flamed. "Reluctant! Don't you believe it? He hates Father like poison." A flash of inspiration came to her. She rose, slim and tall and purposeful. "Cass Fendrick is the man you want, and he is the man I want. He robbed the express company, and he has killed my father or abducted him. I know now. Arrest him to-night."

"I have to have evidence," Bolt said quietly.

"I can give you a motive. Listen. Father expected to prove up yesterday on his Del Oro claim. If he had done so Cass Fendrick's sheep would have been cut off from the water. Father had to be got out of the way not later than Wednesday, or that man would have been put out of business. He was very bitter about it. He had made threats."

"It would take more than threats to get rid of the best fighting man in Arizona, right in the middle of the day, in the heart of the town, without a soul knowing about it." The officer added with a smile: "I'd hate to undertake the contract, give me all the help I wanted."

"He was trapped somehow, of course," Curly

cut in. For he was sure that in no other way could Luck Cullison have been overcome.

"If you'll only tell me how, Flandrau," Bolt returned.

"I don't know how, but we'll find out."

"I hope so."

Kate felt his doubt, and it was like a spark to powder.

"Fendrick is your friend. You were elected by his influence. Perhaps you want to prove that Father did this."

"The people elected me, Miss Cullison," answered Bolt, with grave reproach. "I haven't any friends or any enemies when it comes to doing what I've sworn to do."

"Then you ought to know Father couldn't have done this. There is such a thing as character. Luck Cullison simply *couldn't* be a thief."

Mackenzie's faith had been strengthened by the insistent loyalty of the girl. "That's right, Nick. Let me tell you something else. Fendrick knew Luck was going to prove up on Thursday. He heard him tell us at the Round-Up Club Tuesday morning."

The sheriff summed up. "You've proved Cass had interests that would be helped if Mr. Cullison were removed. But you haven't shaken the evidence against Luck."

"We've proved Cass Fendrick had to get Father out of the way on the very day he disappeared. One day later would have been too late. We've shown his enmity. Any evidence that rests on his word is no good. The truth isn't in the man."

"Maybe not, but he didn't make this evidence."

Kate had another inspirational flash. "He did— some of it. Somehow he got hold of father's hat, and he manufactured a story about shooting it from the robber's head. But to make his story stick he must admit he was on the ground at the time of the hold-up. So he must have known the robbery was going to take place. It's as plain as old Run-A-Mile's wart that he knew of it because he planned it himself."

Bolt's shrewd eyes narrowed to a smile. "You prove to me that Cass had your father's hat *before the hold-up,* and I'll take some stock in the story."

"And in the meantime," suggested Curly.

"I'll keep right on looking for Luck Cullison, but I'll keep an eye on Cass Fendrick, too."

Kate took up the challenge confidently. "I'll prove he had the hat—at least I'll try to pretty hard. It's the truth, and it must come out some-how."

After he had left her at the hotel, Curly walked the streets with a sharp excitement tingling his blood. He had lived his life among men, and he knew little about women and their ways. But his imagination seized avidly upon this slim, dark girl with the fine eyes that could be both tender and ferocious, with the look of combined delicacy and strength in every line of her.

"Ain't she the gamest little thoroughbred ever?" he chuckled to himself. "Stands the acid every crack. Think of her standing pat so game—just like she did for me that night out at the ranch. She's the best argument Luck has got."

CHAPTER VI

TWO HATS ON A RACK

One casual remark of Mackenzie had given Kate a clew. Even before she had explained it, Curly caught the point and began to dig for the truth. For though he was almost a boy, the others leaned on him with the expectation that in the absence of Maloney he would take the lead. Before they separated for the night he made Mackenzie go over every detail he could remember of the meeting between Cullison and Fendrick at the Round-Up Club. This was the last time the two men had been seen together in public, and he felt it important that he should know just what had taken place.

In the morning he and Kate had a talk with his uncle on the same subject. Not content with this, he made the whole party adjourn to the club rooms so that he might see exactly where Luck had sat and the different places the sheepman had stood from the time he entered until the poker players left.

Together Billie Mackenzie and Alec Flandrau dramatized the scene for the young people. Mac personated the sheepman, came into the room, hung up his hat, lounged over to the poker table, said his little piece as well as he could remember it, and passed into the next room. Flandrau, Senior, taking the rôle of Cullison, presently got up, lifted his hat from the rack, and went to the door.

With excitement trembling in her voice, the girl asked an eager question. "Were their hats side by side like that on adjoining pegs?"

Billie turned a puzzled face to his friend. "How about that, Alec?"

"That's how I remember it."

"Same here, my notion is."

"Both gray hats?" Curly cut in.

His uncle looked helplessly at the other man. "Can't be sure of that. Luck's was gray all right."

"Cass wore a gray hat too, seems to me," Mackenzie contributed, scratching his gray hair.

"Did Father hesitate at all about which one to take?"

"No-o. I don't reckon he did. He had turned to ask me if I was coming—wasn't looking at the hats at all."

Curly looked at Kate and nodded. "I reckon we know how Cass got Mr. Cullison's hat. It was left on the rack."

"How do you mean?" his uncle asked.

"Don't you see?" the girl explained, her eyes shining with excitement. "Father took the wrong hat. You know how absent-minded he is some-times."

Mackenzie slapped his knee. "I'll bet a stack of blues you've guessed it."

"There's a way to make sure," Curly said.

"I don't get you."

"Fendrick couldn't wear Mr. Cullison's hat around without the risk of someone remembering it later. What would he do then?"

Kate beamed. "Buy another at the nearest store."

"That would be my guess. And the nearest store is the New York Emporium. We've got to find out whether he did buy one there on Tuesday some time after nine o'clock in the morning."

The girl's eyes were sparkling. She bustled with businesslike energy. "I'll go and ask right away."

"Don't you think we'd better let Uncle Alec find out? He's not so likely to stir up curiosity," Curly suggested.

"That's right. Let me earn my board and keep," the owner of the Map of Texas volunteered.

Within a quarter of an hour Alec Flandrau joined the others at the hotel. He was beaming like a schoolboy who has been given an unexpected holi-day.

"You kids are right at the head of the class in the detective game. Cass bought a brown hat, about 9:30 in the mo'ning. Paid five dollars for it. Wouldn't let them deliver the old one but took it with him in a paper sack."

With her lieutenants flanking her Kate went straight to the office of the sheriff. Bolt heard the story out and considered it thoughtfully.

"You win, Miss Cullison. You haven't proved Fendrick caused your father's disappearance by foul play, and you haven't proved he committed the robbery. Point of fact I don't think he did either one. But it certainly looks like he may possibly have manufactured evidence."

Curly snorted scornfully. "You're letting your friend down easy, Mr. Bolt. By his own story he was on the ground a minute after the robbery took place. How do we know he wasn't there a minute before? For if he didn't know the hold-up was going to occur why did he bring Mr. Cullison's hat with him, punctured so neatly with bullet holes?"

"I'll bet a thousand dollars he is at the bottom of this whole thing," Mackenzie added angrily.

The sheriff flushed. "You gentlemen are entitled to your opinions just as I'm entitled to mine. You haven't even proved he took Mr. Cullison's hat; you've merely showed he may have done it."

"We've given you a motive and some evidence. How much more do you want?" Curly demanded.

"Hold your hawses a while, Flandrau, and look

at this thing reasonable. You're all prejudiced for Cullison and against Fendrick. Talk about evidence! There's ten times as much against your friend as there is against Cass."

"Then you'll not arrest Fendrick?"

"When you give me good reason to do it," Bolt returned doggedly.

"That's all right, Mr. Sheriff. Now we know where you stand," Flandrau, Senior, said stiffly.

The harassed official mopped his face with a bandanna. "Sho! You all make me tired. I'm not Fendrick's friend while I'm in this office any more than I'm Luck's. But I've got to use my judgment, ain't I?"

The four adjourned to meet at the Del Mar for a discussion of ways and means.

"We'll keep a watch on Fendrick—see where he goes, who he talks to, what he does. Maybe he'll make a break and give himself away," Curly said hopefully.

"But my father—we must rescue him first."

"As soon as we find where he is. Me, I'm right hopeful all's well with him. Killing him wouldn't help Cass any, because you and Sam would prove up on the claim. But if he could hold your father a prisoner and get him to sign a relinquishment to him he would be in a fine position."

"But Father wouldn't sign. He ought to know that."

"Not through fear your father wouldn't. But if Fendrick could get at him some way he might put down his John Hancock. With this trouble of Sam still unsettled and the Tin Cup hold-up to be pulled off he might sign."

"If we could only have Fendrick arrested——"

"What good would that do? If he's guilty he wouldn't talk. And if he is holding your father somewhere in the hills it would only be serving notice that we were getting warm. No, I'm for a still hunt. Let Cass ride around and meet his partners in this deal. We'll keep an eye on him all right."

"Maybe you're right," Kate admitted with a sigh.

CHAPTER VII

ANONYMOUS LETTERS

Sheriff Bolt, though a politician, was an honest man. It troubled him that Cullison's friends believed him to be a partisan in a matter of this sort. For which reason he met more than half way Curly's overtures. Young Flandrau was in the office of the sheriff a good deal, because he wanted to be kept informed of any new developments in the W. & S. robbery case.

It was on one of those occasions that Bolt tossed across to him a letter he had just opened.

"I've been getting letters from the village cut-up or from some crank, I don't know which. Here's a sample."

The envelope, addressed evidently in a disguised hand, contained one sheet of paper. Upon this was lettered roughly,

"Play the Jack of Hearts."

Flandrau looked up with a suggestion of eagerness in his eyes.

"What do you reckon it means?" he asked.

"Search me. Like as not it don't mean a thing. The others had just as much sense as that one."

"Let's see the others."

"I chucked them into the waste paper basket. One came by the morning mail yesterday and one by the afternoon. I'm no mind reader, and I've got no time to guess fool puzzles."

Curly observed that the waste paper basket was full. Evidently it had not been emptied for two or three days.

"Mind if I look for the others?" he asked.

Bolt waved permission. "Go to it."

The young man emptied the basket on the floor and went over its contents carefully. He found three communications from the unknown writer. Each of them was printed by hand on a sheet of cheap lined paper torn from a scratch pad. He smoothed them out and put them side by side on the table. This was what he read:

HEARTS ARE TRUMPS

WHEN IN DOUBT PLAY TRUMPS

PLAY TRUMPS *NOW*

There was only the one line to each message, and all of them were plainly in the same hand. He could make out only one thing, that someone was trying to give the sheriff information in a guarded way.

He was still puzzling over the thing when a boy came with a special delivery letter for the sheriff. Bolt glanced at it and handed the note to Curly.

"Another *billy doo* from my anxious friend."

This time the sender had been in too much of a hurry to print the words. They were written in a stiff hand by some uneducated person.

The Jack of Trumps, to-day

"Mind if I keep these?" Curly asked.

"Take 'em along."

Flandrau walked out to the grandstand at the fair grounds and sat down by himself there to think out what connection, if any, these singular warnings might have with the vanishing of Cullison or the robbery of the W. & S. He wasted three precious hours without any result. Dusk was falling before he returned.

"Guess I'll take them to my little partner and give her a whack at the puzzle," he decided.

Curly strolled back to town along El Molino street and down Main. He had just crossed the old Spanish plaza when his absorbed gaze fell on a sign that brought him up short. In front of a cigar store stretched across the sidewalk a painted picture of a jack of hearts. The same name was on the window.

Fifty yards behind him was the Silver Dollar saloon, where Luck Cullison had last been seen on his way to the Del Mar one hundred and fifty yards in front of him. Somewhere within that distance of two hundred yards the owner of the Circle C had vanished from the sight of men. The evidence showed he had not reached the hotel, for a cattle buyer had been waiting there to talk with him. His testimony, as well as that of the hotel clerk, was positive.

Could this little store, the Jack of Hearts, be the central point of the mystery? In his search for information Curly had already been in it, had bought a cigar, and had stopped to talk with Mrs. Wylie, the proprietor. She was a washed-out little woman who had once been pretty. Habitually she wore a depressed, hopeless look, the air of pathetic timidity that comes to some women who have found life too hard for them. It had been easy to alarm her. His first question had evidently set her heart a-flutter, but Flandrau had reassured her cheerfully. She had protested with absurd earnestness that she had seen nothing of Mr. Cullison. A single glance had been enough to dismiss her from any possible suspicion.

Now Curly stepped in a second time. **The**

frightened gaze of Mrs. Wylie fastened upon him instantly. He observed that her hand moved instinctively to her heart. Beyond question she was in fear. A flash of light clarified his mind. She was a conspirator, but an unwilling one. Possibly she might be the author of the anonymous warnings sent Bolt.

The young *vaquero* subscribed for a magazine and paid her the money. Tremblingly she filled out the receipt. He glanced at the slip and handed it back.

"Just write below the signature 'of the Jack of Hearts,' so that I'll remember where I paid the money if the magazine doesn't come," he suggested.

She did so, and Curly put the receipt in his pocket carelessly. He sauntered leisurely to the hotel, but as soon as he could get into a telephone booth his listlessness vanished. Maloney had returned to town and he telephoned him to get Mackenzie at once and watch the Jack of Hearts in front and rear. Before he left the booth Curly had compared the writing of Mrs. Wylie with that on the sheet that had come by special delivery. The loop of the J's, the shape of the K's, the formation of the capital H in both cases were alike. So too was the general lack of character common to both, the peculiar hesitating drag of the letters.

Beyond question the same person had written both.

Certainly Mrs. Wylie was not warning the sheriff against herself. Then against whom? He must know her antecedents, and at once. There was no time for him to mole them out himself. Calling up a local detective agency, he asked the manager to let him know within an hour or two all that could be found out about the woman without alarming her.

"Wait a moment. I think we have her on file. Hold the 'phone." The detective presently returned. "Yes. We can give you the facts. Will you come to the office for them?"

Fifteen minutes later Curly knew that Mrs. Wylie was the divorced wife of Lute Blackwell. She had come to Saguache from the mountains several years before. Soon after there had been an inconspicuous notice in the *Sentinel* to the effect that Cora Blackwell was suing for divorce from Lute Blackwell, then a prisoner *in* the penitentiary at Yuma. Another news item followed a week later stating that the divorce had been granted together with the right to use her maiden name. Unobtrusively she had started her little store. Her former husband, 'paroled from the penitentiary a few months before the rustling episode, had at intervals made of her shop a loafing place since that time.

Curly returned to the Del Mar and sent his name

up to Miss Cullison. With Kate and Bob there was also in the room Alec Flandrau.

The girl came forward lightly to meet him with the lance-straight poise that always seemed to him to express a brave spirit ardent and unafraid.

"Have you heard something?" she asked quickly.

"Yes. Tell me, when did your father last meet Lute Blackwell so far as you know?"

"I don't know. Not for years, I think. Why?"

The owner of the Map of Texas answered the question of his nephew. "He met him the other day. Let's see. It was right after the big poker game. We met him downstairs here. Luck had to straighten out some notions he had got."

"How?"

Flandrau, Senior, told the story of what had occurred in the hotel lobby.

"And you say he swore to get even?"

"That's what he said. And he looked like he meant it too."

"What is it? What have you found out?" Kate implored.

The young man told about the letters and Mrs. Wylie.

"We've got to get a move on us," he concluded. "For if Lute Blackwell did this thing to your father it's mighty serious for him."

Kate was white to the lips, but in no danger of

breaking down. "Yes, if this man is in it he would not stop at less than murder. But I don't believe it. I know Father is alive. Cass Fendrick is the man we want. I'm sure of it."

Curly had before seen women hard as nails, gaunt strong mountaineers as tough as hickory withes. But he had never before seen that quality dwelling in a slim girlish figure of long soft curves, never seen it in a face of dewy freshness that could melt to the tenderest pity. She was like flint, and yet she could give herself with a passionate tenderness to those she loved. He had seen animals guard their young with that same alert eager abandon. His conviction was that she would gladly die for her father if it were necessary. As he looked at her with hard unchanging eyes, his blood quickened to a fierce joy in her it had known for no other woman.

"First thing is to search the Jack of Hearts and see what's there. Are you with me, Uncle Alec?"

"I sure am, Curly;" and he reached for his hat.

Bob too was on his feet. "I'm going. You needn't any of you say I ain't, for I am."

Curly nodded. "If you'll do as you're told, Bob."

"I will. Cross my heart."

"May I come too?" Kate pleaded.

She was a strongwilled impulsive young woman, and her deference to Curly flattered him; but he shook his head none the less.

"No. You may wait in the parlor downstairs and I'll send Bob to you with any news. There's just a chance this may be a man's job and we want to go to it unhampered." He turned at the door with his warm smile. "By the way, I've got some news I forgot. I know where your father got the money to pay his poker debts. Mr. Jordan of the Cattlemen's National made him a personal loan. He figured it would not hurt the bank because the three men Luck paid it to would deposit it with the bank again."

"By George, that's what we did, too, every last one of us," his uncle admitted.

"Every little helps," Kate said, and her little double nod thanked Curly.

The young man stopped a moment after the others had gone. "I'm not going to let Bob get into danger," he promised.

"I knew you wouldn't," was her confident answer.

At the corner of the plaza Curly gave Bob instructions.

"You stay here and keep an eye on everyone that passes. Don't try to stop anybody. Just size them up."

"Ain't I to go with you? I got a gun."

"You're to do as I say. What kind of a soldier would you make if you can't obey orders? I'm running this. If you don't like it trot along home."

"Oh, I'll stay," agreed the crestfallen youth.

Maloney met them in front of the Jack of Hearts.

"Dick, you go with me inside. Uncle Alec, will you keep guard outside?"

"No, bub, I won't. I knew Luck before you were walking bowlegged," the old cattleman answered brusquely.

Curly grinned. "All right. Don't blame me if you get shot up."

Mrs. Wylie's startled eyes told tales when she saw the three men. Her face was ashen.

"I'm here to play trumps, Mrs. Wylie. What secret has the Jack of Hearts got hidden from us?" young Flandrau demanded, his hard eyes fastened to her timorous ones.

"I—I—I don't know what you mean."

"No use. We're here for business. Dick, you stay with her. Don't let her leave or shout a warning."

He passed into the back room, which was a kind of combination living room, kitchen and bedroom. A door led from the rear into a back yard littered with empty packing cases, garbage cans and waste paper. After taking a look around the yard he locked the back door noiselessly. There was no other apparent exit from the kitchen-bedroom except the one by which he and his uncle had entered from the shop. But he knew the place must have a cellar, and his inspection of the yard had showed no entrance there. He drew back the Navajo rug that covered the floor and found one of the old-fashioned trap doors some cheap houses have. Into this was fitted an iron ring with which to lift it.

From the darkness below came no sound, but Curly's imagination conceived the place as full of shining eyes glaring up at him. Any bad men down there already had the drop on them. Therefore neither Curly nor his uncle made the mistake of drawing a weapon.

"I'm coming down, boys," young Flandrau announced in a quiet confident voice. "The place is surrounded by our friends and it won't do you a whole lot of good to shoot me up. I'd advise you not to be too impulsive."

He descended the steps, his face like a stone wall for all the emotion it recorded. At his heels came the older man. Curly struck a match, found an electric bulb above his head, and turned the button. Instantly the darkness was driven from the cellar.

The two Flandraus were quite alone in the room. For furniture there was a table, a cot which had been slept in and not made up, and a couple of rough chairs. The place had no windows, no means of ventilation except through the trap door. Yet there were evidences to show that it had recently been inhabited. Half smoked cigars littered the floor. A pack of cards lay in disorder on the table. The *Sentinel* with date line of that day lay tossed in a corner.

The room told Curly this at least: There had been a prisoner here with a guard or guards. Judging by the newspaper they had been here within a few hours. The time of sending the special delivery letter made this the more probable. He had missed the men he wanted by a very little time. If he had had the gumption to understand the hints given by the letters Cullison might now be eating supper with his family at the hotel.

"Make anything out of it?" the older Flandrau asked.

"He's been here, but they've taken him away. Will you cover the telephoning? Have all the ranches notified that Luck is being taken into the hills so they can picket the trails."

"How do you know he is being taken there?"

"I don't know. I guess. Blackwell is in it. He knows every nook of the hills. The party left here not two hours since, looks like."

Curly put the newspaper in his pocket and led the way back to the store.

"The birds have flown, Dick. Made their getaway through the alley late this afternoon, probably just after it got dark." He turned to the woman.

"Mrs. Wylie, murder is going to be done, I shouldn't wonder. And you're liable to be held guilty of it unless you tell us all you know."

She began to weep, helplessly, but with a sort of stubbornness too. Frightened she certainly was, but some greater fear held her silent as to the secret. "I don't know anything about it," she repeated over and over.

"Won't do. You've got to speak. A man's life hangs on it."

But his resolution could not break hers, incomparably stronger than she though he was. Her conscience had driven her to send veiled warnings to the sheriff. But for very fear of her life she dared not commit herself openly.

Maloney had an inspiration. He spoke in a low voice to Curly. "Let's take her to the hotel. Miss Kate will know how to get it out of her better than we can."

Mrs. Wylie went with them quietly enough. She was shaken with fears but still resolute not to speak. They might send her to prison. She would tell them nothing—nothing at all. For someone who had made terror the habit of her life had put the fear of death into her soul.

CHAPTER VIII

A MESSAGE IN CIPHER

While Kate listened to what Curly had to tell her the dark eyes of the girl were fastened upon the trembling little woman standing near the door.

"Do you mean that she is going to let my father be killed rather than tell what she knows?" Her voice was sharply incredulous, touched with a horror scarcely realized.

"So she says."

Mrs. Wylie wrung her hands in agitation. Her lined face was a mirror of distress.

"But that's impossible. She must tell. What has Father ever done to hurt her?"

"I—I don't know anything about it," the harassed woman iterated.

"What's the use of saying that when we know you do? And you'll not get out of it by sobbing. You've *got* to talk."

Kate had not moved. None the less her force, the upblaze of feminine energy in her, crowded the little storekeeper to the wall. "You've got to tell—you've just got to," she insisted.

The little woman shrank before the energy of a passion so vital. No strength was in her to fight.

213

But she could and did offer the passive resistance of obstinate silence.

Curly had drawn from his pocket the newspaper found in the cellar. His eyes had searched for the date line to use as cumulative evidence, but they had remained fastened to one story. Now he spoke imperatively.

"Come here, Miss Kate."

She was beside him in an instant. "What is it?"

"I'm not sure yet, but—— Look here. I believe this is a message to us."

"A message?"

"From your father perhaps."

"How could it be?"

"I found the paper in the cellar where he was. See how some of these words are scored. Done with a finger nail, looks like."

"But how could he know we would see the paper, and if we did see it would understand?"

"He couldn't. It would be one chance in a million, but all his life he's been taking chances. This couldn't do any harm."

Her dark head bent beside his fair one with the crisp sun-reddened curls.

"I don't see any message. Where is it?"

"I don't see it myself—not much of it. Gimme time."

This was the paragraph upon which his gaze had

fastened, and the words and letters were scored sharply as shown below, though in the case of single letters the mark ran through them instead of underneath, evidently that no mistake might be made as to which was meant.

> J. P. Kelley of the ranger force reports over the telephone that by unexpected good <u>luck</u> he has succeeded in taking <u>prisoner</u> the notorious Jack Foster of Hermosilla and the Rincons notoriety and is <u>now</u> bringing him to <u>Saguache</u> where he will be locked up <u>pending</u> a disposition of his case. Kelley <u>succeeded in surprising him</u> while he was eating dinner at a Mexican roadhouse just this side of the border.

"Do you make it out?" Maloney asked, looking over their shoulders.

Curly took a pencil and an envelope from his pocket. On the latter he jotted down some words and handed the paper to his friend. This was what Maloney read:

```
. . . . . . . . . . . . . . . . . . . . . . . . . . . . . . . . . .
. . . . . . . . . . . . . . . . . . . luck . . . . . . . . .
. . . . prisoner . . . . Jack . . . . of He . . . . a
. . . . R . . . . . . t . . . . . . s now . . . . . . . . . . .
Saguache . . . . . . locked up pending a dis-
position of his case.  . . . . succeeded in
surprising him . . . . . . . . . . . . . . . . . . .
. . . . . . . . . . . . . . . . . . . . . . . . . . . . . . . . . . . . .
. . . . . . . . . . . . . .
```

215

"Read that right ahead."

Dick did not quite get the idea, but Kate, tense with excitement, took the envelope and read aloud.

"Luck——prisoner——Jack of Hearts——now Saguache——locked up pending a disposition of his case——succeeded in surprising him." She looked up with shining eyes. "He tells us everything but the names of the people who did it. Perhaps somewhere else in the paper he may tell that too."

But though they went over it word for word they found no more. Either he had been interrupted, or he had been afraid that his casual thumb nail pressures might arouse the suspicion of his guards if persisted in too long.

"He's alive somewhere. We'll save him now." Kate cried it softly, all warm with the joy of it.

"Seems to let our friend Fendrick out," Maloney mused.

"Lets him out of kidnapping Uncle Luck but maybe not out of the robbery," Bob amended.

"Doesn't let him out of either. Somebody was in this with Blackwell. If it wasn't Cass Fendrick then who was it?" Kate wanted to know.

"Might have been Soapy Stone," Dick guessed.

"Might have been, but now Sam has gone back into the hills to join Soapy; the gang would have to keep it from Sam. He wouldn't stand for it."

"No, not for a minute," Kate said decisively.

Curly spoke to her in a low voice. "You have a talk with Mrs. Wylie alone. We'll pull our freights. She'll tell you what she knows." He smiled in his gentle winning way. "She's sure had a tough time of it if ever a woman had. I reckon a little kindness is what she needs. Let her see we're her friends and will stand by her, that we won't let her come to harm because she talks. Show her we know everything anyhow but want her to corroborate details."

It was an hour before Kate joined them, and her eyes, though they were very bright, told tales of tears that had been shed.

"That poor woman! She has told me everything. Father has been down in that cellar for days under a guard. They took him away to-night. She doesn't know where. It was she sent the warnings to Sheriff Bolt. She wanted him to raid the place, but she dared not go to him."

"Because of Blackwell?"

"Yes. He came straight to her as soon as he was freed from the penitentiary. He had her completely terrorized. It seems she has been afraid to draw a deep breath ever since he returned. Even while he was in the hills she was always looking for him to come. The man used to keep her in a hell and he began bullying her again. So she gave him money, and he came for more—and more."

Curly nodded. He said nothing, but his strong jaw clamped.

"He was there that day," the girl continued. "She plucked up courage to refuse him what little she had left because she needed it for the rent. He got hold of her arm and twisted it. Father heard her cry and came in. Blackwell was behind the door as it opened. He struck with a loaded cane and Father fell unconscious. He raised it to strike again, but she clung to his arm and called for help. Before he could shake her off another man came in. He wrenched the club away."

"Fendrick?" breathed Curly.

"She doesn't know. But the first thing he did was to lock the outer door and take the key. They carried Father down into the cellar. Before he came to himself his hands were tied behind his back."

"And then?"

"They watched him day and night. Fendrick himself did not go near the place—if it was Fendrick. Blackwell swore to kill Mrs. Wylie if she told. They held him there till to-night. She thinks they were trying to get Father to sign some paper."

"The relinquishment of course. That means the other man was Fendrick."

Kate nodded. "Yes."

Curly rose. The muscles stood out in his jaw hard as steel ropes.

"We'll rake the Rincons with a fine tooth comb. Don't you worry. I've already wired for Bucky O'Connor to come and help. We'll get your Father out of the hands of those hell hounds. Won't we, Dick?"

The girl's eyes admired him, a lean hard-bitten Westerner with eyes as unblinking as an Arizona sun and with muscles like wire springs. His face still held its boyishness, but it had lost forever the irresponsibility of a few months before. She saw in him an iron will, shrewdness, courage and resource. All of these his friend Maloney also had. But Curly was the prodigal son, the sinner who had repented. His engaging recklessness lent him a charm from which she could not escape. Out of ten thousand men there were none whose voice drummed on her heart strings as did that of this youth.

CHAPTER IX

"THE FRIENDS OF L. C. SERVE NOTICE"

Two men sat in a log cabin on opposite sides of a cheap table. One of them was immersed in a newspaper. His body was relaxed, his mind apparently at ease. The other watched him malevolently. His fingers caressed the handle of a revolver that protruded from the holster at his side. He would have liked nothing better than to have drawn it and sent a bullet crashing into the unperturbed brain of his prisoner.

There were reasons of policy why it were better to curb this fascinating desire, but sometimes the impulse to kill surged up almost uncontrollably. On these occasions Luck Cullison was usually "deviling" him, the only diversion that had been open to the ranchman for some days past. Because of its danger—for he could never be quite sure that Blackwell's lust for swift vengeance would not overpower discretion—this pastime made a peculiar appeal to the audacious temper of the owner of the Circle C.

From time to time as Luck read he commented genially on the news.

"I see Tucson is going to get the El Paso & Southwestern extension after all. I'll bet the boys in that burg will be right tickled to hear it. They sure have worked steady for it."

Blackwell merely scowled. He never relaxed to the give and take of casual talk with his captive. Given his way, Cullison would not be here to read the *Sentinel*. But the brains of the conspiracy had ruled otherwise and had insisted too upon decent treatment. With one ankle securely tied to a leg of the table there was no danger in freeing the hands of the cattleman, but his hosts saw that never for an instant were hands and feet at liberty together. For this man was not the one with whom to take chances.

"Rudd has been convicted of forgery and taken to Yuma. Seems to me you used to live there, didn't you?" asked the cattleman with cool insolence, looking up from his paper to smile across at the furious convict.

Blackwell was livid. The man who had sent him to the territorial prison at Yuma dared to sit there bound and unarmed and taunt him with it.

"Take care," he advised hoarsely.

Cullison laughed and went back to the paper.

" 'Lieutenant O'Connor of the Arizona Rangers left town to-day for a short trip into the hills where he expects to spend a few days hunting.' Hunting what, do you reckon? Or hunting who, I should say. Ever meet Bucky O'Connor, Blackwell? No, I reckon not. He's since your time. A crackerjack too! Wonder if Bucky ain't after some friends of mine."

"Shut up," growled the other.

"Sure you'll be shut up—when Bucky lands you," retorted Luck cheerfully. Then, with a sudden whoop: "Hello, here's a personal to your address. Fine! They're getting ready to round you up, my friend. Listen. 'The friends of L. C. serve notice that what occurred at the Jack of Hearts is known. Any violence hereafter done to him will be paid for to the limit. No guilty man will escape.' So the boys are getting busy. I figured they would be. Looks like your chance of knocking me on the head has gone down Salt River. I tell you nowadays a man has to grab an opportunity by the tail when it's there."

The former convict leaned forward angrily. "Lemme see that paper."

His guest handed it over, an index finger pointing out the item. "Large as life, Blackwell. No, sir. You ce'tainly didn't ride herd proper on that opportunity."

"Don't be too sure it's gone, Mr. Sheriff."

The man's face was twisted to an ugly sneer back

of which lurked cruel menace. The gray eyes of Cullison did not waver a hair's breadth.

"It's gone. I'm as safe as if I were at the Circle C."

"Don't you think it."

"They've got you dead to rights. Read that personal again. Learn it by heart. 'The friends of L. C. give warning.' You better believe they're rounding up your outfit. They know I'm alive. They know all about the Jack of Hearts. Pretty soon they'll know where you've got me hidden."

"You'd better pray they won't. For if they find the nest it will be empty."

"Yes?" Luck spoke with ironical carelessness, but he shot an alert keen glance at the other.

"That's what I said. Want to know where you will be?" the other triumphed.

"I see you want to tell me. Unload your mind."

Triumph overrode discretion. "Look out of that window behind you."

Luck turned. The cabin was built on a ledge far up on the mountain side. From the back wall sloped for a hundred feet an almost perpendicular slide of rock.

"There's a prospect hole down there," Blackwell explained savagely. "You'd go down the Devil's Slide—what's left of you, I mean—deep into that

223

prospect hole. The timberings are rotted and the whole top of the working ready to cave in. When your body hits it there will be an avalanche—with Mr. Former-sheriff Cullison at the bottom of it. You'll be buried without any funeral expenses, and I reckon your friends will never know where to put the headstone."

The thing was devilishly simple and feasible. Luck, still looking out of the window, felt the blood run cold down his spine, for he knew this fellow would never stick at murder if he felt it would be safe. No doubt he was being well paid, and though in this workaday world revenge has gone out of fashion there was no denying that this ruffian would enjoy evening the score. But his confederate was of another stripe, a human being with normal passions and instincts. The cattleman wondered how he could reconcile it to his conscience to go into so vile a plot with a villain like the convict.

"So you see I'm right; you'd better pray your friends *won't* find you. They can't reach here without being heard. If they get to hunting these hills you sure want to hope they'll stay cold, for just as soon as they get warm it will be the signal for you to shoot the chutes."

Luck met his triumphant savagery with an impassive face. "Interesting if true. And where will you be when my friends arrive. I reckon it won': be a pleasant meeting for Mr. Blackwell."

"I'll be headed for Mexico. I tell you because you ain't liable to go around spreading the news. There's a horse saddled in the dip back of the hill crest. Get it?"

"Fine," Cullison came back. "And you'll ride right into some of Bucky O'Connor's rangers. He's got the border patroled. You'd never make it."

"Don't worry. I'd slip through. I'm no tenderfoot."

"What if you did? Bucky would drag you back by the scruff of the neck in two weeks. Remember Chavez."

He referred to a murderer whom the lieutenant of rangers had captured and brought back to be hanged later.

"Chavez was a fool."

"Was he? You don't get the point. The old days are gone. Law is in the saddle. Murder is no longer a pleasant pastime." And Cullison stretched his arms and yawned.

From far below there came through the open window the faint click of a horse's hoofs ringing against the stones in the dry bed of a river wash. Swiftly Blackwell moved to the door, taking down a rifle from its rack as he did so. Cullison rose noiselessly in his chair. If it came to the worst he meant to shout aloud his presence and close with this fellow. Hampered as he was by the table, the man would get him without question. But if he could only sink his fingers into that hairy throat while there was still life in him he could promise that the Mexican trip would never take place.

Blackwell, from his place by the door, could keep an eye both on his prisoner and on a point of the trail far below where horsemen must pass to reach the cabin.

"Sit down," he ordered.

Cullison's eyes were like fine.y-tempered steel. "I'd rather stand."

"By God, if you move from there——" The man did not finish his sentence, but the rifle was already half lifted. More words would have been super-fluous.

A rider came into sight and entered the mouth of the cañon. He was waving a white handker-chief. The man in the doorway answered the sig-nal.

"Not your friends this time, Mr. Sheriff," Black-well jeered.

"I get a stay of execution, do I?" The cool drawling voice of the cattleman showed nothing of the tense feeling within.

He resumed his seat and the reading of the newspaper. Presently, to the man that came over the threshold he spoke with a casual nod.

"Morning, Cass."

Fendrick mumbled a surly answer. The manner of ironical comradeship his captive chose to employ was more than an annoyance. To serve his ends it was necessary to put the fear of death into this man's heart, which was a thing he had found impossible to do. His foe would deride him, joke with him, discuss politics with him, play cards with him, do anything but fear him. In the meantime the logic of circumstances was driving the sheepman into a corner. He had on impulse made the owner of the Circle C his prisoner. Seeing him lie there unconscious on the floor of the Jack of Hearts, it had come to him in a flash that he might hold him and force a relinquishment of the Del Oro claim. His disappearance would explain itself if the rumor spread that he was the W. & S. express robber. Cass had done it to save himself from the ruin of his business, but already he had regretted it fifty times. Threats could not move Luck in the least. He was as hard as iron.

So the sheepman found himself between the upper and the nether millstones. He could not drive his prisoner to terms and he dared not release him. For if Cullison went away unpledged he would surely send him to the penitentiary. Nor could he hold him a prisoner indefinitely. He had seen the "personal" warning in both the morning and the afternoon papers. He guessed that the presence of the ranger Bucky O'Connor in Saguache was not a chance. The law was closing in on him. Somehow Cullison must be made to come through with a relinquishment and a pledge not to prosecute. The only other way out would be to let Blackwell wreak his hate on the former sheriff. From this he shrank with every instinct. Fendrick was a hard man. He would have fought it out to a finish if necessary. But murder was a thing he could not do.

He had never discussed the matter with Blackwell. The latter had told him of this retreat in the mountains and they had brought their prisoner here. But the existence of the prospect hole at the foot of the Devil's Slide was unknown to him. From the convict's revenge he had hitherto saved Luck. Blackwell was his tool rather than his confederate, but he was uneasily aware that if the man yielded to the elemental desire to kill his enemy the law would hold him, Cass Fendrick, guilty of the crime.

"Price of sheep good this week?" Cullison asked amiably.

"I didn't come here to discuss the price of sheep with you." Fendrick spoke harshly. A dull anger against the scheme of things burned in him. For somehow he had reached an *impasse* from which there was neither advance nor retreat.

"No. Well, you're right there. What I don't know about sheep would fill several government reports. Of course I've got ideas. One of them is——"

"I don't care anything about your ideas. Are you going to sign this relinquishment?"

Luck's face showed a placid surprise. "Why no, Cass. Thought I mentioned that before."

"You'd better." The sheepman's harassed face looked ugly enough for anything.

"Can't figure it out that way."

"You've got to sign it. By God, you've no option."

"No?" Still with pleasant incredulity.

"Think I'm going to let you get away from here now. You'll sign and you'll promise to tell nothing you know against us."

"No, I don't reckon I will."

Cullison was looking straight at him with his fearless level gaze. Fendrick realized with a sinking heart that he could not drive him that way to surrender. He knew that in the other man's place he would have given way, that his enemy was gamer than he was.

He threw up his hand in a sullen gesture that

disclaimed responsibility. "All right. It's on your own head. I've done all I can for you."

"What's on my head?"

"Your life. Damn you, don't you see you're driving me too far?"

"How far?"

"I'm not going to let you get away to send us to prison. What do you expect?"

Luck's frosty eyes did not release the other for a moment. "How are you going to prevent it, Cass?"

"I'll find a way."

"Blackwell's way—the Devil's Slide?"

The puzzled look of the sheepman told Cullison that Blackwell's plan of exit for him had not been submitted to the other.

"Your friend from Yuma has been explaining how he has arranged for me to cross the divide," he went on. "I'm to be plugged full of lead, shot down that rock, and landed in a prospect hole at the bottom."

"First I've heard of it." Fendrick wheeled upon his accomplice with angry eyes. He was in general a dominant man, and not one who would stand much initiative from his assistants.

"He's always deviling me," complained the convict surlily. Then, with a flash of anger: "But

I stand pat. He'll get his before I take chances of getting caught. I'm nobody's fool."

Cass snapped him up. "You'll do as I say. You'll not lift a finger against him unless he tries to escape."

"Have you seen the *Sentinel?* I tell you his friends know everything. Someone's peached. They're hot on our trail. Bucky O'Connor is in the hills. Think I'm going to be caught like a rat in a trap?"

"We'll talk of that later. Now you go look after my horse while I keep guard here."

Blackwell went, protesting that he was no "nigger" to be ordered about on errands. As soon as he was out of hearing Fendrick turned his thin lip-smile on the prisoner.

"It's up to you, Cullison. I saved your life once. I'm protecting you now. But if your friends show up he'll do as he says. I won't be here to stop him. Sign up and don't be a fool."

Luck's answer came easily and lightly. "My friend, we've already discussed that point."

"You won't change your mind?"

"Your arguments don't justify it, Cass."

The sheepman looked at him with a sinister significance. "Good enough. I'll bring you one that will justify it *muy pronto.*"

"It will have to be a mighty powerful one. Sorry I can't oblige you and your friend, the convict."

"It'll be powerful enough." Fendrick went to the door and called Blackwell. "Bring back that horse. I'm going down to the valley."

CHAPTER X

CASS FENDRICK MAKES A CALL

Kate was in her rose garden superintending the stable boy as he loosened the dirt around the roots of some of the bushes. She had returned to the Circle C for a day or two to give some directions in the absence of her father. Buck and the other riders came to her for orders and took them without contempt. She knew the cattle business, and they knew she knew it. To a man they were proud of her, of her spirit, her energy, and her good looks.

This rose garden was one evidence of her enterprise. No ranch in the county could show such a riot of bloom as the Circle C. The American Beauty, the Duchess, the La France bowed gracefully to neighbors of a dozen other choice varieties. Kate had brought this glimpse of Eden into the desert. She knew her catalogues by heart and she had the loving instinct that teaches all gardeners much about growing things.

The rider who cantered up to the fence, seeing her in her well-hung corduroy skirt, her close-fitting blouse, and the broad-rimmed straw hat that shielded her dark head from the sun, appreciated the fitness of her surroundings. She too was a flower of the desert, delicately fashioned, yet vital with the bloom of health.

At the clatter of hoofs she looked up from the bush she was trimming and at once rose to her feet. With the change in position she showed slim and tall, straight as a young poplar. Beneath their long lashes her eyes grew dark and hard. For the man who had drawn to a halt was Cass Fendrick.

From the pocket of his shirt he drew a crumpled piece of stained linen.

"I've brought back your handkerchief, Miss Cullison."

"What have you done with my father?"

He nodded toward the Mexican boy and Kate dismissed the lad. When he had gone she asked her question again in exactly the same words.

"If we're going to discuss your father you had better get your quirt again," the sheepman suggested, touching a scar on his face.

A flush swept over her cheeks, but she held her voice quiet and even. "Where is Father? What have you done with him?"

He swung from the horse and threw the rein to the ground. Then, sauntering to the gate, he let himself in.

"You've surely got a nice posy garden here.

234

Didn't know there was one like it in all sunbaked Arizona."

She stood rigid. Her unfaltering eyes, sloe-black in the pale face, never lifted from him.

"There's only one thing you can talk to me about. Where have you hidden my father?"

"I've heard folks say he did himself all the hiding that was done."

"You know that isn't true. That convict and you have hidden him somewhere. We have evidence enough to convict you both."

"Imagination, most of it, I expect." He was inspecting the roses and inhaling their bloom.

"Fact enough to send you to the penitentiary."

"I ought to be scared. This is a La France, ain't it?"

"I want you to tell me what you have done with my father."

He laughed a little and looked at her with eyes that narrowed like those of a cat basking in the sun. He had something the look of the larger members of the cat family—the soft long tread, the compact rippling muscles of a tame panther, and with these the threat that always lies behind its sleepy wariness.

"You're a young lady of one idea. No use arguing with you, I reckon."

"Not the least use. I've talked with Mrs. Wylie."

He raised his eyebrows. "Do I know the lady?"

"She will know you. That is more to the point."

"Did she say she knew me?" he purred.

"She will say it in court—if it ever comes to that."

"Just what will she say, if you please."

Kate told him in four sentences with a stinging directness that was the outstanding note of her, that and a fine self-forgetful courage.

"Is. that all? Comes to this then, that she says I heard her scream, ran in, and saved your father's life. Is that a penitentiary offense? I don't say it oughtn't to be, but is it?"

"You helped the villain take his body into the cellar. You plotted with him to hold Father a prisoner there."

"Says that, does she—that she overheard us plotting?"

"Of course she did not overhear what you said. You took good care of that. But she knew you were conspiring."

"Just naturally knew it without overhearing," he derided. "And of course if I was in a plot I must have been Johnny-on-the-spot a good deal of the time. Hung round there a-plenty, I expect?"

He had touched on the weak spot of Mrs. Wylie's testimony. The man who had saved Cullison's life, after a long talk with Blackwell, had gone out of the Jack of Hearts and had not returned so far as she knew. For her former husband had sent her on an errand just before the prisoner was taken away and she did not know who had helped him.

Kate was silent.

"How would this do for an explanation?" he suggested lazily. "We'll say just for the sake of argument that Mrs. Wylie's story is true, that I did save your father's life. We'll put it that I did help carry him downstairs where it was cooler and that I did have a long talk with the fellow Blackwell. What would I be talking to him about, if I wasn't reading the riot act to him? Ain't it likely too that he would be sorry for what he did while he was angry at your father for butting in as he was having trouble with his wife? And after he had said he was sorry why shouldn't I hit the road out of there? There's no love lost between me and Luck Cullison. I wasn't under any obligations to wrap him up in cotton and bring him back this side up with care to his anxious friends. If he chose later to take a hike out of town on p.d.q. hurry up business I ain't to blame. And I reckon you'll find a jury will agree with me."

She had to admit to herself that he made out a plausible case. Not that she believed it for a moment. But very likely a jury would. As for his subsequent silence that could be explained by his desire not to mix himself in the affairs of one with whom he was upon unfriendly terms. The irrefutable fact that he had saved the life of Cullison would go a long way as presumptive proof of his innocence.

"I see you are wearing your gray hat again. What have you done with the brown one?"

She had flashed the question at him so unexpectedly that he was startled, but the wary mask fell again over the sardonic face.

"You take a right friendly interest in my hats, seems to me."

"I know this much. Father took your hat by mistake from the club. You bought a brown one half an hour later. You used Father's to manufacture evidence against him. If it isn't true that he is your prisoner how does it come that you have your gray hat again? You must have taken it from him."

He laughed uneasily. She had guessed the exact truth.

"In Arizona there are about forty thousand gray hats like this. Do you figure you can identify this one, Miss Cullison? And suppose your fairy tale of the Jack of Hearts is true, couldn't I have swapped hats again while he lay there unconscious?"

She brushed his explanation aside with a woman's superb indifference to logic.

"You can talk of course. I don't care. It is all lies—lies. You have kidnapped Father and are holding him somewhere. Don't you dare to hurt him. If you should—Oh, if you should—you will wish you had never been born." The fierceness of her passion beat upon him like sudden summer hail.

He laughed slowly, well pleased. A lazy smoldering admiration shone in his half shuttered eyes.

"So you're going to take it out of me, are you?"

A creature of moods, there came over her now a swift change. Every feature of her, the tense pose, the manner of defiant courage, softened indescribably. She was no longer an enemy bent on his destruction but a girl pleading for the father she loved.

"Why do you do it? You are a man. You want to fight fair. Tell me he is well. Tell me you will set him free."

He forgot for the moment that he was a man with the toils of the law closing upon him, forgot that his success and even his liberty were at stake. He saw only a girl with the hunger of love in her wistful eyes, and knew that it lay in his power to bring back the laughter and the light into them.

"Suppose I can't fight fair any longer. Suppose

239

I've let myself get trapped and it isn't up to me but to somebody else."

"How do you mean?"

"Up to your father, say."

"My father?"

"Yes. How could I turn him loose when the first thing he did would be to swear out a warrant for my arrest?"

"But he wouldn't—not if you freed him."

He laughed harshly. "I thought you knew him. He's hard as nails."

She recognized the justice of this appraisal. "But he is generous too. He stands by his friends."

"I'm not his friend, not so you could notice it." He laughed again, bitterly. "Not that it matters. Of course I was just putting a case. Nothing to it really."

He was hedging because he thought he had gone too far, but she appeared not to notice it. Her eyes had the faraway look of one who communes with herself.

"If I could only see him and have a talk with him."

"What good would that do?" he pretended to scoff.

But he watched her closely nevertheless.

"I think I could get him to do as I ask. He nearly always does." Her gaze went swiftly back to him. "Let me talk with him. There's a reason why he ought to be free now, one that would appeal to him."

This was what he had come for, but now that she had met him half way he hesitated. If she should not succeed he would be worse off than before. He could neither hold her a prisoner nor free her to lead the pack of the law to his hiding place. On the other hand if Cullison thought they intended to keep her prisoner he would have to compromise. He dared not leave her in the hands of Lute Blackwell. Fendrick decided to take a chance. At the worst he could turn them both free and leave for Sonora.

"All right. I'll take you to him. But you'll have to do as I say."

"Yes," she agreed.

"I'm taking you to back my play. I tell you straight that Blackwell would like nothing better than to put a bullet through your father. But I've got a hold on the fellow that ties him. He's got to do as I say. But if I'm not there and it comes to a showdown—if Bucky O'Connor for instance happens to stumble in—then it's all off with Luck Cullison. Blackwell won't hesitate a second. He'll kill your father and make a bolt for it. That's one reason why I'm taking you. I want to pile up witnesses against the fellow so as to make him go

slow. But that's not my main object. You've got
to persuade Luck to come through with an agreement to let go of that Del Oro homestead and to
promise not to prosecute us. He won't do it to
save his own life. He's got to think you come there
as my prisoner. See? He's got to wrestle with
the notion that you're in the power of the damnedest
villain that ever went unhung. I mean Blackwell.
Let him chew on that proposition a while and see
what he makes of it."

She nodded, white to the lips. "Let us go at
once, please. I don't want to leave Father alone
with that man." She called across to the corral.
"Manuel, saddle the pinto for me. Hurry!"

They rode together through the wind-swept sun-
lit land. From time to time his lazy glance em-
braced her, a supple graceful creature at perfect
ease in the saddle. What was it about her that
drew the eye so irresistibly? Prettier girls he had
often seen. Her features were irregular, mouth and
nose too large, face a little thin. Her contour lacked
the softness, the allure that in some women was
an unconscious invitation to cuddle. Tough as
whipcord she might be, but in her there flowed a
life vital and strong; dwelt a spirit brave and un-
conquerable. She seemed to him as little subtle as
any woman he had ever met. This directness came
no doubt from living so far from feminine in-

fluences. But he had a feeling that if a man once wakened her to love, the instinct of sex would spring full-grown into being.

They talked of the interests common to the country, of how the spring rains had helped the range, of Shorty McCabe's broken leg, of the new school district that was being formed. Before she knew it Kate was listening to his defense of himself in the campaign between him and her father. He found her a partisan beyond chance of conversion. Yet she heard patiently his justification.

"I didn't make the conditions that are here. I have to accept them. The government establishes forest reserves on the range. No use ramming my head against a stone wall. Uncle Sam is bigger than we are. Your father and his friends got stubborn. I didn't."

"No, you were very wise," she admitted dryly.

"You mean because I adapted myself to the conditions and made the best of them. Why shouldn't I?" he flushed.

"Father's cattle had run over that range thirty years almost. What right had you to take it from him?"

"Conditions change. He wouldn't see it. I did. As for the right of it—well, Luck ain't king of the valley just because he thinks he is."

She began to grow angry. A dull flush burned through the tan of her cheeks.

"So you bought sheep and brought them in to ruin the range, knowing that they would cut the feeding ground to pieces, kill the roots of vegetation with their sharp hoofs, and finally fill the country with little gullies to carry off the water that ought to sink into the ground."

"Sheep ain't so bad if they are run right."

"It depends where they run. This is no place for them."

"That's what you hear your father say. He's prejudiced."

"And you're not, I suppose."

"I'm more reasonable than he is."

"Yes, you are," she flung back at him irritably.

Open country lay before them. They had come out from a stretch of heavy underbrush. Catclaw had been snatching at their legs. Cholla had made the traveling bad for the horses. Now she put her pony to a canter that for the time ended conversation.

CHAPTER XI

. A COMPROMISE

Luck lay stretched full length on a bunk, his face to the roof, a wreath of smoke from his cigar traveling slowly toward the ceiling into a filmy blue cloud which hung above him. He looked the personification of vigorous full-blooded manhood at ease. Experience had taught him to take the exigencies of his turbulent life as they came, nonchalantly, to the eye of an observer indifferently, getting all the comfort the situation had to offer.

By the table, facing him squarely, sat José Dominguez, a neatly built Mexican with snapping black eyes, a manner of pleasant suavity, and an ever-ready smile that displayed a double row of shining white teeth. That smile did not for an instant deceive Luck. He knew that José had no grudge against him, that he was a very respectable citizen, and that he would regretfully shoot him full of holes if occasion called for so drastic a termination to their acquaintanceship. For Dominguez had a third interest in the C. F. ranch, and he was the last man in the world to sacrifice his business for sentiment. Having put the savings of a lifetime into the sheep business, he did not propose to let anybody deprive him of his profits either legally or illegally.

Luck was talking easily, in the most casual and amiable of voices.

"No, Dominguez, the way I look at it you and Cass got in bad this time. Here's the point. In this little vendetta of ours both sides were trying to keep inside the law and win out. When you elected Bolt sheriff that was one to you. When you took out that grazing permit and cut me off the reserve that was another time you scored heavy. A third time was when you brought 'steen thousand of Mary's little lambs baaing across the desert. Well, I come back at you by deeding the Circle C to my girl and taking up the Del Oro homestead. You contest and lose. Good enough. It's up to you to try another move."

"Si, Señor, and we move immediate. We persuade you to visit us at our summer mountain home where we can talk at leisure. We suggest a compromise."

Luck grinned. "Your notion of a compromise and mine don't tally, José. Your idea is for me to give you the apple and stand by while you eat it. Trouble is that both parties to this quarrel are grabbers."

"True, but Señor Cullison must remember his hands are tied behind him. He will perhaps not find the grabbing good," his opponent suggested politely.

"Come to that, your hands are tied too, my friend. You can't hold me here forever. Put me out of business and the kid will surely settle your hash by proving up on the claim. What are you going to do about it?"

"Since you ask me, I can only say that it depends on you. Sign the relinquishment, give us your word not to prosecute, and you may leave in three hours."

Cullison shook his head. "That's where you get in wrong. Buck up against the law and you are sure to lose."

"If we lose you lose too," Dominguez answered significantly.

The tinkle of hoofs from the river bed in the gulch below rose through the clear air. The Mexican moved swiftly to the door and presently waved a handkerchief.

'What gent are you wig-wagging to now?" Luck asked from the bed. "Thought I knew all you bold bad bandits by this time. Or is it Cass back again?"

"Yes, it's Cass. There's someone with him too. It is a woman," the Mexican discovered in apparent surprise.

"A woman!" Luck took the cigar from his mouth in vague unease. "What is he doing here with a woman?"

247

The Mexican smiled behind his open hand. "Your question anticipates mine, Señor. I too ask the same."

The sight of his daughter in the doorway went through the cattleman with a chilling shock. She ran forward and with a pathetic cry of joy threw herself upon him where he stood. His hands were tied behind him. Only by the turn of his head and by brushing his unshaven face against hers could he answer her caresses. There was a look of ineffable tenderness on his face, for he loved her more than anything else on earth.

"Mr. Fendrick brought me," she explained when articulate expression was possible.

"He brought you, did he?" Luck looked across her shoulder at his enemy, and his eyes grew hard as jade.

"Of my own free will," she added.

"I promised you a better argument than those I'd given you. Miss Cullison is that argument," Fendrick said.

The cattleman's set face had a look more deadly than words. It told Fendrick he would gladly have killed him where he stood. For Luck knew he was cornered and must yield. Neither Dominguez nor Blackwell would consent to let her leave otherwise.

"He brought me here to have a talk with you,

Dad. You must sign any paper he wants you to sign."

"And did he promise to take you back home after our talk?"

"Miss Cullison would not want to leave as long as her father was here," Fendrick answered for her glibly with a smile that said more than the words.

"I'm going to hold you responsible for bringing her here."

Fendrick could not face steadily the eyes of his foe. They bored into him like gimlets.

"And responsible for getting her back home just as soon as I say the word," Luck added, the taut muscles standing out in his clenched jaw.

"I expect your say-so won't be final in this matter, Luck. But I'll take the responsibility. Miss Cullison will get home at the proper time."

"I'm not going home till you do," the girl broke in. "Oh, Dad, we've been so worried. You can't think."

"You've played a rotten trick on me, Fendrick. I wouldn't have thought it even of a sheepman."

"No use you getting crazy with the heat, Cullison. Your daughter asked me to bring her here, and I brought her. Of course I'm not going to break my neck getting her home where she can 'phone Bolt or Bucky O'Connor and have us rounded up. That ain't reasonable to expect. But I aim to do what's right. We'll all have supper together like sensible folks. Then José and I will give you the cabin for the night if you'll promise not to attempt to escape. In the morning maybe you'll see things different."

Fendrick calculated not without reason that the best thing to do would be to give Kate a chance for a long private talk with her father. Her influence would be more potent than any he could bring to bear.

After supper the door of the cabin was locked and a sentry posted. The prisoners were on parole, but Cass did not on that account relax his vigilance. For long he and his partner could hear a low murmur of voices from within the cabin. At length the lights went out and presently the voices died. But all through the night one or the other of the sheepmen patroled a beat that circled around and around the house.

Fendrick did not broach the subject at issue next morning till after breakfast.

"Well, what have you decided?" he asked at last.

"Let's hear about that compromise. What is it you offer?" Luck demanded gruffly.

"You sign the relinquishment and agree not to make us any trouble because we brought you here, and you may go by two o'clock."

"You want to reach Saguache with the relinquishment in time to file it before I could get to a 'phone. You don't trust me."

Fendrick smiled. "When we let you go we're trusting you a heap more than we would most men. But of course you're going to be sore about this and we don't want to put temptation in your way."

"I see. Well, I accept your terms. I'll make you no *legal* trouble. But I tell you straight this thing ain't ended. It's only just begun. I'm going to run you out of this country before I'm through with you."

"Go to it. We'll see whether you make good."

"Where is that paper you want me to sign?"

Luck dashed off his signature and pushed the document from him. He hated the necessity that forced him to surrender. For himself he would have died rather than give way, but he had to think of his daughter and of his boy Sam who was engaged in a plot to hold up a train.

His stony eyes met those of the man across the table. "No need for me to tell you what I think of this. A white man wouldn't have done such a trick. It takes sheepherders and greasers to put across a thing so damnable as dragging a woman into a feud."

Fendrick flushed angrily. "It's not my fault; you're a pigheaded obstinate chump. I used the only weapon left me."

Kate, standing straight and tall behind her father's chair, looked at their common foe with uncompromising scorn. "He is not to blame, Dad. He can't help it because he doesn't see how despicable a thing he has done."

Again the blood rushed to the face of the sheepman. "I reckon that will hold me hitched for the present, Miss Cullison. In the meantime I'll go file that homestead entry of mine. Nothing like living up to the opinion your friends have of you."

He wheeled away abruptly, but as he went out of the door one word came to him.

"Friends!" Kate had repeated, and her voice told fully the contempt she felt.

At exactly two o'clock Dominguez set the Cullisons on the homeward road. He fairly dripped apologies for the trouble to which he and his friends had been compelled to put them.

Blackwell, who had arrived to take his turn as guard, stood in the doorway and sulkily watched them go.

From the river bed below the departing guests

SHE WAS THANKING GOD THE AFFAIR WAS ENDED

Page 253

looked up at the cabin hidden in the pines. The daughter was thanking God in her heart that the affair was ended. Her father was vowing to himself that it had just begun.

CHAPTER XII

AN ARREST

After half a week in the saddle Lieutenant Bucky O'Connor of the Arizona Rangers and Curly Flandrau reached Saguache tired and travel-stained. They had combed the Rincons without having met hide or hair of the men they wanted. Early next morning they would leave town again and this time would make for Soapy Stone's horse ranch.

Bucky O'Connor was not disheartened. Though he was the best man hunter in Arizona, it was all in the day's work that criminals should sometimes elude him. But with Curly the issue was a personal one. He owed Luck Cullison a good deal and his imagination had played over the picture of that moment when he could go to Kate and tell her he had freed her father.

After reaching town the first thing each of them did was to take a bath, the second to get shaved. From the barber shop they went to the best restaurant in Saguache. Curly was still busy with his pie *à la mode* when Burridge Thomas, United States Land Commissioner for that district, took the seat opposite and told to O'Connor a most interesting piece of news.

They heard him to an end without interruption. Then Curly spoke one word. "Fendrick."

"Yes, sir, Cass Fendrick. Came in about one o'clock and handed me the relinquishment just as I've been telling you."

"Then filed on the claim himself, you said."

"Yes, took it up himself."

"Sure the signature to the relinquishment was genuine?"

"I'd take oath to it. As soon as he had gone I got out the original filing and compared the two. Couldn't be any possible mistake. Nobody could have forged the signature. It is like Luck himself, strong and forceful and decided."

"We're not entirely surprised, Mr. Thomas," Lieutenant O'Connor told the commissioner. "In point of fact we've rather been looking for something of the kind."

"Then you know where Luck is?" Thomas, a sociable garrulous soul, leaned forward eagerly.

"No, we don't. But we've a notion Fendrick knows." Bucky gave the government appointee his most blandishing smile. "Of course we know *you* won't talk about this, Mr. Thomas. Can we depend on your deputies?"

"I'll speak to them."

"We're much obliged to you. This clears up a point that was in doubt to us. By the way, what was the date when the relinquishment was signed?"

"To-day."

"And who was the notary that witnessed it?"

"Dominguez. He's a partner of Fendrick in the sheep business."

"Quite a family affair, isn't it. Well, I'll let you know how things come out, Mr. Thomas. You'll be interested to know. Have a cigar."

Bucky rose. "See you later, Curly. Sorry I have to hurry, Mr. Thomas, but I've thought of something I'll have to do right away."

Bucky followed El Molino Street to the old plaza and cut across it to the Hotel Wayland. After a sharp scrutiny of the lobby and a nod of recognition to an acquaintance he sauntered to the desk and looked over the register. There, among the arrivals of the day, was the entry he had hoped to see.

Cass Fendrick, C. F. Ranch, Arizona.

The room that had been assigned to him was 212.

"Anything you want in particular, Lieutenant?" the clerk asked.

"No-o. Just looking to see who came in to-day."

He turned away and went up the stairs, ignoring the elevator. On the second floor he found 212. In answer to his knock a voice said "Come in."

Opening the door, he stepped in, closed it behind him, and looked at the man lying in his shirt sleeves on the bed.

"Evening, Cass."

Fendrick put down his newspaper but did not rise. "Evening, Bucky."

Their eyes held to each other with the level even gaze of men who recognize a worthy antagonist.

"I've come to ask a question or two."

"Kick them out."

"First, I would like to know what you paid Luck Cullison for his Del Oro claim."

"Thinking of buying me out?" was the ironical retort of the man on the bed.

"Not quite. I've got another reason for wanting to know."

"Then you better ask Cullison. The law says that if a man *sells* a relinquishment he can't file on another claim. If he surrenders it for nothing he can. Now Luck may have notions of filing on another claim. You can see that we'll have to take it for granted he gave me the claim."

It was so neat an answer and at the same time so complete a one that O'Connor could not help appreciating it. He smiled and tried again.

"We'll put that question in the discard. That paper was signed by Luck to-day. Where was he when you got it from him?"

"Sure it was signed to-day? Couldn't it have been ante-dated?"

"You know better than I do. When was it signed?"

Fendrick laughed. He was watching the noted officer of rangers with narrowed wary eyes. "On advice of counsel I decline to answer."

"Sorry, Cass. That leaves me only one thing to do. You're under arrest."

"For what?" demanded the sheepman sharply.

"For abducting Luck Cullison and holding him prisoner without his consent."

Lazily Cass drawled a question. "Are you right sure Cullison can't be found?"

"What do you mean?"

"Are you right sure he ain't at home attending to his business?"

"Has he come back?"

"Maybe so. I'm not Luck Cullison's keeper."

Bucky thought he understood. In return for the relinquishment Cullison had been released. Knowing Luck as he did, it was hard for him to see how pressure enough had been brought to bear to move him.

"May I use your 'phone?" he asked.

"Help yourself."

Fendrick pretended to have lost interest. He returned to his newspaper, but his ears were alert to catch what went on over the wires. It was always possible that Cullison might play him false and break the agreement. Cass did not expect this, for the owner of the Circle C was a man whose word was better than most men's bond. But the agreement had been forced upon him through a trick. How far he might feel this justified him in ignoring it the sheepman did not know.

O'Connor got the Circle C on long distance. It was the clear contralto of a woman that answered his "Hello!"

"Is this Miss Cullison?" he asked. Almost at once he added: O'Connor of the rangers is speaking. I've heard your father is home again. Is that true?"

An interval followed during which the ranger officer was put into the rôle of a listener. His occasional "Yes——Yes——Yes" punctuated the rapid murmur that reached Fendrick.

Presently Bucky asked a question. "On his way to town now?"

Again the rapid murmur.

"I'll attend to that, Miss Cullison. I am in Fendrick's room now. Make your mind easy."

Bucky hung up and turned to the sheepman. The latter showed him a face of derision. He had gathered one thing that disquieted him, but he did not intend to let O'Connor know it.

"Well?" he jeered. "Find friend Cullison in tolerable health?"

"I've been talking with his daughter."

"I judged as much. Miss Spitfire well?"

"Miss Cullison didn't mention her health. We were concerned about yours."

"Yes?"

"Cullison is headed for town and his daughter is afraid he is on the warpath against you."

"You don't say."

"She wanted me to get you out of her father's way until he has cooled down."

"Very kind of her."

"She's right, too. You and Luck mustn't meet yet. Get out of here and hunt cover in the hills for a few days. You know why better than I do."

"How can I when I'm under arrest?" Fendrick mocked.

"You're not under arrest. Miss Cullison says her father has no charge to bring against you."

"Good of him."

"So you can light a shuck soon as you want to."

"Which won't be in any hurry."

"Don't make any mistake. Luck Cullison is a dangerous man when he is roused."

The sheepman looked at the ranger with opaque stony eyes. "If Luck Cullison is looking for me he is liable to find me, and he won't have to go into the hills to hunt me either."

Bucky understood perfectly. According to the code of the frontier no man could let himself be driven from town by the knowledge that another man was looking for him with a gun. There are in the Southwest now many thousands who do not live by the old standard, who are anchored to law and civilization as a protection against primitive passions. But Fendrick was not one of these. He had deliberately gone outside of the law in his feud with the cattleman. Now he would not repudiate the course he had chosen and hedge because of the danger it involved. He was an aspirant to leadership among the tough hard-bitted denizens of the sunbaked desert. That being so, he had to see his feud out to a fighting finish if need be.

"There are points about this case you have overlooked," Bucky told him.

"Maybe so. But the important one that sticks out like a sore thumb is that no man living can serve notice on me to get out of town because he is coming on the shoot."

"Luck didn't serve any such notice. All his daughter knows is that he is hot under the collar. Look at things reasonably, Cass. You've caused that young lady a heap of trouble already. Are

261

you going to unload a lot more on her just because you want to be pigheaded. Only a kid struts around and hollers 'Who's afraid?' No, it's up to you to pull out, not because of Luck Cullison but on account of his daughter."

"Who is such a thorough friend of mine," the sheepman added with his sardonic grin.

"What do you care about that? She's a girl. I don't know the facts, but I can guess them. She and Luck will stand pat on what they promised you. Don't you owe her something for that? Seems to me a white man wouldn't make her any more worry."

"It's because I am a white man that I can't dodge a fight when it's stacked up for me, Bucky."

He said it with a dogged finality that was unshaken, but O'Connor made one more effort.

"Nobody will know why you left."

"I would know, wouldn't I? I've got to go right on living with myself. I tell you straight I'm going to see it out."

Bucky's jaw clamped. "Not if I know it. You're under arrest."

Fendrick sat up in surprise. "What for?" he demanded angrily.

"For robbing the W. & S. Express Company."

"Hell, Bucky. You don't believe that."

"Never mind what I believe. There's some evidence against you—enough to justify me."

"You want to get me out of Cullison's way. That's all."

"If you like to put it so."

"I won't stand for it. That ain't square."

"You'll stand for it, my friend. I gave you a chance to clear out and you wouldn't take it."

"I wouldn't because I couldn't. Don't make any mistake about this. I'm not looking for Luck. I'm attending to my business. Arrest *him* if you want to stop trouble."

There came a knock on the door. It opened to admit Luck Cullison. He shut it and put his back to it, while his eyes, hard as hammered iron, swept past the officer to fix on Fendrick.

The latter rose quickly from the bed, but O'Connor flung him back.

"Don't forget you're my prisoner."

"He's your prisoner, is he?" This was a turn of affairs for which Luck was manifestly unprepared: "Well, I've come to have a little settlement with him."

Fendrick, tense as a coiled spring, watched him warily. "Can't be any too soon to suit me."

Clear cut as a pair of scissors through paper Bucky snapped out his warning. "Nothing stirring, gentlemen. I'll shoot the first man that makes a move."

"Are you in this, Bucky?" asked Cullison evenly.

"You're right I am. He's my prisoner."

"What for?"

"For robbing the W. & S."

Luck's face lit. "Have you evidence enough to cinch him?"

"Not enough yet. But I'll take no chances on his getting away."

The cattleman's countenance reflected his thoughts as his decision hung in the balance. He longed to pay his debt on the spot. But on the other hand he had been a sheriff himself. As an outsider he had no right to interfere between an officer and his captive. Besides, if there was a chance to send Fendrick over the road that would be better than killing. It would clear up his own reputation, to some extent under a cloud.

"All right, Bucky. If the law wants him I'll step aside for the time."

The sheepman laughed in his ironic fashion. His amusement mocked them both. "Most as good as a play of the movies, ain't it? But we'd ought all to have our guns out to make it realistic."

But in his heart he did not jeer. For the situation had been nearer red tragedy than melodrama. The resource and firmness of Bucky O'Connor had alone made it possible to shave disaster by a hair's breadth and no more.

CHAPTER XIII

A CONVERSATION

Bucky O'Connor and his prisoner swung down the street side by side and turned in at the headquarters of the rangers. The officer switched on the light, shut the door, and indicated a chair. From his desk he drew a box of cigars. He struck a match and held it for the sheepman before using it himself.

Relaxed in his chair, Fendrick spoke with rather elaborate indolence.

"What's your evidence, Bucky? You can't hold me without any. What have you got that ties me to the W. & S. robbery?"

"Why, that hat play, Cass? You let on you had shot Cullison's hat off his head while he was making his getaway. Come to find out you had his hat in your possession all the time."

"Does that prove I did it myself?"

"Looks funny you happened to be right there while the robbery was taking place and that you had Luck's hat with you."

The sleepy tiger look lay warily in the sheepman's eyes. "That's what the dictionaries call a coincidence, Bucky."

"They may. I'm not sure I do."

"Fact, just the same."

"I've a notion it will take some explaining."

"Confidentially?"

"Confidentially what?"

"The explanation. You won't use it against me."

"Not if you weren't in the hold-up."

"I wasn't. This is the way it happened. You know Cullison was going to prove up on that Del Oro claim on Thursday. That would have put the C. F. ranch out of business. I knew he was in town and at the Del Mar, but I didn't know where he would be next day. He had me beat. I couldn't see any way out but to eat crow and offer a compromise. I hated it like hell, but it was up to me to hunt Luck up and see what he would do. His hat gave me an excuse to call. So I started out and came round the corner of San Mateo Street just in time to see the robber pull out. Honest, the fellow did shape up a little like Luck. Right then I got the darned fool notion of mixing him up in it. I threw his hat down and shot a hole in it, then unlocked the door of the express office carrying the hat in my hand. That's all there was to it."

"Pretty low-down trick, wasn't it, to play on an innocent man?"

"He was figuring to do me up. I don't say it

was exactly on the square, but I was sore at him clear through. I wanted to get him into trouble. I *had* to do something to keep his mind busy till I could turn round and think of a way out."

Bucky reflected, looking at the long ash on his cigar. "The man that made the raid of the W. & S. shaped up like Luck, you say?"

"In a general way."

The ranger brushed the ash from the end of the cigar into the tray. Then he looked quietly at Fendrick. "Who was the man, Cass?"

"I thought I told you———"

"You did. But you lied. It was a moonlight night. And there's an arc light at that corner. By your own story, the fellow took his mask off as he swung to his horse. You saw his face just as distinctly as I see yours now."

"No, I reckon not," Fendrick grinned.

"Meaning you won't tell?"

"That's not how I put it, Bucky. You're the one that says I recognized him. Come to think of it, I'm not sure the fellow didn't wear his mask till he was out of sight."

"I am."

"You are."

"Yes. The mask was found just outside the office where the man dropped it before he got into the saddle."

"So?"

"That's not all. Curly and I found something else, too—the old shirt from which the cloth was cut."

The sheepman swept him with one of his side-ong, tiger-cat glances. "Where did you find it?"

"In a barrel back of the Jack of Hearts."

"Now, if you only knew who put it there," suggested Cass, with ironic hopefulness.

"It happens I do. I have a witness who saw a man shove that old shirt down in the barrel after tearing a piece off."

"Your witness got a name, Bucky?"

"I'll not mention the name now. If it became too well known something might happen to my witness."

Fendrick nodded. "You're wiser there. She wouldn't be safe, not if a certain man happened to hear what you've just told me."

"I didn't say *she,* Cass."

"No, I said it. Your witness is Mrs. Wylie."

"Maybe, then, you can guess the criminal, too."

"Maybe I could, but I'm not going to try."

"Then we'll drop that subject. I'll ask you a question. Can you tell me where I can find a paroled convict named Blackwell?"

Fendrick shook his head. "Don't know the gentleman. A friend of yours?"

"One of yours. Better come through, Cass. I'm satisfied you weren't actually in this robbery, but there is such a thing as accessory after the fact. Now, I'm going to get that man. If you want to put yourself right, it's up to you to give me the information I want. Where is he?"

"Haven't got him in *my* pocket."

The officer rose, not one whit less amiable. "I didn't expect you to tell me. That's all right. I'll find him. But in the meantime I'll have to lock you up till this thing is settled."

From his inside coat pocket, Fendrick drew a sealed envelope, wrote the date across the front, and handed it to O'Connor.

"Keep this, Bucky, and remember that I gave it to you. Put it in a safe place, but don't open the envelope till I give the word. Understand?"

"I hear what you say, but I don't understand what you mean—what's back of it."

"It isn't intended that you should yet. I'm protecting myself. That's all."

"I guessed that much. Well, if you're ready, I'll arrange your lodgings for the night, Cass. reckon I'll put you up at a hotel with one of the boys."

"Just as you say."

Fendrick rose, and the two men passed into the street.

CHAPTER XIV

A TOUCH OF THE THIRD DEGREE

Cullison was not the man to acknowledge himself beaten so long as there was a stone unturned. In the matter of the Del Oro homestead claim he moved at once. All of the county commissioners were personal friends of his, and he went to them with a plan for a new road to run across the Del Oro at the point where the cañon walls opened to a valley.

"What in Mexico is the good of a county road there, Luck? Can't run a wagon over them mountains and down to the river. Looks to me like it would be a road from nowhere to nowhere," Alec Flandrau protested, puzzled at his friend's request.

"I done guessed it," Yesler announced with a grin. "Run a county road through, and Cass Fendrick can't fence the river off from Luck's cows. Luck ain't aiming to run any wagon over that road."

The Map of Texas man got up and stamped with delight. "I get you. We'll learn Cass to take a joke, by gum. Luck sure gets a county road for his cows to amble over down to the water. Cass can have his darned old homestead now."

When Fendrick heard that the commissioners had condemned a right of way for a road through his homestead he unloaded on the desert air a rich vocabulary. For here would have been a simple way out of his trouble if he had only thought of it. Instead of which he had melodramatically kidnapped his enemy and put himself within reach of the law and of Cullison's vengeance.

Nor did Luck confine his efforts to self-defense. He knew that to convict Fendrick of the robbery he must first lay hands upon Blackwell.

It was, however, Bucky that caught the convict. The two men met at the top of a mountain pass. Blackwell, headed south, was slipping down toward Stone's horse ranch when they came face to face. Before the bad man had his revolver out, he found himself looking down the barrel of the ranger's leveled rifle.

"I wouldn't," Bucky murmured genially.

"What you want me for?" Blackwell demanded sulkily.

"For the W. & S. robbery."

"I'm not the man you want. My name's Johnson."

"I'll put up with you till I find the man I do want, Mr. Johnson," Bucky told him cheerfully. "Climb down from that horse. No, I wouldn't try that. Keep your hands up."

With his prisoner in front of him, O'Connor turned townward. They jogged down out of the hills through dark gulches and cactus-clad arroyos. The sharp catclaw caught at their legs. Tangled mesquite and ironwood made progress slow. They reached in time Apache Desert, and here Bucky camped. He hobbled his prisoner's feet and put around his neck a rope, the other end of which was tied to his own waist. Then he built a small fire of greasewood and made coffee for them both. The prisoner slept, but his captor did not. For he could take no chances of an escape.

The outlines of the mountain ranges loomed shadowy and dim on both sides. The moonlight played strange tricks with the mesquit and the giant cactus, a grove of which gave to the place an awesome aspect of some ghostly burial ground of a long vanished tribe.

Next day they reached Saguache. Bucky took his prisoner straight to the ranger's office and telephoned to Cullison.

"Don't I get anything to eat?" growled the convict while they waited.

"When I'm ready."

Bucky believed in fair play. The man had not eaten since last night. But then neither had he. It happened that Bucky was tough as whipcord, as supple and untiring as a hickory sapling. Well,

Blackwell was a pretty hard nut to crack, too. The lieutenant did not know anything about book psychology, but he had observed that hunger and weariness try out the stuff that is in a man. Under the sag of them many a will snaps that would have held fast if sustained by a good dinner and a sound night's sleep. This is why so many "bad men," gun fighters with a reputation for gameness, wilt on occasion like whipped curs. In the old days this came to nearly every terror of the border. Some day when he had a jumping toothache, cr when his nerves were frayed from a debauch, a silent stranger walked into his presence, looked long and steadily into his eyes, and ended forever his reign of lawlessness. Sometimes the two-gun man was "planted," sometimes he subsided into innocuous peace henceforth.

The ranger had a shrewd instinct that the hour had come to batter down this fellow's dogged resistance. Therefore he sent for Cullison, the man whom the convict most feared.

The very look of the cattleman, with that grim, hard, capable aspect, shook Blackwell's nerve.

"So you've got him, Bucky."

Luck looked the man over as he sat handcuffed beside the table and read in his face both terror and a sly, dogged cunning. Once before the fellow had been put through the third degree. Something of the sort he fearfully expected now. Villainy is usually not consistent. This hulking bully should have been a hardy ruffian. Instead, he shrank like a schoolgirl from the thought of physical pain.

"Stand up," ordered Cullison quietly.

Blackwell got to his feet at once. He could not help it, even though the fear in his eyes showed that he cowered before the anticipated attack.

"Don't hit me," he whined.

Luck knew the man sweated under the punishment his imagination called up, and he understood human nature too well to end the suspense by making real the vision. For then the worst would be past, since the actual is never equal to what is expected.

"Well?" Luck watched him with the look of tempered steel in his hard eyes.

The convict flinched, moistened his lips with his tongue, and spoke at last.

"I—I—Mr. Cullison, I want to explain. Every man is liable to make a mistake—go off half cocked. I didn't do right. That's a fac'. I can explain all that, but I'm sick now—awful sick."

Cullison laughed harshly. "You'll be sicker soon."

"You promised you wouldn't do anything if we

turned you loose," the man plucked up courage to remind him.

"I promised the law wouldn't do anything. You'll understand the distinction presently."

"Mr. Cullison, please—— I admit I done wrong. I hadn't ought to have gone in with Cass Fendrick. He wanted me to kill you, but I wouldn't."

With that unwinking gaze the ranchman beat down his lies, while fear dripped in perspiration from the pallid face of the prisoner.

Bucky had let Cullison take the center of the stage. He had observed a growing distress mount and ride the victim. Now he stepped in to save the man with an alternative at which Blackwell might be expected not to snatch eagerly perhaps, but at least to be driven toward.

"This man is my prisoner, Mr. Cullison. From what I can make out you ought to strip his hide off and hang it up to dry. But I've got first call on him. If he comes through with the truth about the W. & S. Express robbery, I've got to protect him."

Luck understood the ranger. They were both working toward the same end. The immediate punishment of this criminal was not the important issue. It was merely a club with which to beat him into submission, and at that a moral rather than a physical one. But the owner of the Circle C knew better than to yield to Bucky too easily. He fought the point out with him at length, and finally yielded reluctantly, in such a way as to aggravate rather than relieve the anxiety of the convict.

"All right. You take him first," he finally conceded harshly.

Bucky kept up the comedy. "I'll take him, Mr. Cullison. But if he tells me the truth—and if I find out it's the whole truth—there'll be nothing doing on your part. He's my prisoner. Understand that."

Metaphorically, Blackwell licked the hand of his protector. He was still standing, but his attitude gave the effect of crouching.

"I aim to do what's right, Captain O'Connor. Whatever's right. You ask me any questions."

"I want to know all about the W. & S. robbery, everything, from start to finish."

"Honest, I wish I could tell you. But I don't know a thing about it. Cross my heart, I don't."

"No use, Blackwell. If I'm going to stand by you against Mr. Cullison, you'll have to tell the truth. Why, man, I've even got the mask you wore and the cloth you cut it from."

"I reckon it must a-been some one else, Major. Wisht I could help you, but I can't."

Bucky rose. "All right. If you can't help me, I

can't help you." Apparently he dismissed the matter from his mind, for he looked at his watch and turned to the cattleman. "Mr. Cullison, I reckon I'll run out and have some supper. Do you mind staying here with this man till I get back?"

"No. That's all right, Bucky. Don't hurry. I'll keep him entertained." Perhaps it was not by chance that his eye wandered to a blacksnake whip hanging on the wall.

O'Connor sauntered to the door. The frightened gaze of the prisoner clung to him as if for safety.

"Major—Colonel—you ain't a-going," he pleaded.

"Only for an hour or two. I'll be back. I wouldn't think of saying good-by—not till **we** reach Yuma."

With that the door closed behind him. Blackwell cried out, hurriedly, eagerly. "Mister O'Connor!"

Bucky's head reappeared. "What! Have you reduced me to the ranks already? I was looking to be a general by the time I got back," he complained whimsically.

"I—I'll tell you everything—every last thing. Mr. Cullison—he's aiming to kill me soon as you've gone."

"I've got no time to fool away, Blackwell. I'm

hungry. If you mean business get to it. But re-member that whatever you say will be used against you."

"I'll tell you any dog-goned thing you want to know. You've got me beat. I'm plumb wore out—sick. A man can't stand everything."

O'Connor came in and closed the door. "Let's have it, then—the whole story. I want it all: how you came to know about this shipment of money, how you pulled it off, what you have done with it, all the facts from beginning to the end."

"Lemme sit down, Captain. I'm awful done up. I reckon while I was in the hills I've been under-fed."

"Sit down. There's a good dinner waiting for you at Clune's when you get through."

Even then, though he must have known that lies could not avail, the man sprinkled his story with them. The residuum of truth that remained after these had been sifted out was something like this.

He had found on the street a letter that had in-advertently been dropped. It was to Jordan of the Cattlemen's National Bank, and it notified him that $20,000 was to be shipped to him by the W. & S. Express Company on the night of the rob-bery. Blackwell resolved to have a try for it. He hung around the office until the manager and the guard arrived from the train, made his raid upon them, locked the door, and threw away his mask. He dived with the satchel into the nearest alley, and came face to face with the stranger whom he later learned to be Fendrick. The whole story of the horse had been a myth later invented by the sheepman to scatter the pursuit by making it appear that the robber had come from a distance. As the street had been quite deserted at the time this detail could be plausibly introduced with no chance of a denial.

Fendrick, who had heard the shouting of the men locked in the express office, stopped the robber, but Blackwell broke away and ran down the alley. The sheepman followed and caught him. After another scuffle the convict again hammered himself free, but left behind the hand satchel containing the spoils. Fendrick (so he later explained to Blackwell) tied a cord to the handle of the bag and dropped it down the chute of a laundry in such a way that it could later be drawn up. Then he hurried back to the express office and released the prisoners. After the excitement had subsided, he had returned for the money and hid it. The original robber did not know where.

Blackwell's second meeting with the sheepman had been almost as startling as the first. Cass had run into the Jack of Hearts in time to save the life of his enemy. The two men recognized each other and entered into a compact to abduct Cullison, for his share in which the older man was paid one thousand dollars. The Mexican Dominguez had later appeared on the scene, had helped guard the owner of the Circle C, and had assisted in taking him to the hut in the Rincons where he had been secreted.

Both men asked the same question as soon as he had finished.

"Where is the money you got from the raid on the W. & S. office?"

"Don't know. I've been at Fendrick ever since to tell me. He's got it salted somewhere. You're fixing to put me behind the bars, and he's the man that really stole it."

From this they could not shake him. He stuck to it vindictively, for plainly his malice against the sheepman was great. The latter had spoiled his coup, robbed him of its fruits, and now was letting him go to prison.

"I reckon we'd better have a talk with Cass," Bucky suggested in a low voice to the former sheriff.

Luck laughed significantly. "When we find him."

For the sheepman had got out on bail the morning after his arrest.

"We'll find him easily enough. And I rather

think he'll have a good explanation, even if this fellow's story is true."

"Oh, he'll be loaded with explanations. I don't doubt that for a minute. But it will take a hell of a lot of talk to get away from the facts. I've got him where I want him now, and by God! I'll make him squeal before the finish."

"Oh, well, you're prejudiced," Bucky told him with an amiable smile.

"Course I am; prejudiced as old Wall-eyed Rogers was against the vigilantes for hanging him on account of horse stealing. But I'll back my prejudices all the same. We'll see I'm right, Bucky."

CHAPTER XV

BOB TAKES A HAND

Fendrick, riding on Mesa Verde, met Bob Cullison, and before he knew what had happened found a gun thrown on him.

"Don't you move," the boy warned.

"What does this tommyrot mean?" the sheepman demanded angrily.

"It means that you are coming back with me to the ranch. That's what it means."

"What for?"

"Never you mind what for."

"Oh, go to Mexico," Cass flung back impatiently. "Think we're in some fool moving-picture play, you blamed young idiot. Put up that gun."

Shrilly Bob retorted. He was excited enough to be dangerous. "Don't you get the wrong idea. I'm going to make this stick. You'll turn and go back with me to the Circle C."

"And you'll travel to Yuma first thing you know, you young Jesse James. What *you* need is a pair of leather chaps applied to your hide,"

"You'll go home with me, just the same."

"You've got one more guess coming, kid. I'll not go without knowing why."

"You're wanted for the W. & S. Express robbery. Blackwell has confessed."

"Confessed that I did it?" Fendrick inquired
scornfully.

"Says you were in it with him. I ain't a-going
to discuss it with you. Swing that horse round,
and don't make any breaks, or there'll be mourning
at the C. F. ranch."

Cass sat immovable as the sphinx. He was thinking that he might as well face the charge now as
any time. Moreover, he had reasons for wanting to
visit the Circle C. They had to do with a tall, slim
girl who never looked at him without scorn in her
dark, flashing eyes.

"All right. I'll go back with you, but not under
a gun."

"You'll go the way I say."

"Don't think it. I've said I'll go. That settles
it. But I won't stand for any gun-play capture."

"You'll have to stand for it."

Fendrick's face set. "Will I? It's up to you,
then. Let's see you make me."

Sitting there with his gaze steadily on the boy,
Cass had Bob at a disadvantage. If the sheep
owner had tried to break away into the chaparral,
Bob could have blazed away at him, but he could
not shoot a man looking at him with cynical,
amused eyes. He could understand the point of

283

view of his adversary. If Fendrick rode into the Circle C under compulsion of a gun in the hands of a boy he would never hear the end of the laugh on him.

"You won't try to light out, will you?"

"I've got no notion of lighting out."

Bob put up his big blue gun reluctantly. Never before had it been trained on a human being, and it was a wrench to give up the thought of bringing in the enemy as a prisoner. But he saw he could not pull it off. Fendrick had declined to scare, had practically laughed him out of it. The boy had not meant his command as a bluff, but Cass knew him better than he did himself.

They turned toward the Circle C.

"Must have been taking lessons on how to bend a gun. You in training for sheriff, or are you going to take Bucky's place with the rangers?" Fendrick asked with casual impudence, malicious amusement gleaming from his lazy eyes.

Bob, very red about the ears, took refuge in a sulky silence. He was being guyed, and not by an inch did he propose to compromise the Cullison dignity.

"From the way you go at it, I figure you an old hand at the hold-up game. Wonder if you didn't pull off the W. & S. raid yourself."

284

Bob writhed impotently. At this sort of thing he was no match for the other. Fendrick, now in the best of humors, planted lazily his offhand barbs.

Kate was seated on the porch sewing. She rose in surprise when her cousin and the sheepman appeared. They came with jingling spurs across the plaza toward her. Bob was red as a turkeycock, but Fendrick wore his most devil-may-care insouciance.

"Where's Uncle Luck, sis? I've brought this fellow back with me. Caught him on the mesa," explained the boy sulkily.

Fendrick bowed rather extravagantly and flashed at the girl a smiling double-row of strong white teeth. "He's qualifying for a moving-picture show actor, Miss Cullison. I hadn't the heart to disappoint him when he got that cannon trained on me. So here I am."

Kate looked at him and then let her gaze travel to her cousin. She somehow gave the effect of judging him of negligible value.

"I think he's in his office, Bob. I'll go see."

She went swiftly, and presently her father came out. Kate did not return.

Luck looked straight at Cass with the uncompromising hostility so characteristic of him. Neither of the men spoke. It was Bob who made the necessary explanations. The sheepman heard them with a polite derision that suggested an impersonal amusement at the situation.

"I've been looking for you," Luck said bluntly, after his nephew had finished.

"So I gathered from young Jesse James. He intimated it over the long blue barrel of his cannon. Anything particular, or just a pleasant social call?"

"You're in bad on this W. & S. robbery. I reckoned you would be safer in jail till it's cleared up."

"You still sheriff, Mr. Cullison? Somehow I had got a notion you had quit the job."

"I'm an interested party. There's new evidence, not manufactured, either."

"Well, well!"

"We'll take the stage into town and see what O'Connor says—that is, if you've got time to go." Luck could be as formal in his sarcasm as his neighbor.

"With such good company on the way I'll have to make time."

The stage did not usually leave till about half past one. Presently Kate announced dinner. A little awkwardly Luck invited the sheepman to join them. Fendrick declined. He was a Fletcherite, he informed Cullison ironically, and was in the habit of missing meals occasionally. This would be one of the times.

His host hung in the doorway. Seldom at a loss to express himself, he did not quite know how to put into words what he was thinking. His enemy understood.

"That's all right. You've satisfied the demands of hospitality. Go eat your dinner. I'll be right here on the porch when you get through."

Kate, who was standing beside her father, spoke quietly.

"There's a place for you, Mr. Fendrick. We should be very pleased to have you join us. People who happen to be at the Circle C at dinner time are expected to eat here."

"Come and eat, man. You'll be under no obligations. I reckon you can hate us, just as thorough after a square meal as before. Besides, I was your guest for several days."

Fendrick looked at the young mistress of the ranch. He meant to decline once more, but unaccountably found himself accepting instead. Something in her face told him she would rather have it so.

Wherefore Cass found himself with his feet under the table of his foe discussing various topics that had nothing to do with sheep, homestead claims, abductions, or express robberies. He looked at Kate but rarely, yet he was aware of her all the time. At his ranch a Mexican did the cooking in haphazard fashion. The food was ill prepared and worse served. He ate only because it was a necessity, and he made as short a business of it as he could. Here were cut roses on a snowy table-cloth, an air of leisure that implied the object of dinner to be something more than to devour a given quantity of food. Moreover, the food had a flavor that made it palatable. The rib roast was done to a turn, the mashed potatoes whipped to a flaky lightness. The vegetable salad was a triumph, and the rice custard melted in his mouth.

Presently a young man came into the dining room and sat down beside Kate. He looked the least in the world surprised at sight of the sheep-man.

"Mornin', Cass," he nodded.

"Morning, Curly," answered Fendrick. "Didn't know you were riding for the Circle C."

"He's my foreman," Luck explained.

Cass observed that he was quite one of the family. Bob admired him openly and without shame, because he was the best rider in Arizona; Kate seemed to be on the best of terms with him, and Luck treated him with the offhand bluffness he might have used toward a grown son.

If Cass had, in his bitter, sardonic fashion, been interested in Kate before he sat down, the feeling had quickened to something different before he rose. It was not only that she was competent to devise such a meal in the desert. There was something else. She had made a *home* for her father and cousin at the Circle C. The place radiated love, domesticity, kindly good fellowship. The casual give and take of the friendly talk went straight to the heart of the sheepman. This was living. It came to him poignantly that in his scramble for wealth he had missed that which was of far greater importance.

The stage brought the two men to town shortly after sundown. Luck called up O'Connor, and made an appointment to meet him after supper.

"Back again, Bucky," Fendrick grinned at sight of the ranger. "I hear I'm suspected of being a bad hold-up."

"There's a matter that needs explaining, Cass. According to Blackwell's story, you caught him with the goods at the time of the robbery, and in making his get-away he left the loot with you. What have you done with it?"

"Blackwell told you that, did he?"

"Yes."

"Don't doubt your word for a moment, Bucky, but before I do any talking I'd like to hear him say so. I'll not round on him until I know he's given himself away."

The convict was sent for. He substantiated the

ranger reluctantly. He was so hemmed in that he did not know how to play his cards so as to make the most of them. He hated Fendrick. But much as he desired to convict him, he could not escape an uneasy feeling that he was going to be made the victim. For Cass took it with that sarcastic smile of his that mocked them all in turn. The convict trusted none of them. Already he felt the penitentiary walls closing on him. He was like a trapped coyote, ready to snarl and bite at the first hand he could reach. Just now this happened to belong to Fendrick, who had cheated him out of the money he had stolen and had brought this upon him.

Cass heard him out with a lifted upper lip and his most somnolent tiger-cat expression. After Blackwell had finished and been withdrawn from circulation he rolled and lit a cigarette.

"By Mr. Blackwell's say-so I'm the goat. By the way, has it ever occurred to you gentlemen that one can't be convicted on the testimony of a single accomplice?" He asked it casually, his chair tipped back, smoke wreaths drifting lazily ceilingward.

"We've got a little circumstantial evidence to add, Cass." Bucky suggested pleasantly.

"Not enough—not nearly enough."

"That will be for a jury to decide," Cullison chipped in.

Fendrick shrugged. "I've a notion to let it go to

that. But what's the use? Understand this. I wasn't going to give Blackwell away, **but** since he has talked, I may tell what I know. It's true enough what he says. I did relieve him of the plunder."

"Sorry to hear that, Cass," Bucky commented gravely. "What did you do with it?"

The sheep owner flicked his cigarette ash into the tray, and looked at the lieutenant out of half-shuttered, indolent eyes. "Gave it to you, Bucky."

O'Connor sat up. His blue Irish eyes were dancing. "You're a cool customer, Cass."

"Fact, just the same. Got that letter I handed you the other day?"

The officer produced it from his safe.

"Open it."

With a paper knife Bucky ripped the flap and took out a sheet of paper.

"There's something else in there," Fendrick suggested.

The something else proved to be a piece of paper folded tightly, which being opened disclosed a key.

O'Connor read aloud the letter:

To NICHOLAS BOLT, SHERIFF, OR BUCKY O'CONNOR, LIEUTENANT OF RANGERS: Having come into possession of a little valise which is not mine, I am getting rid of it in the following manner. I have

rented a large safety-deposit box at the
Cattlemen's National Bank, and have put
into it the valise with the lock still un-
broken. The key is inclosed herewith.
Shaw, the cashier, will tell you that when
this box was rented I gave explicit orders
it should be opened only by the men
whose names are given in an envelope left
with him, not even excepting myself.
The valise was deposited at exactly 10:30
A. M. the morning after the robbery, as
Mr. Shaw will also testify. I am writing
this the evening of the same day.

CASS FENDRICK.

"Don't believe a word of it," Cullison exploded.

"Seeing is believing," the sheepman murmured.
He was enjoying greatly the discomfiture of his
foe.

"Makes a likely fairy tale. What for would you
keep the money and not turn it back?'"

"That's an easy one, Luck. He wanted to throw
the burden of the robbery on you," Bucky explained.

"Well, I've got to be shown."

In the morning he was shown. Shaw confirmed
exactly what Fendrick had said. He produced a
sealed envelope. Within this was a sheet of paper, upon which were written two lines.

Box 2143 is to be opened only by Sheriff Bolt or Lieutenant Bucky O'Connor of
the Rangers, and before witnesses.

CASS FENDRICK.

From the safety-deposit vault Bucky drew a
large package wrapped in yellow paper. He cut the
string, tore away the covering, and disclosed a
leather satchel. Perry Hawley, the local manager
of the Western & Southern Express Company, fitted to this a key and took out a sealed bundle. This
he ripped open before them all. Inside was found
the sum of twenty thousand dollars in crisp new
bills.

CHAPTER XVI

A CLEAN UP

A slight accident occurred at the jail, one so unimportant that Scanlan the jailer did not think it worth reporting to his chief. Blackwell, while eating, knocked a glass from the table and broke it on the cement floor of his cell. There is a legend to the effect that for want of a nail a battle was lost. By reason of a bit of glass secreted in his bed something quite as important happened to the convict.

From the little table in his room he pried loose one of the corner braces. At night he scraped away at this with his bit of glass until the wood began to take the shape of a revolver. This he carefully blacked with the ink brought him by his guard. To the end of his weapon he fitted an iron washer taken from the bedstead. Then he waited for his opportunity.

His chance came through the good nature of Scanlan. The jailer was in the habit of going down town to loaf for an hour or two with old cronies after he had locked up for the night. Blackwell pretended to be out of chewing tobacco and asked the guard to buy him some. About ten o'clock Scanlan returned and brought the tobacco to his prisoner. The moon was shining brightly, and he did not bring a lantern with him. As he passed the plug through the grating Blackwell's fingers closed around his wrist and drew the man close to the iron lattice work. Simultaneously a cold rim was pressed against the temple of the guard.

"Don't move, or I'll fill you full of holes," the convict warned.

Scanlan did not move, not until the man in the cell gave the word. Then he obeyed orders to the letter. His right hand found the bunch of keys, fitted the correct one to the door, and unlocked it according to instructions. Not until he was relieved of his weapon did Blackwell release him. The jailer was backed into the cell, gagged with a piece of torn bedding, and left locked up as securely as the other had been a few minutes earlier.

The convict made his way downstairs, opened the outer door with the bunch of keys he had taken from Scanlan, locked it behind him, and slipped into the first alley that offered refuge. By way of the Mexican quarters he reached the suburbs and open country. Two hours later he stole a horse from an irrigated ranch near town. Within twenty-four hours he had reached the Soapy Stone horse ranch and safety.

After this the plans for the raid on the Texas, Arizona & Pacific Flyer moved swiftly to a head. Soapy Stone and Sam dropped into Saguache inconspicuously one evening. Next day Stone rode down to Tin Cup to look over the ground. Maloney telephoned their movements to the Circle C and to the Hashknife. This brought to Saguache Luck Cullison, Curly Flandrau, and Slats Davis. Bucky O'Connor had been called to Douglas on important business and could not lend his help.

Curly met Sam in front of Chalkeye's Place. They did the town together in a mild fashion and Flandrau proposed that they save money by taking a common room. To this young Cullison agreed.

Luck, Curly and Dick Maloney had already ridden over the country surrounding the scene of the projected hold-up. They had decided that the robbery would probably take place at the depot, so that the outlaws could get the agent to stop the Flyer without arousing suspicion. In a pocket of the hills back of the station a camp had been selected, its site well back from any trail and so situated that from it one could command a view of Tin Cup.

The owner of the Circle C selected three of his closemouthed riders—Sweeney, Jake and Buck were the ones he chose—to hold the camp with him until after the robbery. The only signal they needed was the stopping of the Flyer at Tin Cup. Then they would come pounding down from the hills in time to catch the robbers before they had got through with their work. Maloney or Curly would be on the train to take a hand in the battle. Caught by surprise, Soapy's gang would surely be trapped.

So they planned it, but it happened that Soapy Stone had made his arrangements differently.

Luck and his riders took their blankets and their traps down to Tin Cup according to agreement, while Davis, Maloney and Flandrau looked after the Saguache end of the business. All of them were very friendly with Sam. The boy, younger than any of them, was flattered that three of the best known riders in the territory should make so much of him. Moreover, Stone had given him instructions to mix with Curly's crowd as much as he could. He had given as a reason that it would divert suspicion, but what he really wanted was to throw the blame of the hold-up on these friends after Sam was found dead on the scene.

Young Cullison had stopped drinking, but he could not keep his nerves from jumping. His companions pretended not to notice how worried he was, but they watched him so closely that he was never out of the sight of at least one of them. Soapy had decreed the boy's death by treachery, but his friends were determined to save him and to end forever the reign of Stone as a bad man.

It was one day when the four young cowpunchers were sitting together in Curly's room playing poker that a special delivery letter came to Sam. The others, to cover their excitement, started an argument as to whether five aces (they were playing with the joker) beat a straight flush. Presently Sam spoke, as indifferently as he could.

"Got the offer of a job down the line. Think I'll run down to-night far as Casa Grande and see what's doing."

"If they need any extra riders here's some more out of a job," Dick told him.

"Heard to-day of a freighter that wants a mule-skinner. I'm going to see him to-morrow," Slats chipped in.

"Darn this looking for a job anyhow. It's tur'ble slow work," Curly followed up, yawning. "Well, here's hoping you land yours, Sam."

This was about two o'clock in the afternoon. The game dragged on for a while, but nobody took any interest in it. Sam had to get ready for the work of the night, and the rest were anxious to get out and give him a chance. So presently Dick threw down his cards.

"I've had enough poker for one session. Me, I'm going to drift out and see what's moving in town."

"Think I'll snooze for a while," Sam said, stretching sleepily.

The others trooped out and left him alone. From the room rented by Davis the three watched to see that Sam did not leave without being observed. He did not appear, and about six o'clock Curly went back to his room.

"Time to grub," he sang out.

"That's right," Sam agreed.

They went to the New Orleans Hash House, and presently Davis and Maloney also arrived. The party ordered a good dinner and took plenty of time to eat it. Sam was obviously nervous, but eager to cover his uneasiness under a show of good spirits.

Curly finished eating just as Sam's second cup of coffee came. Flandrau, who had purposely chosen a seat in the corner where he was hemmed in by the chairs of the others, began to feel in his vest pockets.

"Darned if I've got a cigar. Sam, you're young and nimble. Go buy me one at the counter."

"Sure." Cullison was away on the instant.

Curly's hand came out of his pocket. In it was a paper. Quickly he shook the contents of the paper into the steaming cup of coffee and stirred the liquid with a spoon.

Sam brought back the cigar and drank his coffee. Without any unnecessary delay they returned to his room. Before the party had climbed the stairs the boy was getting drowsy.

"Dunno what's the matter with me. I'm feeling awful sleepy," he said, sitting on the bed.

"Why don't you take a snooze? You've got lots of time before the train goes."

"No, I don't reckon I better."

He rubbed his eyes, yawned, and slumped down. His lids wavered, shut, jerked open again, and closed slowly.

"Wake me, Curly—time for train." And with that he was sound asleep.

They took off his boots and settled him comfortably. In his pocket they found a black mask big enough to cover his whole face. The registered letter could not be found and they decided he must have destroyed it.

The sight of the mask had given Curly an idea. He was of about the same build as Sam. Why not go in his place? It would be worth doing just to catch sight of Soapy's face when he took the mask off after the robbers had been captured.

"What's the use?" Davis protested. "It's an unnecessary risk. They might shoot you in place of Sam."

"I'll look out for myself. Don't worry about

that. Before the time for getting rid of Sam comes Mr. Soapy and his bunch will be prisoners."

They argued it out, but Curly was set and could not be moved. He dressed in young Cullison's clothes and with Maloney took the express at 9:57. Davis remained to guard Sam.

Curly's watch showed 10:17 when the wheels began to grind from the setting of the air brakes. He was in the last sleeper, Dick in the day coach near the front. They had agreed that Dick was to drop off as soon as the train slowed down enough to make it safe, whereas Curly would go on and play Sam's part until the proper time.

The train almost slid to a halt from the pressure of the hard-jammed brakes. A volley of shots rang out. Curly slipped the mask over his face and rose with a revolver in each hand. He had been sitting at the end of the car, so that nobody noticed him until his voice rang out with a crisp order.

"Hands up! Don't anybody move!"

An earthquake shock could not have alarmed the passengers more. The color was washed completely from the faces of most of them.

"Reach for the roof. Come, punch a hole in the sky!" To do it thoroughly, Curly flung a couple of shots through the ceiling. That was enough. Hands went up without any argument, most of them quivering as from an Arkansas chill.

Presently Cranston herded the passengers in from the forward coaches. With them were most of the train crew. The front door of the car was locked so that they could not easily get out.

"We're cutting off the express car and going forward to 'Dobe Wells with it. There we can blow open the safe uninterrupted," Bad Bill explained. "You ride herd on the passengers here from the outside till you hear two shots, then hump yourself forward and hop on the express car."

Fine! Curly was to stand out there in the moonlight and let anybody in the car that had the nerve pepper away at him. If they did not attend to the job of riddling him, his false friends would do it while he was running forward to get aboard. Nothing could have been simpler—if he had not happened to have had inside information of their intent.

He had to think quickly, for the plans of him and his friends had been deranged. They had reckoned on the express car being rifled on the spot. This would have given Cullison time to reach the scene of action. Now they would be too late. Maloney, lying snugly in the bear grass beside the track, would not be informed as to the arrangement. Unless Curly could stop it, the hold-up would go through according to the program of Soapy and not of his enemies.

The decision of Flandrau was instantaneous. He slid down beside the track into the long grass. Whipping up one of his guns, he fired. As if in answer to the first shot his revolver cracked twice. Simultaneously, he let out a cry of pain, wriggled back for a dozen yards through the grass, and crossed the track in the darkness. As he crouched down close to the wheels of the sleeper someone came running back on the other side.

"What's up, Sam? You hit?" he could hear Blackwell whisper.

No answer came. The paroled convict was standing close to the car for fear of being hit himself and he dared not move forward into the grass to investigate.

"Sam," he called again; then, "He's sure got his."

That was all Curly wanted to know. Softly he padded forward, keeping as low as he could till he reached the empty sleepers. A brakeman was just uncoupling the express car when Curly dived underneath and nestled close to the trucks.

From where he lay he could almost have reached out and touched Soapy standing by the car.

"What about the kid?" Stone asked Blackwell as the latter came up.

"They got him. Didn't you hear him yelp?"

"Yes, but did they put him out of business? See his body?"

Blackwell had no intention of going back into the fire zone and making sure. For his part he was satisfied. So he lied.

"Yep. Blew the top of his head off."

"Good," Soapy nodded. "That's a receipt in full for Mr. Luck Cullison."

The wheels began to move. Soon they were hitting only the high spots. Curly guessed they must be doing close to sixty miles an hour. Down where he was the dust was flying so thickly he could scarce breathe, as it usually does on an Arizona track in the middle of summer.

Before many minutes the engine began to slow down. The wheels had hardly stopped moving when Curly crept out, plowed through the sand, up the rubble of a little hill, and into a draw where a bunch of scrub oaks offered cover.

A voice from in front called to him. Just then the moon appeared from behind drifting clouds.

"Oh, it's you, Sam. Everything all right?"

"Right as the wheat. We're blowing open the safe now," Flandrau answered.

Moving closer, he saw that his questioner was the man in charge of the horses. Though he knew the voice, he could not put a name to its owner. But this was not the point that first occupied his mind. *There were only four horses for five riders.* Curly knew now that he had not been mistaken. Soapy had expected one of his allies to stay on the field of battle, had prepared for it from the beginning. The knowledge of this froze any remorse the young *vaquero* might have felt.

He pushed his revolver against the teeth of the horse wrangler.

"Don't move, you handy-legged maverick, or I'll fill your hide full of holes. And if you want to keep on living padlock that mouth of yours."

In spite of his surprise the man caught the point at once. He turned over his weapons without a word.

Curly unwound a rope from one of the saddles and dropped a loop round the neck of his prisoner. The two men mounted and rode out of the draw, the outlaw leading the other two horses. As soon as they reached the bluff above Flandrau outlined the next step in the program.

"We'll stay here in the *tornilla* and see what happens, my friend. Unless you've a fancy to get lead poisoning keep still."

"Who in Mexico are you?" the captured man asked.

"It's your showdown. Skin off that mask."

The man hesitated. His own revolver moved a few inches toward his head. Hastily he took off the mask. The moon shone on the face of the man called Dutch. Flandrau laughed. Last time they had met Curly had a rope around his neck. Now the situation was reversed.

An explosion below told them that the robbers had blown open the safe. Presently Soapy's voice came faintly to them.

"Bring up the horses."

He called again, and a third time. The dwarfed figures of the outlaws stood out clear in the moonlight. One of them ran up the track toward the draw. He disappeared into the scrub oaks, from whence his alarmed voice came in a minute.

"Dutch! Oh, Dutch!"

The revolver rim pressed a little harder against the bridge of the horse wrangler's nose.

"He ain't here," Blackwell called back to his accomplices.

That brought Stone on the run. "You condemned idiot, he *must* be there. Ain't he had two hours to get here since he left Tin Cup?"

They shouted themselves hoarse. They wandered up and down in a vain search. All the time Curly and his prisoner sat in the brush and scarcely batted an eye.

At last Soapy gave up the hunt. The engine and the express car were sent back to join the rest of the train and as soon as they were out of sight the robbers set out across country toward the Flat-iron ranch.

Curly guessed their intentions. They would rustle horses there and head for the border. It was the only chance still left them.

After they had gone Curly and his prisoner returned to the road and set out toward Tin Cup. About a mile and a half up the line they met Cullison and his riders on the way down. Maloney was with them. He had been picked up at the station.

Dick gave a shout of joy when he heard Flandrau's voice.

"Oh, you Curly! I've been scared stiff for fear they'd got you."

Luck caught the boy's hand and wrung it hard. "You plucky young idiot, you've got sand in your craw. What the deuce did you do it for?"

They held a conference while the Circle C riders handcuffed Dutch and tied him to a horse. Soon the posse was off again, having left the prisoner in charge of one of the men. They swung round in a wide half circle, not wishing to startle their game until the proper time. The horses pounded up hills, slid into washes, and plowed through sand on a Spanish trot, sometimes in the moonlight, more often in darkness. The going was rough, but they could not afford to slacken speed.

When they reached the edge of the mesa that

307

looked down on the Flatiron the moon was out and the valley was swimming in light. They followed the dip of a road that led down to the corral. Passing the fenced lane leading to the stable, they tied their ponies inside and took the places assigned to them by Cullison.

They had not long to wait. In less than half an hour three shadowy figures slipped round the edge of the corral and up the lane. Each of them carried a rifle in addition to his hip guns.

They slid into the open end of the stable. Cullison's voice rang out coldly.

"Drop your guns!"

A startled oath, a shot, and before one could have lifted a hand that silent moonlit valley of peace had become a battlefield.

The outlaws fell back from the stable, weapons smoking furiously. Blackwell broke into a run, never looking behind him, but Soapy and Bad Bill gave back foot by foot fighting every step of the way.

Dick and Curly rose from behind the rocks where they had been placed and closed the trap on Blackwell. The paroled convict let out one yell.

"I give up. Goddlemighty, don't shoot!"

His rifle he had already thrown away. With his arms reaching above him, his terror-stricken eyes popping from his head, he was a picture of the most frightened "bad man" who had ever done business in Arizona.

Half way down the lane Cranston was hit. He sank to his knees, and from there lopped over sideways to his left elbow. In the darkness his voice could be heard, for the firing had momentarily ceased.

"They've got me, Soapy. Run for it. I'll hold 'em back."

"Hit bad, Bill?"

"I'm all in. *Vamos!*"

Stone turned to run, and for the first time saw that his retreat was cut off. As fast as he could pump the lever his rifle began working again.

The firing this time did not last more than five seconds. When the smoke cleared it was all over. Soapy lay on his back, shot through and through. Blackwell had taken advantage of the diversion to crawl through the strands of barbed wire and to disappear in the chaparral. Bill had rolled over on his face.

Curly crept through the fence after the escaping man, but in that heavy undergrowth he knew it was like looking for a needle in a haystack. After a time he gave it up and returned to the field of battle.

Dick was bending over Stone. He looked up at the approach of his friend and said just one word.

"Dead."

Cullison had torn open Cranston's shirt and was examining his wounds.

"No use, Luck. I've got a-plenty. You sure fooled us thorough. Was it Sam gave us away?"

"No, Bill. Curly overheard Soapy and Blackwell at Chalkeye's Place. Sam stood pat, though you were planning to murder him."

"I wasn't in on that, Luck—didn't know a thing about it till after the boy was shot. I wouldn't a-stood for it."

"He wasn't shot. Curly saved him. He had to give you away to do it."

"Good enough. Serves Soapy right for double crossing Sam. Take care of that kid, Luck. He's all right yet." His eye fell on Flandrau. "You're a game sport, son. You beat us all. No hard feelings."

"Sorry it had to be this way, Bill."

The dying man was already gray to the lips, but his nerve did not falter. "It had to come some time. And it was Luck ought to have done it too." He waved aside Sweeney, who was holding a flask to his lips. "What's the use? I've got mine."

"Shall we take him to the house?" Maloney asked.

"No. I'll die in the open. Say, there's something else, boys. Curly has been accused of that

Bar Double M horse rustling back in the early summer. I did that job. He was not one of us. You hear, boys. Curly was not in it."

A quarter of an hour later he died. He had lied to save from the penitentiary the lad who had brought about his death. Curly knew why he had done it—because he felt himself to blame for the affair. Maybe Bad Bill had been a desperado, a miscreant according to the usual standard, but when it came to dying he knew how to go better than many a respectable citizen. Curly stole off into the darkness so that the boys would not see him play the baby.

By this time the men from the Flatiron were appearing, armed with such weapons as they could hastily gather. The situation was explained to them. Neighboring ranches were called up by telephone and a systematic hunt started to capture Blackwell.

Luck left his three riders to help in the man hunt, but he returned with Curly and Maloney to Saguache. On the pommel of his saddle was a sack. It contained the loot from the express car of the Flyer. Two lives already had been sacrificed to get it, and the sum total taken amounted only to one hundred ninety-four dollars and sixteen cents.

CHAPTER XVII

THE PRODIGAL SON

They found the prodigal son with his sister and Laura London at the Del Mar. Repentance was writ large all over his face and manner. From Davis and from the girls he had heard the story of how Soapy Stone had intended to destroy him. His scheme of life had been broken into pieces and he was a badly shaken young scamp.

When Luck and Curly came into the room he jumped up, very white about the lips.

"Father!"

"My boy!"

Cullison had him by the hand, one arm around the shaking shoulders.

"What——what——?"

Sam's question broke down, but his father guessed it.

"Soapy and Bad Bill were killed, Dutch is a prisoner, and Blackwell escaped. All Spring Valley is out after him."

The boy was aghast. "My God!"

"Best thing for all of us. Soapy meant to murder you. If it hadn't been for Curly——"

"Are you sure?"

"No question about it. He brought no horse for you to ride away on. Bill admitted it, though he didn't know what was planned. Curly heard Soapy ask Blackwell whether he had seen your body."

The boy shuddered and drew a long sobbing breath. "I've been a fool, Father—and worse."

"Forget it, son. We'll wipe the slate clean. I've been to blame too."

It was no place for outsiders. Curly beat a retreat into the next room. The young women followed him. Both of them were frankly weeping. Arms twined about each other's waists, they disappeared into an adjoining bedroom.

"'Don't go,'" Kate called to him over her shoulder.

Curly sat down and waited. Presently Kate came back alone. Her shining eyes met his.

"I never was so happy in all my life before. Tell me what happened—everything please."

As much as was good for her to know Curly told. Without saying a word she listened till he was through. Then she asked a question.

"Won't Dutch tell about Sam being in it?"

"Don't matter if he does. Evidence of an accomplice not enough to convict. Soapy overshot himself. I'm here to testify that Sam and he quarrelled before Sam left. Besides, Dutch won't talk. I drilled it into him thorough that he'd better take his medicine without bringing Sam in."

She sat for a long time looking out of the window without moving. She did not make the least sound, but the young man knew she was crying softly to herself. At last she spoke in a low sweet voice.

"What can we do for you? First you save Father and then Sam. You risked everything for my brother—to win him back to us, to save his life and now his reputation. If you had been killed people would always have believed you were one of the gang."

"Sho! That's nonsense, Miss Kate." He twisted his hat in his hand uneasily. "Honest, I enjoyed every bit of it. And a fellow has to pay his debts."

"Was that why you did it?" she asked softly.

"Yes. I had to make good. I had to show your father and you that I had not thrown away all your kindness. So I quit travelling that downhill road on which I had got started."

"I'm glad—I'm so glad." She whispered it so low he could hardly hear.

"There was one way to prove myself. That was to stand between Sam and trouble. So I butted in and spoiled Soapy's game."

"I wish I could tell you how fine Father thinks it was of you. He doesn't speak of it much, but I know."

314

"Nothing to what I did—nothing at all." A wave of embarrassment had crept to the roots of his curly hair. "Just because a fellow—Oh, shucks!"

"That's all very well for you to say, but you can't help us thinking what we please."

"But that ain't right. I don't want you thinking things that ain't so because——"

"Yes? Because——?"

She lifted her eyes and met his. Then she knew it had to come out, that the feeling banked in him would overflow in words.

"Because you're the girl I love."

He had not intended to say it now, lest he might seem to be urging his services as a claim upon her. But the words had slipped out in spite of him.

She held out her two hands to him with a little gesture of surrender. The light of love was in her starry eyes.

And then——

She was in his arms, and the kisses he had dreamed about were on his lips.

CHAPTER XVIII

CUTTING TRAIL

Kate Cullison had disappeared, had gone out riding one morning and at nightfall had not returned. As the hours passed, anxiety at the Circle C became greater.

"Mebbe she got lost," Bob suggested.

Her father scouted this as absurd. "Lost nothing. You couldn't lose her within forty miles of the ranch. She knows this country like a cow does the range. And say she was lost—all she would have to do would be to give that pinto his head and he'd hit a bee line for home. No, nor she ain't had an accident either, unless it included the pony too."

"You don't reckon a cougar——," began Sweeney, and stopped.

Luck looked at his handy-legged old rider with eyes in which little cold devils sparkled. "A human cougar, I'll bet. This time I'll take his hide off inch by inch while he's still living."

"You thinking of Fendrick?" asked Sam.

"You've said it."

Sweeney considered, rasping his stubbly chin. "I

don't reckon Cass would do Miss Kate a meanness. He's a white man, say the worst of him. But it might be Blackwell. When last seen he was head-ing into the hills. If he met her——"

A spasm of pain shot across Luck's face. "My God! That would be awful."

"By Gum, there he is now, Luck." Sweeney's finger pointed to an advancing rider.

Cullison swung as on a pivot in time to see some-one drop into the dip in the road, just beyond the corral. "Who—Blackwell?"

"No. Cass."

Fendrick reappeared presently and turned in at the lane. Cullison, standing on the porch at the head of the steps looked like a man who was pass-ing through the inferno. But he looked too a per-sonified day of judgment untempered by mercy. His eyes bored like steel gimlets into those of his enemy.

The sheepman spoke, looking straight at his foe. "I've just heard the news. I was down at Yesler's ranch when you 'phoned asking if they had seen anything of Miss Cullison. I came up to ask you one question. When was she seen last?"

"About ten o'clock this morning. Why?"

"I saw her about noon. She was on Mesa Verde, headed for Blue Cañon looked like."

"Close enough to speak to her?" Sam asked.

317

"Yes. We passed the time of day."

"And then?" Luck cut back into the conversation with a voice like a file.

"She went on toward the gulch and I kept on to the ranch. The last I saw of her she was going straight on."

"And you haven't seen her since?"

The manner of the questioner startled Fendrick. "God, man, you don't think I'm in this, do you?"

"If you are you'd better blow your brains out before I learn it. And if you're trying to lead me on a false scent——" Luck stopped. Words failed him, but his iron jaw clamped like a vice.

Fendrick spoke quietly. "I'm willing. In the meantime we'd better travel over toward Mesa Verde, so as to be ready to start at daybreak."

Cullison's gaze had never left him. It observed, weighed, appraised. "Good enough. We'll start."

He left Sweeney to answer the telephone while he was away. All of his other riders were already out combing the hills under supervision of Curly. Luck had waited with Sam only to get some definite information before starting. Now he had his lead. Fendrick was either telling the truth or he was lying with some sinister purpose in view. The cattleman meant to know which.

Morning breaks early in Arizona. By the time they had come to the spot where the sheepman said he had met Kate gray streaks were already lightening the sky. The party moved forward slowly toward the cañon, spreading out so as to cover as much ground as possible. Before they reached its mouth the darkness had lifted enough to show the track of a horse in the sand.

They pushed up the gulch as rapidly as they could. The ashes of a camp fire halted them a few minutes later. Scattered about lay the feathers and dismembered bones of some birds.

Cass stooped and picked up some of the feathers. "Quails, I reckon. Miss Cullison had three tied to her saddle horn when I met her."

"Why did she come up here to cook them?" Sam asked.

Luck was already off his horse, quartering over the ground to read what it might tell him.

"She wasn't alone. There was a man with her. See these tracks."

It was Fendrick who made the next discovery. He had followed a draw for a short distance and climbed to a little mesa above. Presently he called to Cullison.

Father and son hurried toward him. The sheepowner was standing at the edge of a prospect hole pointing down with his finger.

"Someone has been in that pit recently, and he's been there several days."

"Then how did he get out?" Sam asked.

Fendrick knelt on the edge of the pit and showed him where a rope had been dragged so heavily that it had cut deeply into the clay.

"Someone pulled him out."

"What's it mean anyhow? Kate wasn't in that hole, was she?"

Cass shook his head. "This is my guess. Someone was coming along here in the dark and fell in. Suppose Miss Cullison heard him calling as she came up the gulch. What would she do?"

"Come up and help the fellow out."

"Sure she would. And if he was hungry—as he likely was—she would cook her quail for him."

"And then? Why didn't she come home?"

Luck turned a gray agonized face on him. "Boy, don't you see? The man was Blackwell."

"And if you'll put yourself in Blackwell's place you'll see that he couldn't let her go home to tell where she had seen him," Fendrick explained.

"Then where is she? What did he do with her?"

There came a moment's heavy silence. The pale face of the boy turned from the sheepman to his father. "You don't think that—that——"

"No, I don't," Cass answered. "But let's look this thing squarely in the face. There were three things he could do with her. First, he might leave her in the pit. He didn't do that because he hadn't the nerve. She might be found soon and set the hunters on his track. Or she might die in that hole and he be captured later with her pinto. I know him. He always plays a waiting game when he can. Takes no chances if he can help it."

"You think he took her with him then." Luck said.

"Yes. There's a third possibility. He may have shot her when he got a good chance, but I don't think so. He would keep her for a hostage as long as he could."

"That's the way I figure it," agreed Cullison. "He daren't hurt her, for he would know Arizona would hunt him down like a wolf if he did."

"Then where's he taking her?" Sam asked.

"Somewhere into the hills. He knows every pocket of them. His idea will be to slip down and cut across the line into Sonora. He's a rotten bad lot, but he won't do her any harm unless he's pushed to the wall. The fear of Luck Cullison is in his heart."

"That's about it," nodded Luck. "He's somewhere in these hills unless he's broken through. Bolt 'phoned me that one of his posse came on the ashes of a camp fire still warm. They're closing in on him. He's got to get food or starve, unless he can break through."

"There's a chance he'll make for one of my sheep

camps to lay in a supply. Wouldn't it be a good idea to keep a man stationed at each one of them?"

"You're talking sense," Cullison approved. "Sam, ride back and get in touch with Curly. Tell him to do that. And rouse the whole country over the wire. We'll run him down and feed him to the coyotes."

CHAPTER XIX

A GOOD SAMARITAN

Fendrick had told the exact truth. After leaving him Kate had ridden forward to the cañon and entered it. She did not mean to go much farther, but she took her time. More than once she slipped from under a fold of her waist a letter and reread sentences of it. Whenever she did this her eyes smiled. For it was a love letter from Curly, the first she had ever had. It had been lying on the inner edge of the threshold of her bedroom door that morning when she got up, and she knew that her lover had risen early to put it there unnoticed.

They were to be married soon. Curly had wished to wait till after his trial, but she had overruled him. Both her father and Sam had sided with her, for she had made them both see what an advantage it would be with a jury for Flandrau to have his bride sitting beside him in the courtroom.

Faintly there came to her a windswept sound. She pulled up and waited, but no repetition of it reached her ears. But before her pony had moved a dozen steps she stopped him again. This time she was almost sure of a far cry, and after it the bark of a revolver.

With the touch of a rein she guided her horse toward the sound. It might mean nothing. On the other hand it might be a call for help. Her shout brought an answer which guided her to the edge of a prospect hole. In the darkness she made out an indistinct figure.

"Water," a husky voice demanded.

She got her canteen from the saddle and dropped it to him. The man glued his lips to the mouth as if he could never get enough.

"For God's sake get me out of here," he pleaded piteously.

"How long have you been there?"

"Two days. I fell in at night whilst I was cutting acrost country."

Kate fastened her rope to the horn of the saddle, tightened the cinch carefully, and dropped the other end to him. She swung to the back of the horse and braced herself by resting her full weight on the farther stirrup.

"Now," she told him.

The imprisoned man tried to pull himself up, bracing his feet against the rough projections of the rock wall to help him. But he could not manage the climb. At last he gave it up with an oath.

"We'll try another way," the girl told him cheer-fully.

At spaces about a foot distant she tied knots in the rope for about the first six feet.

"This time you'll make it," she promised. "You can get up part way as you did before. Then I'll start my horse forward. Keep braced out from the wall so as not to get crushed."

He growled an assent. Once more she got into the saddle and gave the word. He dragged himself up a few feet and then the cowpony moved for-ward. The legs of the man doubled up under the strain and he was crushed against the wall just as he reached the top. However, he managed to hang on and was dragged over the edge with one cheek scratched and bleeding.

"Might a-known you'd hurt me if you moved so fast," he complained, nursing his wounded face in such a way as to hide it.

"I'm sorry. I did my best to go carefully," the girl answered, stepping forward.

His hand shot forward and caught her wrist. Her startled eyes flashed to his face. The man was the convict Blackwell.

"Got anything to eat with you. I'm starving," he snapped.

"Yes. I shot some quail. Let go my hand."

He laughed evilly, without mirth. "Don't try

any of your sassy ways on me. By God, I'm a wolf on the howl."

In spite of her supple slenderness there was strength in her small wrists. She fought and twisted till she was worn out in her efforts to free herself. Panting, she faced him.

"Let me go, I tell you."

For answer his open hand struck her mouth. "Not till you learn your boss. Before I'm through with you a squaw won't be half so tame as you."

He dragged her to the horse, took from its case the rifle that hung by the saddle, and flung her from him roughly. Then he pulled himself to the saddle.

"March ahead of me," he ordered.

As soon as they had reached the bed of the cañon he called a halt and bade her light a fire and cook him the quail. She gathered ironwood and catclaw while he watched her vigilantly. Together they roasted the birds by holding them over the fire with sharpened sticks thrust through the wings. He devoured them with the voracity of a wild beast.

Hitherto his mind had been busy with the immediate present, but now his furtive shifting gaze rested on her more thoughtfully. It was as a factor of his safety that he considered her. Gratitude was a feeling not within his scope. The man's mind worked just as Fendrick had surmised. He would

not let her go back to the ranch with the news that
he was hidden in the hills so close at hand. He
dared not leave her in the prospect hole. He was
not yet ready to do murder for fear of punishment. That was a possibility to be considered only
if he should be hard pressed. The only alternative
left him was to take her to the border as a companion of his fugitive doublings.

"We'll be going now," he announced, after he
had eaten.

"Going where? Don't you see I'll be a drag to
you? Take my horse and go. You'll get along
faster."

"Do you think so?"

She opened her lips to answer, but there was
something in his face—something at once so cruel
and deadly and wolfish—that made the words die
on her lips. For the first time it came to her that
if he did not take her with him he would kill her
to insure his own safety. None of the arguments
that would have availed with another man were of
any weight here. Her sex, her youth, the service
she had done him—these would not count a straw.
He was lost to all the instincts of honor that govern
even hard desperate men of his class.

They struck into the mountains, following a
cattle trail that wound upward with devious twists.
The man rode, and the girl walked in front with

the elastic lightness, the unconscious flexuous grace of poise given her body by an outdoor life. After a time they left the gulch. Steadily they traveled, up dark arroyos bristling with mesquite, across little valleys leading into timbered stretches through which broken limbs and uprooted trees made progress almost impossible, following always untrodden ways that appalled with their lonely desolation.

By dusk they were up in the headwaters of the creeks. The resilient muscles of the girl had lost their spring. She moved wearily, her feet dragging heavily so that sometimes she staggered when the ground was rough. Not once had the man offered her the horse. He meant to be fresh, ready for any emergency that might come. Moreover, it pleased his small soul to see the daughter of Luck Cullison fagged and exhausted but still answering the spur of his urge.

The moon was up before they came upon a tent shining in the cold silvery light. Beside it was a sheetiron stove, a box, the ashes of a camp fire, and a side of bacon hanging from the limb of a stunted pine. Cautiously they stole forward.

The camp was for the time deserted. No doubt its owner, a Mexican sheepherder in the employ of Fendrick and Dominguez, was out somewhere with his flock.

Kate cooked a meal and the convict ate. The

girl was too tired and anxious to care for food, but she made herself take a little. They packed the saddlebags with bacon, beans, coffee and flour. Blackwell tightened again the cinches and once more the two took the trail.

They made camp in a pocket opening from a gulch far up in the hills. With her own *reata* he fastened her hands behind her and tied the girl securely to the twisted trunk of a Joshua tree. To make sure of her he lay on the rope, both hands clinched to the rifle. In five minutes he was asleep, but it was long before Kate could escape from wakefulness. She was anxious, her nerves were jumpy, and the muscles of arms and shoulders were cramped. At last she fell into troubled catnaps.

From one of these she awoke to see that the morning light was sifting through the darkness. Her bones and muscles ached from the constraint of the position in which the rope held them. She was shivering with the chill of an Arizona mountain night. Turning her body, the girl's eyes fell upon her captor. He was looking at her in the way that no decent man looks at a woman. Her impulse was to scream, to struggle to her feet and run. What did he mean? What was he going to do?

But something warned her this would precipitate the danger. She called upon her courage and tried to still the fearful tumult in her heart. Somehow she succeeded. A scornful, confident pride flashed from her eyes into his. It told him that for his life he dared not lay a finger upon her in the way of harm. And he knew it was true, knew that if he gave way to his desire no hole under heaven would be deep enough to hide him from the vengeance of her friends.

He got sullenly to his feet. "Come. We'll be going."

Within the hour they saw some of his hunters. The two were sweeping around the lip of a mountain park nestling among the summits. A wisp of smoke rose from the basin below. Grouped about it were three men eating breakfast.

"Don't make a sound," warned Blackwell.

His rifle covered her. With all her soul she longed to cry for help. But she dared not take the risk. Even as the two on the edge of the bowl withdrew from sight one of the campers rose and sauntered to a little grove where the ponies were tethered. The distance was too far to make sure, but something in the gait made the girl sure that the man was Curly. Her hands went out to him in a piteous little gesture of appeal.

She was right. It was Curly. He was thinking of her at that moment despairingly, but no bell of warning rang within to tell him she was so near and in such fearful need of him.

Twice during the morning did the refugee attempt to slip down into the parched desert that stretched toward Sonora and safety. But the cordon set about him was drawn too close. Each time a loose-seated rider lounging in the saddle with a rifle in his hands drove them back. The second attempt was almost disastrous, for the convict was seen. The hum of a bullet whistled past his ears as he and his prisoner drew back into the chaparral and from thence won back to cover.

Kate, drooping with fatigue, saw that fear rode Blackwell heavily. He was trapped and he knew that by the Arizona code his life was forfeit and would be exacted of him should he be taken. He had not the hardihood to game it out in silence, but whined complaints, promises and threats. He tried to curry favor with her, to work upon her pity, even while his furtive glances told her that he was wondering whether he would have a better chance if he sacrificed her life.

From gulch to arroyo, from rock-cover to pine-clad hillside he was driven in his attempts to break the narrowing circle of grim hunters that hemmed him. And with each failure, with every passing hour, the terror in him mounted. He would have welcomed life imprisonment, would have sold the last vestige of manhood to save the worthless life that would soon be snuffed out unless he could evade his hunters till night and in the darkness break through the line.

He knew now that it had been a fatal mistake to bring the girl with him. He might have evaded Bolt's posses, but now every man within fifty miles was on the lookout for him. His rage turned against Kate because of it. Yet even in those black outbursts he felt that he must cling to her as his only hope of saving himself. He had made another mistake in lighting a campfire during the morning. Any fool ought to have known that the smoke would draw his hunters as the smell of carrion does a buzzard.

Now he made a third error. Doubling back over an open stretch of hillside, he was seen again and forced into the first pocket that opened. It proved to be a blind gulch, one offering no exit at the upper end but a stiff rock climb to a bluff above.

He whipped off his coat and gave it to Kate.

"Put it on. Quick."

Surprised, she slipped it on.

"Now ride back out and cut along the edge of the hill. You've got time to make it all right before they close in if you travel fast. Stop once— just once—and I'll drop you in your tracks. Now git!"

She saw his object in a flash. Wearing his gray felt hat and his coat, the pursuers would mistake her for him. They would follow her—perhaps shoot her down. Anyhow, it would be a diversion to draw them from him. Meanwhile he would climb the cliff and slip away unnoticed.

The danger of what she had to do stood out quite clearly, but as a chance to get away from him she welcomed it gladly. She swung the pony with a touch of the rein and set him instantly at the canter. It was rough going, but she took it almost blindly.

From the lip of the gulch she swung abruptly to the right. Her horse stumbled and went down just as a bullet flew over her head. Before she was free of the stirrups strong hands pinned her shoulders to the ground. She heard a glad startled cry. The rough hands became immediately gentle. Then things grew black. The last she remembered was that the mountains were dancing up and down in an odd fashion.

Her eyes opened to see Curly. She was in his arms and his face was broken with emotions of love and tenderness.

"You're not hurt," he implored.

"No."

"He didn't—mistreat you?" His voice was trembling as he whispered it.

"No—No."

And at that she broke down. A deep sob shook

her body—and another. She buried her head on his shoulder and wept.

. . . .

Without losing an instant the convict set himself at the climb. His haste, the swift glances shot behind him, the appalling dread that made his nerves ragged, delayed his speed by dissipating the single-ness of his energy. His face and hands were torn with catclaw, his knee bruised by a slip against a sharp jut of quartz.

When he reached the top he was panting and shaken. Before he had moved a dozen steps a man came out of the brush scarce seventy-five yards away and called to him to surrender. He flung his rifle to place and fired twice.

The man staggered and steadied himself. A shell had jammed and Blackwell could not throw it out. He turned to run as the other fired. But he was too late. He stumbled, tripped, and went down full length.

The man that had shot him waited for him to rise. The convict did not move. Cautiously the wounded hunter came forward, his eyes never lifting from the inert sprawling figure. Even now he half expected him to spring up, life and energy in every tense muscle. Not till he stood over him, till he saw the carelessly flung limbs, the uncouth twist to the neck, could he believe that so slight a crook of the finger had sent swift death across the plateau.

The wounded man felt suddenly sick. Leaning against a rock, he steadied himself till the nausea was past. Voices called to him from the plain below. He answered, and presently circled down into the gulch which led to the open.

At the gulch mouth he came on a little group of people. One glance told him all he needed to know. Kate Cullison was crying in the arms of Curly Flandrau. Simultaneously a man galloped up, flung himself from his horse, and took the young woman from her lover.

"My little girl," he cried in a voice that rang with love.

Luck had found his ewe lamb that was lost.

It was Curly who first saw the man approaching from the gulch. "Hello, Cass! Did you get him?"

Fendrick nodded wearily.

"Dead sure?"

"Yep. He's up there." The sheepman's hand swept toward the bluff.

"You're wounded."

"Got me in the shoulder. Nothing serious, I judge."

Cullison swung around. "Sure about that, Cass?" It was the first time for years that he had called the other by his first name except in irony.

335

"Sure."

"Let's have a look at the shoulder."

After he had done what he could for it Luck spoke bluffly. "This dashed feud is off, Cass. You've wiped the slate clean. When you killed Blackwell you put me out of a hostile camp."

"I'm glad—so glad. Now we'll all be friends, won't we?" Kate cried.

Cass looked at her and at Curly, both of them radiant with happiness, and his heart ached for what he had missed. But he smiled none the less.

"Suits me if it does you."

He gave one hand to Luck and the other to his daughter.

Curly laughed gaily. "Everybody satisfied, I reckon."

336

CHAPTER XX

LOOSE THREADS

Curly was right when he said that those who knew about Sam's share in the planning of the Tin Cup hold-up would keep their mouths close. All of the men implicated in the robbery were dead except Dutch. Cullison used his influence to get the man a light sentence, for he knew that he was not a criminal at heart. In return Dutch went down the line without so much as breathing Sam's name.

Luck saw to it that Curly got all the credit of frustrating the outlaws in their attempt on the Flyer and of capturing them afterward. In the story of the rescue of Kate he played up Flandrau's part in the pursuit at the expense of the other riders. For September was at hand and the young man needed all the prestige he could get. The district attorney had no choice but to go on with the case of the State versus Flandrau on a charge of rustling horses from the Bar Double M. But public sentiment was almost a unit in favor of the defendant.

The evidence of the prosecution was not so strong as it had been. All of his accomplices were dead and one of the men implicated had given it out in his last moments that the young man was not a party to the crime. The man who had owned the feed corral had sold out and gone to Colorado. The hotel clerk would not swear positively that the prisoner was the man he had seen with the other rustlers.

Curly had one important asset no jury could forget. It counted for a good deal that Alec Flandrau, Billy Mackenzie, and Luck Cullison were known to be backing him, but it was worth much more that his wife of a week sat beside him in the courtroom. Every time they looked at the prisoner the jurymen saw too her dusky gallant little head and slender figure. They remembered the terrible experience through which she had so recently passed. She had come through it to happiness. Every look and motion of the girl wife radiated love for the young scamp who had won her. And since they were tender-hearted old frontiersmen they did not intend to spoil her joy. Moreover, society could afford to take chances with this young fellow Flandrau. He had been wild no doubt, but he had shown since the real stuff that was in him. Long before they left the box each member of the jury knew that he was going to vote for acquittal.

It took the jury only one ballot to find a verdict of not guilty. The judge did not attempt to stop the uproar of glad cheers that shook the building when the decision was read. He knew it was not the prisoner so much they were cheering as the brave girl who had sat so pluckily for three days beside the husband she had made a man.

From the courtroom Curly walked out under the blue sky of Arizona a free man. But he knew that the best of his good fortune was that he did not go alone. For all the rest of their lives her firm little steps would move beside him to keep him true and steady. He could not go wrong now, for he was anchored to a responsibility that was a continual joy and wonder to him.

The End

There Are Two Sides to Everything—

—including the wrapper which covers every Grosset & Dunlap book. When you feel in the mood for a good romance, refer to the carefully selected list of modern fiction comprising most of the successes by prominent writers of the day which is printed on the back of every Grosset & Dunlap book wrapper.

You will find more than five hundred titles to choose from—books for every mood and every taste and every pocket-book.

Don't forget the other side, but in case the wrapper is lost, write to the publishers for a complete catalog.

Lightning Source UK Ltd.
Milton Keynes UK
UKHW021108220119
335965UK00011B/1209/P